DANGER IN HER WORDS

DEDICATION

TO MY FRIENDS WHO ENCOURAGED ME
TO BE NAUGHTY!
YOU ARE THE BOMB.

EVERY AUTHOR IN SOME WAY
PORTRAYS HIMSELF IN HIS WORKS,
EVEN IF IT BE AGAINST HIS WILL
—JOHANN WOLFGANG VON GOETHE

DANGER
IN
HER
WORDS

A Novel

BARBARA BARTH

When Fantasy and Reality Blur
Fiction Can Be Deadly

ISBN-10: 098317153X
ISBN-13: 978-0-9831715-3-9

First Edition
Gilbert Street Press

Book & Cover Design
pd king design

PROLOGUE

Daisy jumped off the couch and dashed to the kitchen. All seven pounds of fluff in protective mode, her piercing bark echoed down the hallway. It was the second time that week Daisy heard something outside and ran to check on it by the back door.

It was just the two of them in the Victorian farmhouse, the writer and her little dog, an hour away from her friends, in a tiny town where she knew no one. Susan was not the nervous type, but writing this new book had made her uneasy.

The soft light from the monitor gave the room an eerie glow. Susan got up from the computer and looked out the window into her yard. Shadows and moonlight greeted her. For half a minute she expected to see a face staring back at her. But all seemed in order.

Chilled, she pulled her sweater close and went back to her desk. It has only been a few months since the writers' conference. *Sex Sells* was the topic of the day. Writing a steamy book seemed like a fun idea. Now she worried it had changed everything and there was danger in the words she wrote.

REALITY IS A SLIDING DOOR
—RALPH WALDO EMERSON

1
JAMIE

"I hate this." Jamie was mad at herself and the world in general. Tonight was more difficult than she thought it would be. She didn't know if she was lonely or just missing sex. *Has it really been three years?* She walked over to the dresser and picked up the silver frame. Jack's devilish face smiled at her. *Bastard*, she whispered. Today was a special day. One she planned to celebrate in her own way tonight.

It was the third anniversary of her husband's death. She was tired of being alone. Her attempts at dating had been horrible. She had been naïve about the dating game and made every mistake a gal who had been married for twelve years could make. She trusted that men were honest with their words.

She took another look at Jack's photo. "I should have known better. You taught me that early on." Jamie opened the drawer and slipped the frame back in. Their marriage wasn't perfect, but she had been happy. Content was a better word. She smiled for a moment. *Sex. That was what kept us together.*

Now she missed sex to the point it made her irritable. Some days she was downright bitchy. She'd been with a few men since Jack died. She was embarrassed to be naked in front of someone new and couldn't relax. It was more than she could handle. She decided to stop dating a year ago and hadn't had sex since.

No one said being a widow would be easy. She missed being touched more than anything else. Her body ached for affection and she was hungry with lust. On nights like this she took matters into her own hands. She hated the vibrator her best friend gave her when she swore off men.

"I think you'll find this handy." Lynn handed her a beautifully wrapped box. Jamie was horrified when she opened it. Her friend was married. What did she know about being alone in bed?

Jamie smiled at Lynn and resisted the temptation to wag her finger. "You are the devil, my dear!"

Her friend had good intentions. Jamie didn't want to be a butt. They kidded about sex all the time. "Maybe I'll give this a whirl as soon as I get home!" She winked at Lynn who seemed pleased with her gift choice.

The vibrator was too impersonal for Jamie. She did try it, then tossed it in the dresser. She took measures into her own hands. She had learned how to pleasure herself without a mechanical aid and did a fine job of it.

Stripped down she stood in front of the mirror. Jamie took a look at herself with a critical eye. Long strawberry blonde hair framed her youthful face. It was hard to guess her age, people were surprised to hear how old she was, mid-thirties, thirty-eight if you counted. Her body was firm. That came from riding her bike daily. Exercise kept her sane that first year she was on her own.

Jamie reached up and cradled her full breasts then watched her reflection as she moved a hand down her flat stomach to her thighs. She tapped gently on her tan skin, her long red nails looked like tiny kisses in the mirror. She felt the air caress her body and longed to be touched.

The feeling was too intense to ignore. Jamie sat down on the edge of the bed and eased herself into a position where her fingers could play. She closed her eyes and let her imagination run wild. The tension mounted and then gave way as deep waves of pleasure filled her.

The intensity of the moment brought tears to her eyes. She wanted to feel hands on her body, just not her own. She wondered what type of man would make her feel like a woman again. Her fantasy life was her only companion in bed.

Enough! The word echoed in Jamie's head. She wanted to have a real sex life again. Maybe find someone she'd like to spend some time with.

Now that's a fantasy. Jamie shook her head. *A good man may be hard to find, but I bet I can find a hard man who will be good to me.* Her mood lifted as she thought about the night ahead.

Her earlier worries about dating were gone. Just like her marriage was. Time had a way of blurring the past. Perhaps that was not a bad thing. Her only thought now was to find a man and have sex. She hated being this pent up and it was time to change that.

Jamie looked at the clock. It was already after eight. She didn't shower but left the scent of her own sex on her thighs. *Let's see if anyone notices.* She didn't know if she felt naughty or desperate.

She found her favorite dress in the closet, a short silver sundress that shimmered when she moved. The length was youthful but she carried it well. Jamie slipped on her bra, stepped into the dress, and pulled on her tiny white lace thong.

A quick stop by the bathroom to brush her teeth, put on lip-gloss, and run a pick through her hair to untangle it was next. Her face was flushed from her earlier playtime. *You look marvelous.* She smiled in the mirror and blew a kiss to herself.

Jamie stepped into her sandals, grabbed her purse, and locked the door behind her.

Her heart raced with anticipation. She wondered what the night would bring.

2
SUSAN

Susan leaned back in her chair and took a sip of sherry. She looked at what she'd just written. A big grin crossed her face. *That was easier than I thought it would be.* She fanned herself. *Is it hot, or did I get worked up with that scene?* Pleased her first chapter was written, she still felt a bit nervous. *I wonder how my fans are going to like this.* 'This' being a change in her writing genre.

The idea to write an erotic novel came to her after a horrible TV sitcom pitch at the writers' convention a few weeks earlier. The agent did not have the paperwork the writers' club had sent him. She was too nervous to remember the synopsis she had so carefully prepared. Her mind went blank on the logline for her script. Five minutes, out of a ten-minute pitch session, were spent talking about the lost paperwork. He yawned, totally disinterested, as he looked at his watch. His exact words, which Susan felt would echo in her mind for all eternity were, "So, are there any other characters other than you and the dog?"

She had an idea for a TV show based on the dog column she wrote for an online magazine. *Widow*, check, make that *single gal*, and her dog about town. It had all the makings of a fun sitcom, until she had to talk about it.

What a jerk. She was annoyed at his response and toyed with a smart-ass reply, then let it go. Her brain was fried and she couldn't think. Disappointed put it mildly. The plot had so much more to offer and she was not prepared with her delivery. She was mad at him, but madder at herself.

She remembered her late husband. Knew exactly what he would have said.

"Remember the Seven P's." He loved that old military adage, even though he had never been in the service. "Proper Planning and Preparation Prevents Piss Poor Performance."

It was a mouthful. But if she had planned better, she would not have felt like her foot landed in her mouth when she tried to give her pitch.

She came home from the conference determined to try something different. At lunch she'd listened to women authors talk about their books. Sex was the topic of the day. Intriguing plots, good women who were naughty as hell, and sex that sizzled.

"I don't think I can write a novel from beginning to end." That was her lament to all her friends. "I like my essays. Short and sassy." Susan had found a way to weave her personal experiences into stories her readers liked. The online dog column boosted her book sales and everyone loved Daisy's antics. She wrote from real life, not about made-up characters. Writing fiction would be a challenge. Especially if she had to write about sex. She was inexperienced with one and out of practice with the other.

No sex in three years, I hope it's like riding a bike . . . Susan kidded herself, but it was not as funny as it sounded. A widow for four years, she dated that first year trying to come to terms with being single, then stopped cold turkey. Sex seemed surreal to her now. *And now I want to write about it.* There was irony there, Susan felt certain.

Three years ago Susan found the true passion in her life. She started writing. In the dark hours of the evening she created her new reality at the computer. The sadness at being a widow was replaced with the beauty of words. She was a shopkeeper during the day and a *soon to be author* working at night.

Susan wrote two books in two years. Thanks to changes in the publishing industry it was easy to get them in print and into E-book format. The day she held the first paper-back copy of her essays, she smiled like an idiot and called Emily. "It's here. It's beautiful." Everything else paled in comparison. That was when she decided to sell her antique shop and write full time.

She had a loyal fan base that identified with her misadventures and then, *the thing* writers hope for the most, happened. *About Town*, an on-line national magazine, contacted her. One of their editors had read her books. "We'd like you to write a monthly dog-column for us. Pay is small, but there are freelance opportunities too." Susan wanted the work, the pay was a bonus. She wasn't rich, but the sale of her shop and small insurance policy kept her comfortable. The rest was kismet.

She felt successful, but worried her material was getting stale and panicked it would show in her work. She wanted, needed, something new.

I can do this. Susan tried hard to convince herself. *If I can write twelve-hundred word essays about Daisy's bad behavior, maybe putting a naked man between the sheets will inspire me to greatness!*

That dumb ass agent might have been the best thing to happen to her if she used that horrible moment to try something out of her comfort zone. Strong willed and determined, Susan liked to kid her friends that when things went amuck, *lemons into lemonade with a shot of tequila.*

That weekend a story started to form. The name Jamie popped into her mind and her character began to come to life. She didn't know the plot line yet, but she knew it would be loaded with sex. Dirty sex. Fun sex. Page turning sex!

Susan took a sip of sherry. The change came with its own set of fears. For a moment she felt chilled. *Am I opening a can of worms?* She'd only written the first chapter and it embarrassed her, not while she wrote it, but afterwards, when she read it. *How much is too much sex? All that foreplay and no male character. That will raise some eyebrows.*

"When you write about sex, keep it in line with your character, or you will appear foolish." Her writing instructor had emphasized in a lecture on sex in storytelling a few years ago.

She didn't want to look foolish and she didn't want to write about sex just to write about sex. *I want a great story that's just sexy as hell.* It seemed like a good plan in her mind. All she had to do was get over herself, her worries, and just do it.

Susan had not told anyone what she was working on. Perhaps it was time.

She looked at the clock. Almost six. She had to drive to Atlanta to meet her best friend Emily for dinner at seven. At least the drive would be against the traffic.

Susan and Daisy headed down the hall to the bedroom. Daisy jumped up on the bed and curled up. Susan pulled her favorite Bohemian lacy black top out of the closet and grabbed her Milagros heart necklace and silver earrings off the painted dresser. She left on her jeans and slipped her feet into her black flat pumps. A quick trip to the bathroom to brush her teeth, put on her favorite *Kiss Me Pink* lip-gloss, a dab of blush, fluff her long dark hair, a bit of perfume, and she was ready to go.

"You look marvelous, darling." Susan blew a kiss at the mirror, tossed a tiny biscuit at Daisy, grabbed her keys, and flew out the door. *Dressed and on the road in less than ten minutes. That's a record for me.* She gave herself a thumbs up and turned the key in the ignition.

She couldn't wait to hear what Emily would have to say about her book idea and opening chapter. She was excited about the night ahead.

Naughty or Nice? What shall I be? Susan giggled to herself and stepped on the gas pedal.

3
Dinner at a Cozy Bistro

"This is just between us!" Susan blurted out her news as soon as they ordered wine. "I am writing something new. A bit of sexy fiction. Finished my first chapter this afternoon." She caught her breath and raced on. "My book starts with the character Jamie playing with herself." Susan hesitated, leaned closer to Emily, and whispered, "You know, masturbating." Her face heated up and she blushed at the word. She waited for Emily's reaction.

"No way!" Emily slapped her hand over her mouth and let out a huge laugh. "Bite me! What brought this on?" Emily reached for her glass of Chablis, then paused before taking a drink. "Seriously, this is quite a switch from what you usually write. But I am pretty much over all the dog stories."

"Come on, everyone loves my dog stories." Susan grabbed her water glass, her wine could wait. She was nervous and her mouth felt parched. "That writers' conference and I guess that stupid agent. Made me think it was time to branch out, mix it up a bit. Seemed like a plan. Now I wonder…"

"Wonder what, sweetie? I think this is great!" Emily eyed her friend and a devious smile crossed her lips. "I'll be happy to read it for you. Need a bit of excitement myself!"

"Of course. I want you to be my beta reader. Just remember it is *fiction*. Don't think I am doing what I'm writing." Susan's smile lit up her face. "Well, maybe just a tiny bit." She winked at Emily. They always teased each other. This was not the time to become a prude.

"So tell me more. What is the plot? And how much sex are you putting in the book?"

"I don't know yet. A work in progress." Susan thought for a moment and a frown crossed her face. "I'm still not really comfortable with some of the words. Honestly, do you think it is okay for me to do this?"

"Why not? Everyone is writing sex these days. Look at that book that hit it big a year or so ago. Hear they are making a movie out of it. I even saw several features on the six o'clock news about authors and erotica. Who would have thought it was so mainstream?" Emily paused and eyed Susan closely. "You need to get out of that damn dog writing mode. I hope you are not putting a dog in your book. Now that would be sick."

Susan let out a hearty laugh and shook her head. "Now my dog stories have helped pay my bills. But no, Jamie does not have a dog. Happy?"

"So are you doing research or trying to remember what it was like to have sex? You haven't dated now in, let's see, how many years?" Emily liked to prod her friend. "Oh yes, I remember, three. You really need to get a life."

"I like my life! I just want to write something different." Susan felt a little defensive. Emily did not understand some of her choices. She didn't want to overreact and sidetracked the subject.

"As far as sex goes, you got plenty of details that first year after Steve died and I was a bit crazy. So give it up. Admit I've had my share of scandalous sex. And of course, Steve…" Susan's voice drifted off. She never shared sex stories about Steve. That was sacred ground. But her few dates were fair game. "My stories about Carl kept you in a frenzy as I recall."

"Sure did. I miss all those wild details. Felt as if I'd been to bed with him. Not that I met him. But I sure felt as though I knew him!" Emily gave her friend a sly smile. "Looking back, maybe you embellished a bit. He wasn't really all that great. Isn't that what writers do?"

"No way. It was all true. That tongue…" Susan rolled her eyes. They both let out a raucous laugh. She and Emily loved to cut up and act silly. They were the same age, thirty-eight. Their birthdays were a month apart. Their friendship went back to when they were in grade school together. Best friends always.

"Stop it. I'm going to choke on my wine!" Emily roared. She flicked a strand of long blonde hair off her cheek

"Wild ass in bed. That was Carl." Susan took a small sip from her glass. "Now it is just me and Daisy. Is that pitiful? Brought it on my-self." She thought back to Carl and damn if she didn't still get excited remembering the sex.

Carl was never really a boyfriend, she wasn't even sure *friends with benefits* would fit either. She met him through an online dating site a few months after Steve died. She had no kids and no family close by, and the nights were unbearable. She also missed the sex. He was ten years her junior. Every Saturday night he would come over, bring a little weed, some beer, and plop in front of her TV. He worked hard in construction and just wanted a place to crash and have sex. She couldn't talk to him unless he got stoned or a bit drunk, then he would turn into a great lover. His mouth traveled her body and took her plac-es that made her forget everything. Her heart wasn't in being with him after the sex was over. By midnight she sent him packing. That went on for all of two months.

It didn't end well. She realized on that last night, as great as the sex was, he made her nervous. He shrugged when she said it was probably best he not come back. He packed up his cooler, kissed her on the cheek, and walked out the door. "See ya." The last words she heard from him.

She never saw him again.

She hadn't had sex since either.

"Hello, earth to Susan." Emily snapped her back from her thoughts. "Where did you go? Clearly missing in action."

Susan laughed. "Sorry, thinking about my book." She didn't want to talk about Carl again.

"So fill me in with some more details. Are you getting kinky? You don't want to bore your readers with sex in the missionary position." Emily leaned forward, her elbows on the table. "Spill it."

"Nothing wrong with the missionary position!" Susan poked at her friend. "Hey, right now any position would work for me. Feel like a virgin again."

"I think it is official — you are a virgin again. Anyone who has gone without sex for several years gets to be reborn as one. So what are you doing to get inspired?" Emily sat back straight in her chair and shook her head. "Can't believe you aren't nuts without sex!"

"Who says I'm not?" Susan batted her eyes. She lowered her voice a bit. "I've watched a little porn on the computer. It's all inspiring…NOT. I don't know why anyone thinks they look good with all that woo ha showing." Susan blushed. "I have learned a few things, however!"

"Maybe Al and I should watch some porn. Get some life back in the old dog." Emily's nose crinkled. "He's a great guy, but our hot days are definitely behind us."

"At least you're having sex. I'm not." Susan sighed.

"Can I get you ladies something else?" The cute male waiter appeared out of nowhere. Susan looked at the smile on his face and wondered if he'd heard her last comment.

"We're fine!" Emily eyed the slender guy standing next to the table. "We may order in a bit."

"I'll check back in ten. Give you time to finish your conversation." He gave them a mischievous grin and walked away.

"Nice ass. He looks like a young version of Al. Maybe that will put you in the mood when you get home tonight." Susan picked up on her friend's lustful look.

"Shut up!" Emily laughed.

Susan thought about Emily. She'd had a bad divorce eight years ago. She was lucky she found a good guy so soon after. Good guys were hard to come by. Al moved in with her three months after they met and they were still living joyfully unwed. She loved Emily and was happy for her.

"A toast to you and Al. We should order. I'm hungry and need to sober up before my drive home."

During dinner they talked about her book.

"Try to remember to put a guy in bed. We all know how to do it ourselves." Emily had to tease her about that opening chapter. "I want to read Jamie down and dirty with a MALE."

"I'm getting there, don't you worry. I may not be having sex, but Jamie will have all the sex anyone could want. With herself and with any Tom, Dick, or Harry. Well, with any *dick* she wants. That's my story and I'm sticking to it." Susan tapped her empty coffee cup against the table to make her point. Then she shook her head. "How crazy is that?"

"I'm with you, babe. It's time you loosen up and have some fun." Emily squeezed Susan's hand. "I sure wish you'd start dating again. Find someone. I hate that you're alone." Emily teased her friend all the time, but she worried Susan had isolated herself in that big old farmhouse miles from her friends. She never understood the move and Susan rarely talked about why she did it.

"I'm not alone. I have my dog, my writing, and my fabulous dream farmhouse! Dating does not interest me at the moment."

"I stand corrected." Emily looked at Susan and shook her head. "You can stop making those faces."

"Good! Now, I've got to run. It's late and Daisy is alone."

"My treat." Emily grabbed the check from Susan. "Least I can do for all that exciting conversation." She laughed, then got serious. "We need to do this more often."

Susan's worries about her book came back as soon as she sat in her car. Was her first chapter enough to draw in a reader or would it be a turn off? She didn't read erotica and didn't plan to start now. She'd have to figure out her own words. This stressed her more than any dog story did.

The night had a nice feel to it. Susan took a deep breath. *I am over thinking this whole thing.* She shut off the A/C and opened the van's window. The soft breeze toyed with her long dark hair. Susan turned on the radio and cranked up the volume until the music blasted out into the night. All her tension slipped away as she sang at the top of her lungs on the ride home.

THERE IS NO PLACE LIKE HOME
—L. FRANK BAUM

4
THE FARMHOUSE

Susan pulled in her driveway, turned off the ignition, and took a long look at the farmhouse. The house took on a bit of magic at night. The solar lights strung along the porch railing looked like tiny stars. A bit tacky on an old house, but she didn't care. There was a light shining in each of the windows, both downstairs and up. Susan hated coming home to a dark house. She could hear Daisy's piercing bark. That dog knew the minute she was home. She wasn't quite ready to head in.

Visiting with Emily brought back memories of the night she told her friends about the farmhouse. She surprised them with her big announcement last May over dinner at the same place she and Emily met tonight.

"I've got something to tell you, so grab a glass of wine." She was nervous. She wasn't sure how they would take her news. She swallowed, got up her courage, and smiled at Emily, Cheryl, and Diane. "I've bought an old farmhouse in Safe Haven, a tiny town about an hour from here."

Three blank faces stared back at her. She knew this was not good.

Diane was the first to speak. "Is Safe Haven that place where they shot that TV mystery show a few years back? Not much there as I recall."

Cheryl popped in. "That was Cedar Lake. Safe Haven is up by the college. But you are right. Nothing there. Not even a Starbucks."

Emily actually started to cry. "Why would you want to leave your friends and move to the middle of nowhere?"

Susan couldn't answer Emily's question. She was still trying to figure it out herself. Her life was full. She was not unhappy. She just didn't want to be in her house any longer. *Their* house when Steve was alive, that no matter how she tried to make it hers, it never happened. The memories of her life with Steve were too deeply embedded. The house was a constant reminder of what she had lost, but it was also the source of her ability to move on. It sold quickly when she put it on the market.

Susan worked hard to find the perfect house, her dream house. She spent most nights after she finished writing looking at homes on-line. The farmhouse popped up during one of her late night searches. The photos convinced her she needed to see it in person.

She called the realtor the next morning and had an appointment mid-afternoon. It was a straight shot up the expressway, then ten miles on a country road. She saw the railroad tracks, crossed over them, and came face to face with the weathered town sign. *Welcome to Safe Haven, Georgia.* The sign was old, hanging from two tall slate columns, but beneath it a newer placard read *Population 323.* Susan chuckled at the size of the town in comparison to Atlanta.

The downtown area was so small, if she blinked she might miss it. Six one story brick buildings ran flush with the tracks. Two were empty with *For Rent* signs in the windows. The other four were just what you would expect in a postage size town; insurance agent, plumber, beauty shop, and a small café. The charm was undeniable.

Her directions said to follow the main street until you came to the church, then make a turn right. As her van turned the corner the house came in to view. The gray shingled, two story farmhouse, with a huge front wrap around porch and tin roof, matched the online photos perfectly. She parked in the driveway and hopped out of her van. Susan was so excited she didn't see the agent standing behind the *for sale* sign.

"Hi. I'm Ann. Did you have trouble finding your way?" She held out her hand and smiled. "I live twenty minutes up the road by Community College so know the area well. It's easy to miss the turn off if you haven't been here before."

She reached her hand out to shake Ann's. "Easy drive. The place looks lovely."

The yard was picture perfect with its blue hydrangea bushes and pink roses spilling off an old arbor. Short granite walls, topped with rusty white iron fencing, bordered the front yard.

"What smells so lush?" Susan was taken with a sweet odor that was thick and exotic.

"Japanese Honeysuckle." Ann pointed to vines crawling up the porch rails. "I love its fragrance. The creek area is overrun with it." Ann smiled at Susan. "Wait until you see the gardens out back. Let's head there first."

Susan followed Ann through a rusty metal gate at the end of the driveway. "As I told you on the phone, the lot is two acres. The land was originally part of the Miller farm. Mr. Miller gave his daughter, Flora, two acres when she married. This house was built as a wedding present for Flora and her husband. The original family house is on the lot behind you. It's been vacant for years. You'll see it from the back fence line."

The back yard was as charming as the front. Established flower beds with fragrant perennials and scented herbs were in bloom. The left side of the yard was framed with a huge, cobbled stone wall, at least her height. A farm fence ran the length of the back and separated her property from the Miller farm. Tall trees and underbrush made it hard to see anything beyond the fence. A brick patio, with a built in fireplace and chimney, sat outside the kitchen door. The wooded creek area was to the far right.

"The patio is a great place to entertain year round." Ann bent down and plucked a branch off a tall spindly plant, rubbed it with her fingers, and offered it to Susan. "It smells divine. Rosemary. Folklore says, *Rosemary grows where a woman rules*. It's just one of the many herbs the owners grew for cooking."

"It's like a secret garden back here!" Susan looked around the large expanse of land. It was a very private yard for being in the center of a tiny town. She couldn't see any other houses. It was as if she were hidden away from the world. Just what she wanted.

"It *is* a special yard." Ann turned to Susan. "The creek area makes you feel as if you are cut off from civilization. Runs from the side yard to the far street, over a third of the acreage. It's a bit of a jungle. It was left natural for that very reason, privacy."

"What's that small building?" Susan pointed to a wood structure with a tin roof. It was in rough shape compared to everything else.

"The original dry shed for fruits and vegetables. With some work it would make a sweet studio. Right now it's full of old doors and windows. It is beat up looking, but charming, don't you think?" Ann turned to Susan. "There used to be a grand garden by it. Onions, asparagus, tomatoes, can't remember what else. They did a lot of canning too. You'll see the pantry in the house."

Susan shaded her eyes and looked back towards the Miller farm. "Why hasn't someone bought the farmhouse?"

"The owners refuse to sell it. It's sad they are letting the old house go to ruin and the property run wild." Ann shook her head. "The folks around here hold on to their land. It's a fluke this house is on the market. The owner grew up here, married, renovated the house, and then got a job offer on the West coast."

A good sales pitch, Susan thought, but the house didn't need one. Her mind was already calculating what she could get for her place to buy this one.

"Most of the neighbors are elderly. There are the two cottages across the street and the house on the other side of that wall. If you look down the road, you can see the church and smaller bungalows. It's a very quiet area. No one should bother you, I think that was a concern of yours." Ann wasn't sure if Susan was worried about safety or a bit anti-social. Writers could be strange.

"Good to know." Susan replied and smiled. She loved the backyard and was mentally placing all her old garden chairs and tables when Ann interrupted her.

"Ready to see the inside? You're going to love the house!"

Susan followed Ann back to the front door where she fiddled with the lockbox. Ann was right. Susan was smitten as soon as she stepped through the beautifully carved door, with its colored glass inserts, into a huge room with nine foot ceilings, pine floors, and a corner fireplace.

"The house is 2600 square feet, give or take. There are nine foot ceilings and pine floors in all the rooms. Every room has a fireplace, but they have been closed off, except for the one in the kitchen." Ann handed a flyer to Susan. "You can read it all here and in the disclosure. The central heat and air are new too."

She looked at the space and light in the front room and felt at home. Her mind was already made up. Perhaps it had been made up before she got there. She was going to live here. "I want to make an offer before I leave today." She turned to Ann. "Show me the other rooms, but I can tell you right now, I'm buying this place!"

"I'll give you the tour and then we'll get down to business and do the paperwork." Ann ushered Susan through the center hall.

The downstairs was spacious. Living room, dining room, center hall, small second bedroom, master bedroom, bathroom, and a kitchen with a built in pantry. Susan mentally made the small bedroom her office. The large windows with their old wavy glass let in tons of sunlight.

"The kitchen is really the heart of this house." Ann led her to the long wide room, with four tall windows, each with a built-in window seat.

Susan gasped as they entered the kitchen. "It's incredible!"

"I knew you'd love it. The owners did a fantastic job in here." Ann smiled, pleased. "There's even a locking pet door."

Susan was glad the door locked. Daisy never went out alone. She turned her attention to the rest of the kitchen. The room was large enough to place a huge farm table and chairs down the center. The old cabinets with glass doors had been freshly painted white. The stove and refrigerator were new, stainless steel. A sky light let sun flood over the pine floors. A brick fireplace was on the wall opposite the tall windows.

Ann pointed to the white globe light fixtures. "All original, but restored and rewired. The cast iron sink is original, but again restored. The counter tops are salvaged green tiles."

Susan looked around the room. As excited as she was, a calm came over her. She knew her life was about to change. The house was what she'd been waiting for.

"Let's go upstairs." Ann guided her towards the stairs with its graceful curved wood railing.

The second floor kept more of the original features of the house. The bathroom sported a claw foot tub, cast iron sink, beadboard walls, and a window similar to the front door, with its colored glass inserts. The toilet was a newer addition. There were two more bedrooms, a sitting room, and a large landing with a window at one end. Susan did a quick run through in her mind. The house would hold all her antiques and art, plus she could still buy a few special pieces when the shopping urge hit.

"I love everything about the house. Let's do it." Susan didn't want to waste another minute. How could she go wrong buying her dream farmhouse in a tiny town called Safe Haven?

"We can write up the offer in the kitchen, if you like. I've got all the papers with me." Ann patted her briefcase.

That was a year ago. She never regretted the move.

Daisy was in a barking frenzy when she unlocked the door. Susan plopped her purse on the counter, lifted Daisy for a kiss, then put her back on the floor.

"Come on, girl. Let's go out!"

Daisy, a seven pound mixed breed puff of fur, twirled around her feet, yapping out of control. Susan followed her outside and waited on the patio until Daisy finished her business. "All done?" Susan scooped the little pooch up and headed back in.

Her computer beckoned to her. She grabbed a glass and her bottle of sherry and sat down. Talking to Emily earlier had energized her. And as much as she hated to admit it, thinking of Carl turned her on. She felt pleasure thinking of his hands and mouth on her and wanted to capture the essence of him in her writing before it faded away.

Susan's fingers moved to the keyboard. Jamie was going to have the time of her life tonight.

5
Jim

Jim looked at the clock. It was after eleven. His neighbor was back. He wasn't spying on her, but he always knew when she got home. Couldn't miss the yapping of her little dog. It was a sharp, shrill sound that floated across the expanse of ground between the houses, over the stone wall, and into his open window. Irritating, but the dog was never out long.

She had moved in a year ago, six months after he did. He had not met her, nor had any of the neighbors had a proper introduction. Rumor had it she was a writer who liked her privacy. A widow from Atlanta. Unfriendly. She kept to herself and no one intruded on her.

Occasionally he caught a glimpse of her coming and going in her van or cutting flowers in her front yard. On a rare occasion he saw her from his upstairs window when she was out in the back with her dog. She looked like a beauty from afar, with her long dark hair and athletic build. It was hard to believe she had such a bad reputation with the locals.

I wonder if she has any idea she is the talk of the town. Jim shook his head. She had replaced the gossip about him. He'd been the center of interest when he moved into his father's place. He hadn't been home in years. He was glad no one knew the real truth why he came back.

His dad closed up the house five years earlier. He was tired of living along, rambling from room to room in his old age. His health was not the best either. He moved into an assisted living apartment closer to the college and his son. When Jim suggested he sell or rent the place, his dad, like most of the homeowners in that small community, refused to sell and was not open to renters. His final words on that subject were clear. "I'll be damned if I let strangers in my house!" The house sat vacant. Jim inherited it when his dad died. At forty he was renovating the old homestead.

He never planned to move back home, but his old girlfriend caused so many problems for him, he needed a break from all the scandal. The gossip in this small community was minor compared to what he had endured after Monica started rumors about him at the college. He taught writing at Community College. She was an instructor there too. They had a whirlwind romance and she moved in with him. When they broke up, she went about trying to ruin his reputation. She damn near came close to it too

They lived together a few months when he realized she was not the gal he thought she was. As easy-going as he considered himself, she was the opposite. She pushed him to the limits. Her jealousy scared him. She stalked him around the campus, convinced he was cheating on her with younger students, and pitched a fit when he confronted her about her behavior. One night after she made a horrific scene in front of a colleague, with more of the same accusations, he'd had enough. He told her to move out. She didn't take it well, but she packed her things and left that same week. He was relieved it ended without more fanfare.

Only later did he find out the stories she was telling anyone who would listen. *I moved because he threatened me. He hit me more than once.* His good friends stood by him, but strangers gave him strange looks. The police questioned him once and then dropped it. None of it was true, but protesting too much only made him look worse. He let it ride its course, lost a few so-called acquaintances, and was lucky it didn't cause him problems with his teaching position. He heard from a friend Monica had moved in with another instructor and started the same crap with him. *Poor guy*, Jim shook his head remembering it all. *At least she's not my problem anymore.*

This house was his escape. He kept his apartment by the college. The house was still full of the family furnishings, so he only packed some clothes and books to bring with him. Working on the house was the distraction he needed.

His neighbor Mildred kept him filled in on the latest gossip about himself. He also figured she started most of it. Mildred was in her early seventies, had short curly gray hair, and a portly figure. She lived in polyester pants and a T-shirt with tulips embroidered on it. She was his neighbor directly across the street and was especially keen on keeping an eye on him. He'd pull in his drive around dinner and by the time he hopped out of his pick-up truck, Mildred was on her front lawn waving to him.

He remembered the evening she introduced herself with a batch of cookies.

"Just finished baking these. Thought you'd enjoy them." She thrust a paper plate full of oatmeal raisin cookies at him. The plastic wrap was still warm to the touch. "So, you're Emmett's son? I heard he passed. What happened to him?" Mildred caught her breath then continued before he could answer. "We liked him when he lived here, but he moved so suddenly. Then let the place just gather dust."

"These are great!" Jim took a huge bite out of one of the cookies. "Sorry, hungry, and these looked too good to wait. Still warm and soft." He did his best to avoid her nosy questions. Whatever he said he knew would be passed on as soon as he went inside.

"You are avoiding my question." Mildred smiled at him as she pressured him for details. "Your dad, what happened to him?"

"Heart attack in his sleep." Jim couldn't ignore Mildred any longer. He was glad his dad went quickly. He'd been ill, but not in pain. Then his heart just gave out. "A surprise to everyone when it happened."

"We never heard about a service for him. Neighbors here would have gone." Mildred shook her head, full of sympathy, but one ear still cocked for gossip. "Glad you came back home."

"I inherited the old home place and decided I'd like to give a run at country life. Seems so quiet here. No crime to speak of. Nice change of pace. The drive to work is easy too." Jim took another bite from the cookie he had started. "You sure know how to bake a mean cookie."

Months later he wished Mildred could share some news about Susan, but she kept her distance from Susan's front door. "You don't go barging in where you ain't welcomed. That Realtor told it like it was." Mildred cornered Ann the day she took her sign down, before Susan moved in. "She wants us to stay clear, have her privacy, so be it."

As much as he wanted to meet her, caution prevailed. He decided to let her make the first move if their paths crossed. He wasn't timid, but he didn't want to step in where all the signs pointed to stay clear. He'd had all the women woes he cared to deal with.

Small town life gave him an opportunity to get away from his problems, but it was lonely at night. He never brought anyone to his house, especially a date. Mildred would certainly have lots to talk about if he did. She even questioned him on his sexual preference after a few months.

"You're a good looking guy. How come we don't see any gals over here? You date girls, don't you?" She was as subtle as a train wreck. He didn't think of himself as good looking. He felt rather average. Six feet tall, thin, with dark hair that curled if he let it grow. He did not stand out in a crowd, yet women were drawn to him. His apartment was where he entertained if the occasion presented itself. A strange woman spending the night with him in Safe Haven would surely raise the level of gossip

His life had changed since the incident with Monica. As much as he thought he'd put everything behind him, there were times it still haunted him, made him angry. That's when he worked late at night, pounding away with his hammer until he was too tired to care.

The dog's yapping stopped. *She must be back in the house,* Jim decided. He had to find a way to meet her. The quiet nights were driving him crazy and he spent too much time thinking about a neighbor he knew very little about. The only real life he had in the old house was his renovation and a growing fantasy on the girl next door.

6
JAMIE'S NIGHT OUT

Jamie sat in her Mustang, a 1966 dark green metallic coupe, and cranked the engine. The car purred as she backed down the drive. Her destination was Harry's, a local bar and dance club. Harry's had a reputation as the local pick-up spot for the over thirty crowd. Jamie's plan for the evening was a simple one. Pick up a man and have sex.

She wiggled in her bucket seat and tugged at the hem of her dress. It rode up on her when she got in the car. She resisted the urge to touch herself as she pulled her hem over her tan thighs. The last thing she needed to do was run the Mustang off the road. Her senses heightened as she thought of the evening ahead. Now if she could just find someone to accommodate her desires, the night would be hers for the asking.

Jamie saw the *valet parking* sign as she turned into the drive. She was glad she had cash on her. Normally she only carried her debit card, but for some reason she opted for cash back when she paid for her groceries earlier that week. *Maybe that's a good sign I'm supposed to be here!* Jamie liked to think signs guided her somewhat erratic behavior.

She smiled as the valet walked towards her. He eyed her Mustang with approval. When Jamie moved her legs to the side to step out of the car, the valet reached for her hand to help her. She could have gotten herself out, but his touch was welcomed. Touch was her goal for the night. She smiled sweetly at him.

"Take care of my baby, hon. I don't want to see a scratch on her when I come back later."

"I'll be good to her. Be good to you too if you'd let me." The valet winked at her. Jamie figured he was in his late twenties. She guessed he flirted with all the older women for his tips.

She liked his looks. His bald head, slightly unshaven face, and dark eyes made him look hot, sizzling hot. *I'd like for him to be good to me too.* Jamie glanced back at him as she headed towards the bar.

Two tall, heavy set men in suits flanked the doorway. They pulled the double doors open for her. "Enjoy your evening." They seemed to say this in unison. It was dark in the large room. The only light came from candles on the table and the large disco ball over the dance floor. She let her eyes adjust to the room. The tables were packed with couples, except for a group of younger women wearing paper hats at the large round table close to the dance floor. *A party,* Jamie thought. She turned her interest to the bar. That is where she needed to be if she was going to meet someone. The lights were dim there too. Just enough light for the bartender to mix and serve drinks.

"Excuse me." Jamie pushed her way between two men at the bar. They were not talking to each other, so she didn't feel she was being rude. "What's a girl got to do to get a drink here?" She sounded perkier than she felt. But it was already late and she didn't have time to wait for someone to approach her.

"This one's on me." The man on her right touched her arm to get her attention. "What will it be young lady?"

Jamie turned and gave him her best smile. "I'll have whatever you're drinking." She hoped it was something strong.

"Bartender! Another shot of Jack Black!"

Jamie took a good look at him. Early forties. It was hard to tell in the low light. His dark hair had a hint of gray peppered through it and his face weathered, like he'd been in the sun too long. *Tan and tough looking,* Jamie thought. He was dressed in jeans, a casual blazer over a black T-shirt, and black boots. She decided he had a well-worn cowboy look to him. *Not really my type,* she eyed him closely, *but certainly someone to flirt with.*

"What are you doing out by yourself tonight, pretty lady?" The man was tall as he smiled down at her. His smile was friendly, but his eyes took in her low top.

"Just out for a bit of fun." Jamie had to raise her voice, the record that started to play was louder than the last. "And you?"

"In town for a meeting, then fly back out to Memphis tomorrow afternoon. I'm in town a few times a month." He took a quick shot and moved in closer to her.

Jamie had no room to back away and decided to enjoy the intimacy of the moment. He had a presence that fascinated her. She tilted her head and smiled up at him. "What type of meeting?"

She hated small talk, but she was at a bar trying to get picked up. Her smile must have encouraged him. She felt his hand touch her lower back and slide down to her butt.

"Well, Jamestown is a friendly place, but not quite that much." Jamie reached for his hand, placed it back on the counter, and gently slapped it. She'd hoped that made her point.

He pushed back closer to her. This time his smile was not so nice. "You come in here flaunting that body like you want something more than a shot of whiskey. I just paid good money for that Black. Least you can do is let me put my arm around you."

Jamie didn't know what she wanted to do. She hadn't been around a man in so long, anyone who showed interest might just get lucky tonight. She toyed with the idea of going further with him.

"I'm not gonna hurt you. Just want my money's worth." His hand was back on her. This time he slid it down the front of her skirt as she faced the bar. She felt his hand touch her thigh and start to move up. Jamie let out a tiny gasp of surprise. No one at the bar could see what he was doing. She did nothing to stop him. Part pleasure, part fear. She didn't want this with him, but the rush she felt as his hand caressed her skin was exciting. She wondered how far he would go. Would she stop him? She didn't know her own mind at that moment.

The music was loud, playing oldies. Jamie looked into the mirror over the bar and saw the dance floor behind her. Couples moved under the rotating disco ball. The flashes of light and the shot of Jack Black made her dizzy. She wanted to go home and go to sleep. In spite of herself, she felt a surge of pleasure. He was stroking her thigh and she was aroused. She was not frightened of him, but afraid of what she might allow him to do in that crowded bar.

"Maybe you'd like to go back to my room, little lady?" His hand squeezed her thigh, moving closer to the space between her legs. She felt his fingers on the edge of her thong. At any moment his fingers could slip inside the lace …

This is so not what I had in mind. Jamie wanted to pull away. She had come in looking for action, but now that she found it, she realized it seemed all wrong. The flash of excitement vanished and panic started to take its place.

"Ah, there you are!" A deep male voice caught her off guard. She turned her head and met the valet's dark eyes. "Got off early and since your car was still here, thought I'd see if I could find you in this dark cavern. That little silver dress shines even in these low lights."

He looked at her stunned face. "My uncle owns the place. I fill in sometimes when there is a huge crowd."

To Jamie's relief, the cowboy moved his hand back to the bar.

"Hey, Jackson." The valet slapped him on the shoulder. "Good to see you. How are things in Memphis and how is the Mrs.?"

Jamie was giddy from relief and ecstatic to have a Prince Charming come to her rescue.

"Was just on my way out. Good to see you Tom. Give your uncle my best."

The valet put out his hand to introduce himself. "Tom. But I think you just heard Jackson say that."

"Jamie." She held his hand for a moment longer than necessary.

"I bet we can get a table. Can I buy you a drink?"

"I'd like that."

He reached for her arm and guided her to an empty table.

"Oh, this is where the party was earlier. A group of girls, maybe ten of them, all in the funniest hats."

"Well, we are party central here. Mid-week the rates are better for drinks and the bar offers specials. Pack them in here all week long."

He pulled a chair out for her and sat down in the one next to her.

"Hey, Tom, what can I get you?" The barmaid came up quickly.

Her tight bodice pushed her already large breasts up in the air. The outfit she wore had a medieval look about it, except the skirt cut off right below her butt.

"Jamie, what will it be?" Tom had the brightest smile she had ever seen.

"Riesling would be perfect. Thanks."

"Usual beer for you, Tom?"

"You got it. Thanks, Midge."

Star struck. That is how she felt. The evening had gone from bad to worse and then, by some miracle, to wonderful.

"So do you buy drinks for all the ladies when you park their cars?"

Tom reached up and moved a strand of hair from her face. "No. I have a thing for cars, especially an older model like yours. Thought you might give me a ride sometime."

The car had been Jack's, but she loved to drive it. "It would be my pleasure." She was glad to know he liked older models. Perhaps he would like her.

"One wine and beer coming up." Midge and her breasts were back. Jamie couldn't miss her perfume as she bent to place their drinks on the table. It was a lovely scent. Jamie wondered if she had a thing for Tom or if the two of them had dated. Had sex to be more specific.

She was already feeling possessive about Tom. He was adorable, young, and just what she needed to fill her lonely nights.

Tom touched her hand. "Want to dance? That way I can hold you close and still be a gentleman."

A slow song played as they moved to the dance floor. The disco ball seemed kinder now that she was under it. Tom had his arm around her and pulled her close, gently. She rested her head on his shoulder. He felt solid and smelled wonderful even after an evening parking cars in the heat. They swayed together more than danced. She felt her face flush with the closeness of his body. His hands locked around her lower back and she tried to move her hips closer to him. She wanted to see if he was hard under those jeans. His grip kept her just far enough away she couldn't tell, but common sense told her his reaction was the same as hers.

The music stopped and Tom stepped back and looked at her. "You move like an angel." His smile was devastating. She forgot her age and enjoyed his more than obvious flirtation.

"Last call." An announcement came over the loud speaker.

"Can I get you anything else?" Tom's voice was deep. A man's voice was important. His had a depth to it that made you take notice. Made you want to wake up to it in the morning.

"I'm fine. This has been fun." Jamie wondered if he might ask to continue the night at her place.

"Got class in the morning. An early one. So I need to run." Tom put his arm around her shoulders. She liked how tall he was next to her. "I've still got your keys. If you wait by the door, I'll get your chariot."

He left her by the two goons at the front door and bolted over the roped area, then disappeared. Within minutes her Mustang appeared in front of her. Tom got out and moved away from the car towards her. He reached for her face with both hands, gently cupped her chin, and placed a kiss on her mouth. His lips lingered on hers, then brushed across her cheek. He buried his face in her neck and gave her a gentle nip. "You are one sexy lady."

Jamie was weak in the knees and her body pulsated with excitement. The stubble on his chin felt rough against her skin and added to the prickly sensations all through her body. She put her arms around his neck and kissed him back. She hoped she would see him again. She imagined him in her bed, his hands on her body.

Tom was the first to break away from the kiss. "I need a phone number. We are going to continue this later."

Jamie grabbed a business card from her purse and handed it to him. "Don't wait too long." She put her hand on his face, gave him a quick peck, and eased herself into the driver's seat.

She was exhausted from the evening. If he wasn't going to come home to her bed tonight, she needed to get home to it herself.

Jamie drove listening to music on the radio. The air felt good on her face. She was happy and relaxed. She had no idea what time it was when she pulled in the driveway. Her thoughts were filled with

Tom and the evening as she entered her house and walked to the bedroom. He was almost too good to be true.

She dropped her dress to the floor and flung her bra and thong on top of it. Still keyed up, a warm shower might be her answer to sleep. Jamie turned the water on and stepped into the tub, sliding the glass door closed. As she scrubbed her arms with oatmeal soap, she thought about the evening. She was crazy about Tom, but Jackson had excited her too. He was aggressive and his hand under her skirt was a memory she couldn't ignore. Her body ached for attention. She flirted with two men in one night and she still was alone with her fantasies.

Jamie tucked her head under the water and let it spill off onto her shoulders, down her back, and over her butt. The soap made her hands slippery and she ran them along her hips, thighs, and between her legs. Her thoughts were on Tom now, as she swayed in the shower, water massaging every inch of her body, moving her hips as she ran soapy hands to and fro, rocking with herself and a melody in her mind that filled her body. The warmth of the water, the excitement of the evening, she was on fire and it didn't take long to reach a climax.

She wrapped the thick towel around her body and grabbed another for her wet hair. The mirror over the sink was steamed up. Jamie wiped her hand across it and looked at her face. She had a glow about her and her cheeks were pink. Under the soft lights in the room, make-up gone, the face of a young girl smiled back at her. She liked the nakedness of her skin, her full lips, and deep blue eyes. The pale green towel, a turban on her head, hid her long hair so her face appeared almost pure and sweet. She laughed, a cat's purr. Romance was in the air and she bloomed from the thought of it.

Jamie slipped into her PJs, hit the bathroom light switch, and headed towards her bed. Tonight she would dream of a hot young valet. Satisfied and tired, but happy and relaxed, she knew she would sleep well. Tomorrow might be the start of something new. She couldn't wait to see Tom again and for the next chapter to begin.

7
STORY SIDETRACKED

"That's disgustingly sweet." Susan pushed back from her desk and took a long look at her monitor. The chapter did not go as she planned. Jamie was to meet a man and have sex. Jackson was that guy. The valet was to be a minor character with just a few sentences. Now he was the romantic lead. Susan took a sip of sherry.

How many authors say the character just wrote itself? Was Jamie letting her know she wanted a relationship, not a quick fling? Have I had too much to drink tonight? Susan was convinced she was a mess at the moment. She'd hoped the sherry would loosen her to let Jamie flow with sex. Instead, she chickened out to write anything more explicit. Jamie was not the problem, she was. Her uptight, out of practice, prudish self. It was bad enough she hadn't had sex in three years, but she couldn't even play with the words to write her book. *I need this book,* Susan reminded herself.

Close to tears she headed out to the patio. She was tired and a bit drunk. The combination brought on a tiny pity party. Daisy trotted behind her. She hoped some fresh air would clear her mind. Maybe she just put too much pressure on herself to be something she was not. This book was definitely out of her range of comfort.

Susan plopped in her favorite antique garden chair and polished off the sherry in her glass. Daisy twirled around her feet, then jumped up and curled into a tight ball on her lap. From habit, Susan ran her hand over Daisy, petting her, and scratching behind her ears. The smell of honeysuckle, sweet and heavy in the warm night air, surrounded her. She felt the tension drain from her body as her mood lightened up.

Susan loved sitting on her patio late at night. She rarely turned on outside lights. The night sky and moonlight were all she needed. She felt safe in her yard, tucked away from the world and its disappointments. She loved the life she had created for herself. It took hard work to find her way back from grief, and she had found her happiness with writing, and now with the farmhouse. She liked living by herself. Her farmhouse was her dream house, decorated exactly as she pleased.

I am happy, Susan reminded herself. For a brief second Susan wondered if she were trying too hard to convince herself of that fact. Her life was so quiet now. Quiet and peaceful, just what she'd wanted. Her social life was non-existent, except for her monthly dinners with Emily. She kept to herself in Safe Haven and had not taken the time to explore the surrounding areas.

Susan held off inviting her friends to the farmhouse. She wanted to be settled, have everything in place, and hang all her art work before they came. She wanted the gardens to be in bloom. It was important they see the house as she did. She had a vision they did not share. For her friends to understand her move, the house had to be perfect. Then they would love it as she did. Now it was a year later and only Emily had been to visit.

Susan invited Emily four months after her move.

"It's so you." She hugged Susan, but her concern about Susan's new life surfaced quickly. "The house is so full there isn't room for anyone else. You've created a private haven for yourself but closed out the world. I love your writing, but, gee, how isolating is that?" She paused to catch her breath.

"Thanks so much! Any other thoughts?" Susan was not mad at her friend. She knew this was coming and remembered how upset Emily was when she first heard about her move. They never discussed it after that. It was time for her to have her say.

Emily smiled at her. "Well, yes. You should at least take your laptop up to the college and work from there. A coffee shop maybe. Meet someone to go out with."

"In good time. Right now I am happy here by myself with Daisy."

Back then she was deliriously happy with her choices. Was that only eight months ago?

"At least promise me you'll meet your neighbors. You can't just hide out by yourself forever."

Susan knew Emily was right. Writing was solitary, even if she loved it. Her friends and old routines kept her busy in Atlanta. At the farmhouse she was alone, but she liked that. Time to write and clear her mind.

She had no desire to meet her neighbors. *How do I explain that to Emily without sounding paranoid?* She didn't want them to know her business, especially if they asked what she was writing. *Been there, done that, got a T-shirt.* She thought about Steve and the ranch house. They'd been so happy, then everything went wrong.

Steve found the house when he worked on a land deal for a developer interested in building condos in the area. They made friends at first, until word got out Steve was involved in the project that robbed them of the wooded area behind their houses. The neighbors ignored them after that. Property values skyrocketed, but the hurt that first year could not be erased. It changed their lives. It still made her sad to think about it.

The books she had written were personal. She didn't want to take a chance that the folks in this small town would frown on the escapades in her memoirs. And what if they thought her new book was sinful? She couldn't deal with that kind of disappointment again. It was just easier to ignore everyone.

Writing about sex was harder than she thought it would be. Memories of Carl inspired her for one chapter, but she couldn't plan a book around sex with him three years ago. She hadn't had sex in so long she could not find the words to put on paper to bring passion to her scenes. She seemed to have trouble putting a man in bed too. Jamie still had not had sex. She needed to up her game if she was going to have an erotic novel and not a sappy romance.

I just have to figure out how to make this work. Susan was never at a loss for long. Getting over hurdles was one of her best characteristics. The first step was admitting there was a problem. *The problem is I am chicken shit to put sex on paper*. She was also out of practice…out of practice having sex. She needed a way to get her juices flowing so her words would flow. It was a simple as that. Tomorrow she would figure it all out. For tonight she was pleased she had started to sort it out.

"Come on, sweetie, let's go in." Susan opened the door and she and Daisy headed for the bedroom. It was late and she was exhausted, not to mention a little drunk. She'd had several glasses of wine with Emily and polished off her bottle of sherry at home. It was time to call it a night.

Susan slipped out of her jeans and T-shirt, tossed her bra across the room, and let her bikini panties drop to the floor. She was too tired to put on her night shirt and bottoms. She crawled under the covers. The sheet felt cool against her bare skin. Daisy curled up in her usual spot.

Thoughts about Jamie swirled through her mind. She replayed those first chapters. *Jamie knows exactly what to do to feel pleasure. Why can't I do the same?* Susan looked up at shadows on her ceiling and moved her hand under the sheet, between her legs. She hadn't done this is way too long. Eyes closed, she touched slowly, savoring every delicious sensation. Words she had written for Jamie guided her as Jamie's reality became her fantasy. She couldn't hold back any longer. Hips arched, her fingers made their final play. Susan cried out into the night and fell back exhausted and satiated. *How naughty was that?* She stuffed her pillow over her face and giggled uncontrollably. *I do declare, my writer's block is gone.*

Relaxed and happy, Susan turned on her side, pulled the quilt close to her chin, and fell into a deep sleep.

DEJA BREW:
THE FEELING THAT
YOU'VE HAD THIS COFFEE BEFORE.
—AUTHOR UNKNOWN

8
Susan, Saturday Morning

"Oh my God." Susan blurted out loud enough Daisy jumped from the bed to the floor. Susan grabbed her head and pushed on her temples. *How much did I drink last night?* She had one nasty hangover.

She threw back her covers and started to giggle in spite of the fact she felt she could puke. *Where the hell are my PJs?* For a second she'd forgotten last night. It was a rare occasion for her to sleep naked. Even when she used to have sex, she would reach around to find her panties, and hike them back on. It was an embarrassing trait of hers, but no undies, no rest for the wicked.

All I need to do now is find a man under the quilt... Susan knew she was being silly as she pulled the quilt up and quickly straightened the bed. She felt sick but was in a great mood. Nothing like ending a pity party with an attitude adjustment. She blushed thinking of what else she did last night. *That Jamie is leading me down a naughty path and I think I approve.*

Susan grabbed her clothes off the floor and wiggled into her jeans and T-shirt. She'd worry about underwear when she took her shower later. Right now, the only thing on her mind was coffee. Couldn't come quick enough. She put on a pot and opened the fridge to see what she could munch on for breakfast. She grabbed an English muffin and popped it in the toaster.

The aroma of the coffee filled the room. It was time to pick her cup. Susan loved to use a different cup every morning. It was a little game she started after she became an antique dealer. It became a ritual after Steve died. Mornings were so bleak, she needed a distraction. It was silly, but did the trick. The cup suited her mood—and there were no cups for a crappy mood, so it was always fun.

Susan looked through the glass door on the cabinet above the counter. She could see all her lovely china, some antique, some more modern, all in floral or chintz patterns. The shape of the cup also depended on how she felt. Some days she wanted a round cup that fit nicely in her hand. The round, open top, allowed coffee to cool quicker when she just wanted to inhale it as fast as she could to wake up. Her small collection of tulip shaped cups, found in second hand shops, retained heat better. Her least favorite were mugs. Susan thought they were clunky and heavy, saved for days she wanted hot chocolate topped with marshmallows.

A lovely chintz cup with tiny multi-colored flowers on a yellow background was her choice this morning. Very English and ladylike. A hangover deserved a fine cup. She filled it close to the top edge. Black, hot coffee. No cream. No sugar. Just the way she loved it.

Daisy danced around the kitchen door to go out. Susan walked outside with her, coffee cup in hand. She was greeted with a banging sound. *At it again.* The pounding noise went on without a break. Susan wondered briefly who lived in the house next door and what kind of remodeling was being done. She never saw anyone outside, just a pick-up truck parked in the driveway some days when she drove by. Susan decided her head might explode if she heard one more thud. "Come on, Daisy, let's go in."

It was Saturday, she had no plans, but then, she rarely did. Her days were her own. Her only plan at the moment was to drink several cups of coffee and then more cups of coffee.

Her cell rang. Susan ignored it and made another pot of coffee. The call could wait, her head could not! She was sure it was Emily. They always talked on Saturday mornings. Was it just last night they had dinner? She still had lots to run by Emily about her book. Coffee first, then she'd call her back.

Droid. Her cell rang again. It still tickled her how the phone alerted her to a call or message. That deep sound that was so serious saying *Droid*. She'd had that model a few years. She wasn't ready to upgrade to something more complicated. This phone was complicated enough and had features that far surpassed her old flip phone. Emily agreed with her. They had the same phone, picked it out together.

"I can't believe how silly you and Emily are with those darn phones." Cheryl teased them over Margaritas right after they bought their Droids. "Goofballs, both of you, imitating the sound of a phone. If I wasn't already drinking, I'd have to start."

"Well you know me. I am easily entertained. I can't speak for Emily." Susan laughed and watched as Emily reached in her bag, pulled out her Droid and kissed it. "I think Emily has just given us her opinion."

A simple gal with simple pleasures, is how Susan described herself. Steve had been just like her, happy with their daily life. Now she had learned how to be happy by herself. A short bark interrupted her thought pattern. Daisy sat by her feet. Susan adjusted her last thought and spoke to Daisy. "Happy not totally by myself, but happy with you, Daisy dear." Daisy twirled around her feet as though she understood.

Susan checked her cell. Two messages. The second one was from Emily. Everyone she needed to talk to now was programmed in her phone. She didn't recognize the first number and was curious. She dialed her voicemail. It was a canned message from an auction house she used to frequent when she had her shop.

Never use your cell for your business. She had made that mistake. Steve have warned her. "Once your cell number is out there for the shop, it's out there forever." She didn't want the expense of a commercial line, so using her cell and a charge service for customers seemed like a plan. When she sold the shop, she thought the calls would stop. But there were still ads on sites with her number on it and people called. If she answered, she always gave them the new owner's number. Most days she let numbers she didn't recognize go straight to voicemail and then deleted them. Which is just what she did with the auction house, deleted it.

Emily was concerned that she used her cell for the shop, too, especially after Steve died. "What if a stalker sees that number and calls you?"

"It's fine." Susan reassured her. "The ads have my shop address, not mine. No one will come looking for me." *Now no one needs a phone number to find me.* Susan thought about it. *I'm all over the web with my books and dog-column.* Susan was pleased her name was out there. That was a good thing.

"Are you hung over?" Emily's voice had a lilt to it on voicemail. "Had a great night with Al. Don't want to make you envious, but I had action and you didn't. I might have some raw material for your book! Give me an hour and call me back. Breakfast is ready here." Emily faked deep breathing and hung up.

Susan grabbed another cup of coffee. *I wonder how Jamie feels this morning.* Jamie had quite the night. In an hour she could knock out a chapter, or at least a good part of one. Daisy was asleep on the couch. She put her lovely chintz cup on the old painted table that was her desk. Susan stretched her arms over her head and took a deep breath. *Okay, Jamie, talk to me.* Susan waited for her muse to speak.

9
Jamie, Saturday Morning

The phone ringing pulled Jamie from her dream. It was a great dream. She and Tom were in bed and had a wild evening of sex. Unfortunately, she couldn't remember any more of the dream. All the drinks last night left her with a bit of a hangover. She reached across the pine end table and grabbed her cell. "Morning." That was all she had to offer.

"Tried to call you last night, but you didn't answer, and you didn't call me back. Did I miss something?" Lynn was up to her old tricks, checking on her.

"Well, I did go out. But I need my coffee before this conversation goes any further." Jamie couldn't decide if her head hurt or if she was just sick from hunger. *All those drinks last night and I forgot to eat.* She needed to get to the kitchen. "Call me later or come on over now and stop for bagels. I'm starving!"

"Oh, you've got me curious. Ben's helping our neighbor fix his lawnmower, so I'm free. Be there in thirty or less. Put the coffee on. I'll stop at Bree's to pick up bagels, cream cheese, and, you know me, got to have one of those great glazed doughnuts!" Lynn hung up before Jamie could say anything else.

Jamie rummaged in her chest of drawers and found fresh cotton bikini briefs. She grabbed her jeans and T-shirt off the floor and headed towards the bathroom. One look in the mirror was all she needed. Flat hair. Washing her long blond hair last night and wrapping it in a towel was fine, but she should have dried it before passing out in bed with her hair still wrapped up. Her normally slightly wild blonde hair was matted flat to her head. Bed head at its worst. She looked creepy the way it pushed up on one side. Jamie reached in the small cabinet under the sink and pulled out her dryer, plugged it in, then turned on the faucet and stuck her head under it. The cold water was a jolt, but one she needed to fully wake up. She pulled her head up, grabbed a towel to keep from dripping all over the floor, and turned on the hair dryer. The warmth of the air made her want to crawl back to bed, but she had to be pulled together for Lynn.

Jamie wanted to see Lynn, but wanted sleep more. The bagels made that decision for her. Within minutes her hair was dry and full around her face. She brushed her teeth, jumped into her clothes, tossed her PJs in the clothes hamper, and made a dash for the kitchen.

Coffee, coffee, coffee. Black and strong—the only way to drink it. *I wonder what kind of coffee Tom likes?* She smiled just thinking about him.

"Hello, are you up and about?" Lynn opened the unlocked door and walked into the kitchen. She placed the brown sack on the counter by Jamie. "Coffee smells good. Why was your door unlocked? Were you so thoughtful to open it for moi?"

"God, I think I was a bit drunk last night. Forgot to lock it. Glad I don't have to worry in this neighborhood." Jamie reached over to grab the bag from her friend. "What do we have here? Oh, and there's a mug on the counter for your coffee. I just got mine and I am not moving any further until I drink my coffee and eat whatever is in this bag."

Jamie grabbed a bagel. Then she reached for a platter and emptied the contents of the bag on it. "A dozen?" She glanced at Lynn who was pouring her coffee. "Oh, they are still warm." She took a bite of the bagel in her hand. Asiago cheese. "Now we're talking!" Jamie had the bagel under her nose, sniffing it like it was a freshly picked flower. "Can you hand me a knife out of the draw please."

"Glad to see you have some manners this morning. Want me to toast it for you?"

"No. I'm just going to slice it and cover it with cream cheese. Maybe toast the next one. Last night gave me quite an appetite."

Jamie smiled slyly at her friend then chomped into the bagel without cutting it or putting cream cheese on it. "Hungry." She smiled sheepishly at Lynn.

"You've had coffee and a hunk of that bagel, now spill it. Where were you last night?" Lynn laughed as Jamie rolled her eyes and stuffed the bagel back in her mouth. "Not a pretty sight." Lynn liked to give Jamie a hard time. They always played off each other's goofy moves. They had been friends since grade school.

Jamie placed the bagel on her plate. "Oh, Lynn, what a night. I met a guy, and it was wonderful. He was wonderful. Nothing really happened. You know I was on a mission to bed someone last night. Just the mood I was in." Jamie felt stupid about her actions the day before. She was so agitated and sex with a stranger seemed like an answer to get her perspective back. Now she was happy how the night ended. "He was really hot and sweet. But didn't ask to come home with me." She took a sip of coffee and continued. "I hope he'll call today and make a date. Can you believe it? I think I have a crush."

"I need more details than that. Don't hold back. You were in a tizzy last I talked to you, so I am happy to hear you didn't get into too much trouble." Lynn worried about Jamie's craziness at times.

"No real trouble. Although there was a guy at the bar that could have been. Honestly, I don't think I was in my right mind last night. I pushed in at the bar and the next thing I know I started talking like a tart. A *slut*. Do you remember we wanted to be sluts in our teens? We thought it was a funny idea. Mother sure straightened me out on that term!"

"I loved your mother. Still think of her from time to time. We had those T-shirts printed for your sweet sixteen birthday. Hot pink with black letters. *Slut* and *Slut in Training*. Which one was I?"

"You were the *slut in training*!" Jamie roared with laughter remembering how silly they had been. "Those shirts didn't last long. You didn't take yours home, afraid of your mom, and mine confiscated them and sent them off with her other bags of things to the Salvation Army. I wonder who finally got them."

"So what happened at the bar, you slut?" Lynn dunked her glazed donut into the warm coffee and slurped down one big bite. "Oh god, I love these things."

"I came on pretty strong. The words just seemed to flow. You know me, I am more passive than aggressive. But I was on a roll last night. Long story short, he put his hand under my skirt and was heading towards heaven." Jamie rolled her eyes again.

"Heading towards heaven? By that I presume you mean…? The guy felt you up in the bar?" Lynn stopped dunking her doughnut and stared at Jamie. "Oh hon, tell me more. How far did he go? And what the hell were you thinking?"

"Well, that is the funny thing. I was worked up, but nervous. Haven't had sex in so long, you know. Then my prince showed up." Jamie waited to see Lynn's reaction.

"Prince. What kind of a metaphor is that?"

"The valet who parked my car. Young guy. Hot as hell. He showed up right as the cowboy at the bar was headed to home base. Seems his uncle owns the place, the other guy was a regular he knew, and things got crazy fast. I ended up on the dance floor with the valet and wanting sex with him. He was so sweet and romantic. A good bit younger, but he didn't seem to notice my age, or mind. We kissed and then he left." Jamie caught her breath. That was a mouthful of words to get out. She decided she needed another bagel and reached towards the platter in the center of the table.

"When you decide to get a little action, you don't fool around. Not sure any of that was wise or safe. Who the hell gets felt up at a bar? And who lets a stranger do that? I mean, someone like you, can't believe it. I'd have made a scene and slapped the tar out of him." Lynn decided she needed to try and find a guy for Jamie. She was out of control. "Just stick to the damn vibrator I gave you and be careful."

Jamie frowned and stuck out her tongue.

Lynn hated sounding like a joy sucker. She worried Jamie would do something stupid and get hurt. Jamie hated her advice and had let her know a few times to keep her thoughts to herself. Lynn quickly back tracked. "Whew, you've made me hot." She fanned herself. "What about the other guy, the valet? I'll bet he liked your Mustang."

"He did. I'm hoping he really liked me too. He seemed pretty sincere. I gave him my card and he said he'd call." Suddenly Jamie's good mood went flat. "If I remember when I dated last, they all said they would call…"

"Hey, stop that. I'll bet you'll hear from him today, or at least in time for the weekend. He'll ask you out on a proper date. Then you'll have to decide how far to take it. Sounds like you are in some serious need behaving like that with two guys in one night."

"You are married, remember. You don't know what it's like to be alone night after night. I am not whining — well, maybe just a little — and I'm not looking for a big romance. I like my work, it keeps me busy, and I like to be my own boss, so not sure I want anyone full time. I just want a bit of sex, while it is still on my mind. I've heard if you don't have sex over a certain period of time, you don't care anymore about it. I am just keeping my brain on a sexual wave-length."

Jamie knew her words were a lie. She wanted a romance. She was tired of being on her own.

"Okay. I hear you. I'm visualizing the phone ringing at any moment." Lynn closed her eyes and put her fingers on her temples. "Ring phone. Ring."

The sound of Jamie's cell ringing startled them both. Jamie looked at Lynn, shrugged her shoulders, and grabbed her cell from the counter. Jamie gave her a thumb's up and mouthed, *it's him.*

"Damn I'm good." Lynn laughed. "If I were writing a book, my timing couldn't be better!"

10
Emily, Saturday Morning

Emily was thrilled it was Saturday and she didn't have to rush. She'd had a great time with Susan last night and then came home and jumped Al. Their lovemaking took on a new dimension as she thought about Susan's book. *Quite a night,* Emily smiled to herself, pleased she had taken the initiative to be a bit bolder in bed. Al was a smiling idiot before they both passed out. They were in sync with each other on every level in their thoughts and daily life. She was lucky to have found him. She was also happy he was gone for his Saturday golf game with the guys so she could ease into the morning.

Emily placed her favorite breakfast on the kitchen table. Hazelnut coffee, cold cereal, freshly peeled apricots, and skim milk. It was her Saturday morning ritual, one she started after her trip to London with Al a few years ago.

She was not a breakfast person. Give her a slice of leftover pizza, coffee followed by a diet coke, or, on days there were no leftovers, a bagel and cream cheese. Her taste buds preferred something to jolt her into the morning. Breakfast foods, eggs and bacon, they were for the evening. Sometimes she and Al went to the 'The Pancake Palace' around the corner for eggs and stacks of pancakes. They could walk there and back, so she never hesitated to stuff herself and feel she was working off the splurge.

Milk and cereal were never on her food list, until that trip. They stayed at a small European hotel right off Trafalgar Square. Friends from New York met them for a few days before they all took off in different directions. Emily was surprised their friends stayed at one of the larger American chains. She never understood that choice. The room and staff at their hotel made them feel at home and the area was beautiful, with its fountains and statues. Trafalgar Square no longer had its legendary pigeons, the city had cleaned the area up. Emily felt cheated she'd missed them, but it was certainly easier to get to The National Gallery.

Every morning she and Al had the hotel's free continental breakfast. It was such a romantic display of cereals, milk, muffins, jams, and fresh apricots, on a table that sparkled with silver and crystal. A white ironstone pitcher was filled with whole, not skim, milk, the individual small cereal boxes were arranged on a large ornate silver tray as though they were little jeweled boxes. Sugar was in an antique crystal shaker with a silver top. The grand finale for her breakfast, sliced fresh apricots to top the cereal. The coffee was strong like she loved it, and black, the only way to drink it. Caffeine, and plenty of it, kept her moving. She loved the Hazelnut flavor. She made the decision to duplicate the breakfast at home, before they even left London.

Emily had her own Victorian sugar shaker to use too. She found one at Susan's shop when she stopped by after her trip to visit with Susan. It was crystal, etched down the sides, with a sterling top. English too. A perfect addition to her Saturday table.

The only part of the breakfast she didn't duplicate was the starched white cotton table cloth and bud vase with a lovely pink rose. She assumed one day she might stop with this silliness, but for now, she loved remembering her trip this way. Calling Susan was a part of her Saturday ritual too. Totally girly morning.

Sundays were a different ritual. She and Al would go out for brunch together, and then she had her Bloody Mary with the breakfast buffet that served more than breakfast foods. After brunch they would go to a movie. "My time with my gal." Al was a bit of a romantic and she loved that.

"You and your rituals." Diane liked to tease her and Susan.

"You're just a tad jealous." Emily would kid her back, knowing Diane had plans of her own.

"I'm usually with my date from the night before Saturday morning, ready to kick him out, whoever he may be." Diane loved men and was a wild child. She was adorable with that red hair and sparkling personality. She'd broken many hearts over coffee in the morning. Sharing her bed was one thing, but don't try to pin her down in the daylight. "One day the right one will come along, until then..." She would just laugh and wink, "a girl needs a little action." Emily, Cheryl, and Susan cheered her philosophy.

Emily pulled the white wicker chair away from the pine table at the end of the kitchen and eased into it, ready for her breakfast. The view out into the small yard was lovely. She'd bought most of her garden statues and planters from Susan's shop. In fact, the wicker chairs around the table came from Susan too. It was her favorite shop *ever*. It nearly killed her when Susan sold it. She thought the shop made Susan happy, so it surprised her, and everyone close to Susan, when she announced she was selling the shop to devote her time to writing.

They all missed Steve. He and Susan were so happy together. The couples lived a mile apart and hung out most Saturday nights. Steve was an excellent chef and loved to experiment with recipes. After Steve died, all the girls got together at least once a week, sometimes more, to check on Susan.

Emily was even more shocked when Susan moved last year. She missed Susan and once a month dinners did not cut it for her. That's when they started the Saturday morning calls.

She reached for her cell. One day she might upgrade her phone, but for the present she was addicted to her Droid. She and Susan got their phones at the same time. Susan used hers for the shop. Emily used hers for everything. After she bought her Droid she became one of *those people* she'd always made fun of. Always on the phone, texting, and checking for e-mails during the day and night. She even checked her e-mails from work. Lucky no one could see her tucked away in her small office. She worked for the federal government. It was a good job, but she hated telling friends she was a fed. Everyone she knew was in a creative job, she was a caseworker.

"Hey, leave a message, I'm not available." Susan's voicemail greeted her.

Damn, I'm in the mood to talk. Emily had a plan for all the girls to get together and she wanted to run it by Susan first. "Call me in an hour." She left a message for Susan. Breakfast and a shower were next on her agenda.

Like clockwork, her cell rang an hour later. Emily saw Susan's number pop up. "Morning. How was the rest of your night after you left me?"

"Oh no you don't. You left that voicemail about your evening. Spill."

"Well, we had a great night. I told Al about your book and the first chapter. What is it about men getting turned on with the thought of a woman playing with herself? I pulled out all the stops myself. Al says he owes you a bottle of wine!"

"Oh no, you told him what I'm writing?" Susan blushed. She wasn't ready for Al to know, or for anyone other than Emily just yet.

"You bet. I think it's great. You may become the erotica goddess. Stop worrying."

"Glad you got some mileage from my chapter." Susan chuckled. She wasn't sure she would ever qualify to be a goddess, or that her writing was erotica, at least not so far as she could tell.

"I had a great idea. I think the girls and I should come visit you. I've seen the farmhouse and love it, but they haven't. It's been a year. We are thrilled when you come to Atlanta, but a year, now really, what is that all about?"

"You're absolutely right. I'd love to have everyone here."

"Maybe we could spend the night? A girls' slumber party? That way we can drink and not have to drive home." Emily's mind was racing. She loved to put outings together. "We can drive up by the college, shop, do a bit of sight-seeing, and just spend time together. What do you think?"

"Too much too early in the morning." Susan's head was spinning. "Plan it and call me with the details. Any date is fine with me. I have an open calendar."

"I'll get with you first of the week after I talk with the others. Let's look at two weeks from today, three weeks max. See what works so everyone can come."

Everyone meant the two of them and Cheryl and Diane.

"We can read your chapters and give you some feedback if you want." Emily was on a roll.

"Perfect! Can't wait. Now I think I'll get more coffee!" Susan would leave the details to the master.

Emily turned off her cell. She was pleased with herself. Al wouldn't mind her spending a girls' night at Susan's place. That is why she loved him so. Easy going on top of all his other wonderful traits. She still had a glow from last night. Thanks to a bit of sexy writing, she was packing heat at home again. She wondered what Susan's next chapter would be. Now that her love life was back on track she didn't want to lose pace. If it took a bit of steamy writing to inspire her and Al to greatness, well so be it! She knew she'd give Susan's book a five-star review when it came out on Amazon for that reason alone!

DON'T WORRY,
IT ONLY SEEMS KINKY THE FIRST TIME
—AUTHOR UNKNOWN

11
LOVE ME CUPID

"Dream Big Dreams. Be Awesome!" Susan found a saying she liked online while cruising her favorite photo sites. It was written in a lovely black script on a robin's egg blue background. She saved it to her desktop and printed out a copy for her vision board. She was up for anything tonight, except writing.

Susan looked across the room. Her vision board was almost full. She'd added a photo of her house earlier. She'd taken it on her cell, uploaded it to a program that made it look like an old negative, and printed it off. It was tacked right next to the banner that said *Best Seller*. Her eye candy inspiration was next to the banner, a magazine photo of her favorite male actor. He posed naked, except for a short leather fringed vest, and a book placed right in front of his privates. It was an ad campaign for a memoir he had written that was due to be released for the holidays. The photo caption simply read…*Coming Soon*. Susan snickered. *I bet*. She had a habit of looking for double meanings in every word, every phrase. The actor's publicist knew exactly how to draw readers to the book.

Sex sells. That's what everyone says these day. The phrase actually was getting on her nerves. Susan sighed. She was trying to jump on that wagon too. *Does that make me cheap, a book 'ho'?* She didn't need another stupid worry about her book. It wasn't like she had stolen anyone's idea. She needed a break from it all and that was what she was doing.

Her old writing group had another saying. *Butt in chair.* Susan looked down and laughed. *My butt is in my chair, but I'm not writing.* She was having too much fun searching the sites for photos of antiques for her house and cute sayings for her board. A stall technique she had perfected with her first book. It relaxed her while she tried to put the pieces of the puzzle together to move forward with her story.

She was happy she'd made resolutions about her writing while under the influence of alcohol, but that was all she did. Drink and give herself an attitude adjustment the other night. That happy feeling lasted all of twenty-four hours.

Susan wanted to be inspired. She'd forgotten how to be sensual, how to talk the talk. Hell, she didn't even walk the walk anymore. *This sucks. I need to find a way to get turned on, and fast.* Her imagination was stale. She didn't know any single men. She hadn't dated in years. Hadn't Emily reminded her of that the other night? Carl was history, long gone. She got a few paragraphs thinking about him the other night, but he was old news. She wanted to be in a sexual frenzy, capture that on paper. Sex beyond the edge of reason.

She fanned herself with an imaginary fan. *Oh Lordy, don't get your head stuck in my hoop skirt.* Susan burst out laughing. Well, there were a hell of a lot of clothes to get through in the Old South. *I wonder how Rhett would appreciate a thong.* It was hard to be discouraged on such a lovely moonlit evening.

Susan gently tapped her fingers on her keyboard. Perhaps there was a way to get inspired and quickly at that. *What was the name of that dating site I was on when I met Carl?* She typed *online dating* and hit search. Susan scanned the names that popped up until she found it. *Love Me Cupid.*

She'd canceled her profile when she left the site after Carl. It was a simple matter to get back on. It was free. All she had to do was hit their *join now* button and start creating her new profile.

Do I really want to do this? She thought back to the first time she filled out the forms four years ago. *I was certainly naïve.* It was funny now, but she'd horrified herself, embarrassed herself, with her lack of knowledge about dating sites. She'd answered almost five hundred sex related questions giving explicit information on her sexual fantasies. She didn't realize they were voluntary questions, not part of the 'must have' general questions, and would be public to other members. She thought it was just behind the scenes information for *Love Me Cupid* to work their magic. She was half tanked by the time she'd finished. An empty bottle of wine sat next to her keyboard. She went to bed feeling sick but satisfied, anxious to hear from her first match.

The following night, after she'd logged back on to *Love Me Cupid*, an instant message popped up in the lower corner of her monitor. *I'd like to watch you use your vibrator.* The cold reality of what she had done hit her. She spent the next two hours deleting five hundred questions that would keep her from ever running for public office should the chance arise.

The girls had a fit over it when she told them at dinner the next week. She pleaded ignorance to them. "I didn't know, really…"

"Are you looking for a sociopath or some kind of pervert?" Emily gave her no mercy.

Cheryl and Diane just laughed. "Who tells total strangers they have a vibrator, and a purple rabbit at that."

Emily shook her head. "What else did you say?"

"Well, one of the questions asked if I liked to watch."

"Watch what? TV, Porn, Baseball?" Emily rolled her eyes. She was teasing Susan, partially, but concerned some creep would show up at her doorstep.

"Ah, let's see," Susan decided to have some fun with this. She was already embarrassed as much as she could be. "I remember. Did I like to watch my partner grab his dick and, uh, you know I hate that word, masturbate."

"Jack off is the term you want, dear." Diane offered.

"What the F did you answer on that one?" Cheryl's voice hit a high pitch.

"I said *yes*. Don't guys like you to watch? Steve didn't, but you know he was a bit sedate. So yes, I said *I like to watch*. You can also include comments and I did. *I'd like to video it for nights I am home alone.*" Susan looked at her friends' expressions to see if they realized she was kidding about the video part. But actually, she did answer *yes* to that question.

"No way." Emily looked shocked. "I didn't know that about you and Steve."

"Me neither," Cheryl popped in. "Steve never struck me as sedate."

"I always thought he was hot." Diane smiled sheepishly.

"We are not talking about Steve here." Emily decided they should drop that subject. She hoped bringing Steve up wouldn't upset Susan. It had only been a few months since his death. "We are talking about Susan telling total strangers she likes to watch them jack off." She slapped her hand over her mouth and laughed. "Did I say that loud enough?" She turned to Diane. "You put that word in my brain."

"It's a valid expression." Diane smiled and shrugged.

"So what else did you answer?" Cheryl leaned forward, anxious for more.

"Did I like someone to watch me?" Susan blushed on that one. She didn't know, but answered *yes* to that question too.

"And..."

"Yes! It seems rather naughty and fun. You know only my doctor ever sees it now. Perhaps I'd like to flaunt it to a stranger. See if I get an approval."

"Oh my God, you are in need of some sex." Emily shook her head. "So what else?"

"How do I feel about sex in public places?"

"What was your answer to that?"

"I answered the more public, the better, as long as I don't get arrested." Susan took a demure sip from her glass and continued. "In the comments section I added, *if a cop picks us up doing it in a public place, perhaps he'd like to watch, and give us a get out of jail free card.*"

"Enough!" Emily looked at Cheryl and Diane. "I don't think she is taking us seriously."

"I am." Susan groaned. "I can't believe I answered five hundred questions about all kinds of weird stuff. I was up until almost four. I took the answers down the next night. Less than twenty-four hours for anyone to read them. Do you think that kind of thing brings on the wrong type of guy?"

"You're not going to find Prince Charming. And yes, you will find the wrong type of guy. What do you think?"

"Yeah, but most of them just want sex anyway, not a relationship. Been there." Diane rolled her eyes and tossed her red hair with her hand. "Doesn't matter what she answered. The only important question they want answered is *will you have sex with me*."

Susan found two guys to have sex with a few weeks after her dinner with the girls. There was the cute blond doctor and good old Carl. She didn't want any more of an attachment then they did. Just sex for sex and to release her built up tension. It was horrible not having a regular partner. She sure took that part of married life for granted.

She met Andy, a chiropractor, and had a one night stand with him. They did it in a public place in a private gated ranch community where they had dinner with his friends. On the way home, before they exited the ranch, he pulled off the road, spread a blanket on the ground and took off her panties. It was heavenly having him enter her as she watched the stars and moon.

She met Carl a few months later on *Love Me Cupid*. He lasted longer...on and off for a few weeks. On and off, literally. All they did was have sex. Great sex. He liked to look at it and then bury his face in it. Sometimes she wished she hadn't sent him packing. Emily agreed with her decision. It surprised her the other night when she brought him back up.

Susan smiled remembering her wild side back then. It seemed so long ago. Nothing seemed personal or important. It was sex to keep her sane. God, Steve would have been shocked. Not that she was having sex, but so soon after he was gone. She did it to survive. She did it to find herself. Now she'd have to do it for her book. Not really *do it* — but chat about it. *Work, work, work*, Susan smiled as she thought how utterly ridiculous this was. She went back online to complete her profile. *This time maybe I won't be so stupid.*

She had recently read an article about what men look for when they cruise the thousands of female profiles on dating sites. They look for — *looks.* The writer of the article had determined that men didn't care how crazy a gal was, as long as she was pretty and hot. Susan wasn't vain, but she did have a photo that might do the trick. She looked pretty hot in it. At least the photo was easy, but writing her profile, she didn't know where to start.

I'm not looking for a date, Susan reminded herself. *I need to create a profile that will bring me a pervert.* She sucked in her breath and typed:

> *I like to be naughty. I can be naughty by myself or naughty with you. Do you like to watch? I do.*

Again she had her doubts. Did she really think some strange guy would get her worked up enough to write erotica? Her sex life was dead, now she wondered if her brain cells had died too.

Relax. Susan's internal conversation was cranking up. *This is just research. You'll get some great ideas, some phrases to use, and if you keep the right attitude, hey, it might be fun.*

She felt her tension start to ease. It was only a bad idea if it didn't work. Chances are it would. Her earlier experience online proved her point. Guys liked to chat about sex with women they didn't know. They did and said things in front of a computer they would never do or say in public. She would help them with their fantasy and they would help her with her writing. It seemed a fair trade. No one would have any real information on her. How much trouble could she get in doing that?

Next she needed a user ID. This was not an easy task. Every sexy name she came up with was taken. Every plain name she came up with was taken. She went through fifty names. Susan threw her hands up in disgust. *I need a drink if I am going to get to the finish line.* She marched into the kitchen and poured a glass of sherry and brought a biscuit back for Daisy.

Your Face Or Mine. Somehow that phrase popped into her mind. A take-off on *your place or mine* with a huge sexual implication. Susan started to get excited. If she looked at this as a creative adventure, she might just enjoy it.

She answered the basic questions giving her age, hair color, eye color, height, and body type. Susan was pleased she could answer truthfully, toned and slender. It was in her genes. She ate too much junk food and was lucky not to gain weight. She filled out the part of the questionnaire that gave your interests, last book read, and favorite movie. Her excitement disappeared as boredom set in. It was tedious to sign up for a dating site. She'd forgotten that.

The last part of the form wanted to know what you were looking for; relationship, dating, casual sex, friendship, one night stand. Susan thought on it a moment. Casual sex. If she said *one night stand* she'd never get anyone engaged in talking about sex, they would expect to come and actually do it.

She checked *casual sex* and sucked in her breath. Almost done. She was relieved this ordeal had an end in sight.

The photo was easy. She went to her documents on the computer, opened the photo file and found the picture taken with her friends at the Jazz Festival in the park downtown a week before she moved. It was her favorite photo and she wished, prayed, she looked that happy every day. She, Emily, Cheryl, and Diane were sun kissed from sitting out listening to music all afternoon. They had the best day and it showed on their faces. She had cropped herself out of the photo to make an avatar for her blog. It was ready to go on the dating site. Tan, happy, her long dark hair almost to her shoulders, big white sunglasses propped on top of her head, and a low cut T-shirt that gave more than a hint of what it covered. Sexy and happy. That photo might grab some attention.

She finished her profile and hit save. If she were lucky within the week her research would be done and her profile put to rest.

Susan was pleased with herself. She gave herself a thumbs up and turned out the lights to head down the hall to bed. Daisy tracked behind her. Snuggled under her quilt Susan thought about *Love Me Cupid.*

I wonder who will contact me. Susan felt certain she'd draw someone in quickly with her bogus profile. She felt like a spider spinning a web. A black widow? No. Just a crazy widow trying to write a book.

The first thing he noticed were her eyes. Deep blue. Her smile, her hair, that T-shirt that left little to the imagination made him feel special looking at her. She was a new user. Looking for sex. He saved her to his favorites file on Love Me Cupid and her photo to his desktop. He pushed away from his desk. 'Baby, I'm here for you'. He unzipped his jeans and felt how hard her photo had made him. With a swift jerk he pulled himself out and went about with the movement he knew all too well. Soon she could take care of him. He'd see to it.

12
THE MORNING AFTER

Susan sat at her desk and brought in her e-mail. *Nothing.* No one on *Love Me Cupid* had contacted her. She wondered if she should have lied about her age. Maybe she was too old to be looking for sex in all the wrong places. Guys liked them young. She was four years younger when she hit the site the first time. Big difference being under thirty-five than over it. *Over the hill. Am I getting old? Cripes that's all I need now.*

She pushed away from her desk and looked at her legs dangling from her cutoffs. Her legs had always brought compliments. Long, lean, and slightly muscular. She smiled as she wiggled her toes. *Nothing's changed there.* She stopped and check her arms. *Firm and tan.*

The only time Susan really thought about her looks was when she had to dress to go somewhere special. She lived in jeans most days. That was one of the great things she had loved about owning her shop. She dressed as she pleased. She was the boss, after all. She wore jeans and was casual on the days her shop was open. Her *casual* had a bit of style to it, more upscale. She always wore vintage jackets over T-shirts and lots of bold jewelry. Layers of artist made necklaces and thin leather cuff bracelets, or old turquoise pieces, were her signature. For anything more formal, she traded her jeans for a long skirt. She loved resale boutiques. In cooler weather, she lived in sweaters. Her style was a bit bohemian. It worked for her in Atlanta. She wondered if the folks in Safe Haven would find her a bit too funky if she ever mingled with them.

She scooted her chair back to the desk and clicked on the icon on her desktop to take her to *Love Me Cupid*. She reviewed her profile to see what she had written last night. Short and teasing. She didn't think she needed to spell it out any clearer. Her profile photo was supersized on the monitor and her T-shirt seemed to reveal more than she realized. *Am I that big?* Her hands moved from the keyboard to her chest. She didn't have on a bra, and apparently had not worn one the day of the concert when the photo was taken. She cupped her breasts and jiggled herself. *Large and firm.* What guy wouldn't like that?

She clicked to bring in her e-mails one more time. Still nothing. *Doesn't anyone want to have sex with me?* Susan stood up and flipped a bird at her monitor. She had better things to do today than sit and wait for an e-mail. It was as frustrating as waiting for a man to call. No wonder she'd stopped dating.

The office was flooded with sunlight coming in the tall windows. Today would be a good day to explore, hit a few antique shops. There were none in Safe Haven, but she was sure she would find plenty of places open up by the college. She didn't need a thing, her house was packed, but shopping therapy was high on her list of ways to snap out of a crappy mood. She also wanted to make sure the farmhouse was at its best and finding something new might excite her to complete some of her decorating projects.

The girls would be there in two weeks, not this weekend, but next, and Susan wanted to put the finishing touches on the place. Finishing touches to Susan meant adding a new antique or painting to just the right spot. She also had that stack of paintings in the dining room to deal with. She had felt no rush to do it. She liked to see art, and large mirrors, propped against a wall. The decorating magazines liked the image too. The first time she saw the photo in *Romantic Décor* magazine of a room with a huge painting standing, not hung, her guilt about stacking hers was lifted off her conscious. Still, maybe it was time to think about hanging them now.

Susan had more paintings than wall space. She counted them when she packed for the move to the farmhouse. She hired a local company and wanted to be sure none got lost in the shuffle. Two hundred. Some were small, a few were quite large, but all mixed and mingled so she could move them from room to room on a whim. Most of her paintings were of flowers and women in garden settings.

She had sold vintage floral oil paintings in her shop. While all her paintings were old, and she liked their patina, she did not like holes in her artwork. Susan taught herself how to repair oil paintings, and on slow times in the shop, she had her paints and easel out, working on her latest purchase that needed a bit of TLC. When her customers asked if she had a green thumb, she'd answer, "No, it's covered in a rainbow of paint!"

"Your house looks just like your shop." All her friends agreed on that. Her love of old treasures, overflowing at home, got her started in the business. She was overrun with paintings, rusty garden chairs, small painted tables, and old cement garden statues, and let friends buy from her house when they visited. Large primitive painted cupboards were another weakness. It was a hard decision to figure out if a cupboard or group of paintings should fill the wall. Space was limited at her old house, but she had plenty of room for everything at the farmhouse. With the high ceilings she could go up!

Susan felt guilty when she first started to hang all the art. Putting that many nails into the original beadboard walls seemed a sacrilege. She learned to use a small drill to lessen the damage. At least the walls did not crumble like the plaster walls in her ranch house. She never measured where to place a painting. She hung by trial and error, and let her eye tell her when she found the exact spot. Her walls were collages of paintings next to each other. When friends visited her old place they marveled at the art and placement on the walls. She loved to brag about her special technique for hanging art. "There are at least three holes behind every painting. I am lucky the wall is still standing!"

She took a bit more care at the farmhouse. She would make an arrangement on the floor and then duplicate it on her wall. The nine foot ceilings threw her off at first, but she finally got it down to a science. When she hung the paintings in the living room she had amazed herself with the results. Standing in the center of the large room, she was surrounded by Victorian oils of roses, lilacs, wisteria, all mixed in with her favorite vintage ladies holding floral bouquets. Most of the paintings were canvas on stretcher bars and could hang without a frame. Susan usually took the old Victorian frames to her shop and hung the art unframed. If the painting was on board she'd replace an ornate frame with a thin vintage wood one. Frames distracted from the artwork in Susan's opinion, and she was all about the art.

The only time she liked frames were on old Victorian mirrors. She had a collection of painted cottage and Victorian mirrors in white and an array of pastel colors, all chipped to perfection, the silver in the mirrors dark from age, hanging in the center hallway behind the living room. There were no windows in the hallway, but the light from the huge crystal chandelier reflected in all the mirrors and made the area sparkle.

Susan looked at the clock. Noon. Somehow she had killed off more of the morning than she realized. If she were going to have an adventure, she needed to hop to it. She went to the bedroom. Daisy was up from her nap on the sofa and tracked behind her. "What should I wear today, Daisy?"

A quick run through her closet provided a white cotton shirt with a row of antique lace across the bottom, jeans, black sandals with a tiny heel, and silver jewelry. "I think this is appropriate for a day of antique shopping, don't you Daisy?" Susan was glad she wrote a column about life with Daisy. She didn't feel like such a nut job chatting to her.

Her make-up routine was simple. BB cream, a dab of lip-gloss, a quick hint of eye shadow, and lots of mascara. Susan peered in the mirror. *Flawless.* Isn't that what the ads promised? She was a sucker for advertisements in magazines. When she saw the ad for BB cream — *BB cream will leave you looking flawless and hydrated. An all in one miracle* — she bought her first tube the next day. It didn't disappoint.

Susan ran a brush through her long hair, then fluffed it back out with her hands. She grabbed her favorite perfume, a vanilla rose scent, from the old painted cabinet next to the sink, and sprayed like crazy around her neck, shoulders and jeans.

"Perfume freak." Diane had laughed and gave her that hideous title when she saw her perfume ritual. "It does smell heavenly though."

Susan found a line of perfumes that she loved in a small gift shop during one of her shopping sprees. The bottles caught her eye before the fragrance did. Small square milk-glass bottles with hand painted flowers. She was so enamored with the look of the product and the fragrances, she carried the perfumes in her shop that last year. Her favorite was the one she wore today.

Daisy gave a tiny yap and Susan looked down at her. "I know, you need a quick run outside." Susan put her perfume back in the cabinet, closed the door, and pulled a dog bone from the crystal bowl she kept next to the sink. She liked to have biscuits handy for Daisy, but wanted to have them in lovely old containers. The bathroom had the crystal bowl, next to her bed the biscuits were in an antique handmade box with roses painted on it. The theme of the containers depended on the room. Her use of antique containers for dog bones made it to her dog-column too. Waste not, want not. If she did something with Daisy, she could usually turn it into a post for her readers.

"Let's go pee-pee." She knew she sounded like an idiot with her high pitched voice, but Daisy loved the inflection. Most dog owners she knew did the same thing when they called their dogs. *Dog-crazy. That's me.* But it was also the readership of her dog column. When she had written about calling to her dog in such a voice to go pee, the response was amazing. That post got more comments than most she wrote. It seemed everyone talked baby talk to their pooches.

The two went outside and Daisy trotted into the yard. The warmth of the sun embraced Susan and she delighted in the moment. Sometimes she missed her shop, but on days like today, she loved that her time was her own.

Back in the kitchen, Susan locked the door and double-checked the doggie door, even though she knew it was secure. She thought about Emily's remark, "You are so anal about that dog!" Emily was right, but Daisy was her love. She'd already lost Steve. She couldn't deal with anything happening to Daisy.

Susan walked in by the computer and temptation got the best of her. It was a bad habit, and one that made her late on those rare days she had to be somewhere on time, but it was a habit she couldn't break. She always checked her e-mails before she left the house.

One e-mail came in. It was from *Love Me Cupid*. The header read, *someone wants to meet you, click here to read your message.*

Susan felt a rush. *It's about damn time!* She thought a moment, then exited her e-mail. She'd deal with this tonight. One more delay and her afternoon would be shot. *Later, gator.* She blew a kiss to Daisy and headed out.

The beauty of her street was undeniable. Old homes on large lots, gingerbread trim, porches, and flowers everywhere she looked. It was always quiet, the only sign of life, a few vehicles parked in neighboring houses. She liked she could come and go and not run into anyone.

Life is good. Susan felt excited. A day of shopping and this evening . . . who knows. For a brief moment Susan thought about the e-mail and wondered if she should have taken time to answer it. Men had a way of disappearing if you didn't move quickly. She fretted, then let it go. The right *Mr. Wrong* would be there. All she had to do was wait.

He was pleased with his e-mail to her. He held back, didn't want to frighten her coming on too strong, although she was clear that she wanted sex. She'd have plenty of sex with him. Sex until she begged him to stop. He liked the begging. It turned him on. She would be his soon enough, locked away for his eyes only. All he had to do was wait.

13
ROAD TRIP

Road trip! Susan almost hummed the words. Perhaps *road trip* was a bit over zealous today, but anytime she went out to treasure hunt it was a grand adventure. *Maybe day trip is better,* Susan mentally corrected herself and grinned as she drove along the countryside.

She'd always wanted to go on a buying trip, *road trip* as her antique friends called it, for her shop, but in all the years she was in business, she never did. Many of the antique dealers she knew hit the big shows in Ohio and New York. Susan dreamed of doing the same, but could never figure out how to make the finances work.

"I just don't get it. Maybe I am too stupid to be in business." She ran figures by Emily on the phone. "I don't know how I can pay for gas, motel rooms, meals, and make a profit." Susan wanted to have wonderful things for sale at reasonable prices. Those travel expenses would jack her prices up too high for her customers.

"You've got a knack for finding things like I've never seen before." Emily made her feel better. "And you've got an eye for detail. Don't be silly. I love your shop and I am a fussy customer!"

Her years of collecting things kept the shop full the first year. Then she came up with her own buying plan. It was simple and a win-win for everyone. She'd buy from the other dealers when they came back from their road trips. There were plenty of estate sales and yard sales where she lived, but she loved the look of pieces from the Midwest and Northern states best.

"Isn't that weird?" Emily had trouble getting on board with her plan.

"No, it's done all the time. You should see how furniture moves from dealer to dealer on set-up days at the shows. This is no different. I just watch to be sure I can make a profit on what I buy."

Susan purchased close to home, but never close to her shop. When she decided to do all garden items, she included online shopping, hitting *Etsy, EBay*, and other antique sites. It worked for her.

Her shopping then was much like her writing now. Susan found wonderful unique pieces without traveling far. Her writing focused on things close to home. She discussed this with Emily one afternoon over Margaritas. Her final question to Emily, "Does this make me smart or am I just plain lazy?" They never resolved that issue, but had a hell of a good time drinking and thinking.

Today she felt smart and revved up. Her destination was a small town an hour away that she read about in the *Safe Haven News*. There were five large antique shops in a two block radius. All of the shops specialized in architectural pieces and industrial items as well as more traditional antiques. Susan wondered just how much trouble she could get into in five shops over five hours.

The writer in her surfaced too. Susan had a pad of paper on the seat next to her and her cell phone handy for quick photos. She never knew when an article idea might pop up or something she could use in her book.

Susan rolled down her window and inhaled the fresh air. She was giddy being out for the day. Nothing like a drive in the country to clear your mind and excite the senses. *Picture perfect,* Susan smiled as she took in everything around her. *My favorite kind of eye candy!* She loved the white railed fences that outlined large farms, and the horses and cows in pastures. On occasion, she would pass an upscale gated subdivision with huge Victorian style houses. While new houses were not her thing, she had to admit they looked lovely.

The change in the scenery, small buildings that came into view, let Susan know she was close to town. She passed a pizza place and a small market with a sign that read, *Local Farm Produce*. She was surprised to see a tattoo parlor in an old cement block building and a few young girls heading in the door. Susan liked the idea of a tattoo, but never had the nerve to get one. *Go girls.* She silently cheered them on. When she passed the library and sandwich shop she knew the tiny downtown was just ahead.

Susan crossed the railroad tracks and headed down Main Street. Founded in the late 1890's, the area was full of small-town Southern charm. The three blocks included shops that ran flush with the track and offices, a bank, and café on the opposite side. Old windows, screen doors, shutters, and fireplace mantels were stacked against the outside of the brick buildings that housed the antiques. Susan pulled into the first parking space she saw and turned off the ignition.

Deep breath. Deep breath. Susan did a silent chant to herself. It never ceased to amaze her that after all her years as an antique dealer, when she was about to discover a new shop, her heart raced, and her palms got sweaty. Today was no exception.

For the next few hours she made a mental note to stop thinking about her book and enjoy her outing. Each shop had wonderful treasures. If she still owned her business, she would have filled her van. Today she wanted to find something special she could use in the house. Maybe a few special things. She did have her three item rule.

She made it through four shops unscathed. No purchases. She was disappointed, but her hopes were up for the last shop at the end of the street. It was another old brick building with more architectural pieces propped up out front. She opened the heavy carved door and entered a room that was dark, except for light coming in the doorway, and an overhead single Halogen bulb. Her foot caught on something on the floor and she lunged forward. She reached for a dresser and steadied herself so she wouldn't fall.

"Are you okay?" A young girl raced up to her, slightly horrified. "I saw you trip on the rug. We usually don't have rugs on the floor for that very reason, but a customer was looking at it only minutes before you came in."

"I'm fine, thanks." Susan smiled at the girl, who appeared very nervous about her near accident.

"Let me get this out of your way." The girl picked up the rug and moved it to the top of an old trunk.

"Looks like a beauty." Susan went over to take a closer look. It was an early hooked rug in pale robin's egg blue with pink roses. She could picture it in front of the wicker settee across from her bed. She spread it out to see size and condition. Her mind calculated the rug was about 4' x 6'.

"Is she buying the rug?"

"*Thinking about it.* Those were her words." The girl smiled and shook her head. "She already left."

"I know, had my own shop. Hate that phrase. Put it right up there with *I'll be back.*"

They both laughed. The girl held out her hand. "Nancy. I'm the owner. My husband and I do the picking and selling."

"Susan." She shook Nancy's hand. "Well, I'd like to buy the rug and I don't have to think about it." She winked. "Taking it with me today." Susan realized she got a bit carried away. She had no idea the cost of the rug. If that rug had been in her old shop it would be $150. "What is the price?"

"Forty-five. And it's in almost mint condition for its age, as you can see."

"Can you hold it a few minutes while I look at what else is here?" Susan felt another deal was just around the corner. Instinct, she called it. She could feel it in her bones. She also had a shopping rule. Everything in threes. She didn't stop until she found the third item. Then she knew it was time to leave and hit another place.

"Come up to the desk when you are done, or holler if you have any questions. We let you move at your own pace here." Nancy pulled the rug off the trunk and headed up the stairway.

Susan looked around the room. It was an interesting and odd assortment of antiques, old signs, vintage clothing, and records. Boxes full of small items sat on beautiful dressers. Smaller pieces blocked larger pieces. Quilts and vintage dresses hung in old wardrobes. If you dug deep there was no telling what you might find.

Her shop had been a pretty one with its garden items. Everything set up in vignettes to show how it might fit in at home. Then she had old white cupboards full of newer, less expensive gift items. Her customers loved her displays. She kept a space full of beautiful things for others, but she was a picker at heart, and loved to dig in to find her treasures.

A flash of old white paint in the back corner, tucked behind a floral print wing chair, caught Susan's eye. She felt her pulse quicken as she walked over to see exactly what it was. She pulled the chair away and stood staring at a large wood gable from an old Victorian house. It was in incredible condition and very ornate. Susan guessed the base was about five feet long and the piece came to a center point about three feet high in the middle. The gingerbread work was intact and incredibly ornate with spindles that fanned out from the base. The old paint had a wonderful patina. She would have liked to have seen the house this came from, Victorian Gothic. It would be a perfect addition for her farmhouse, somewhere inside or out. She didn't care if it sat against a wall. She had to buy it.

"Love it. Love it." Nancy was back with a box of old china. "That came from a 150 year old house in Mississippi. We bought it at auction last month. It is a beauty, but not many folks have room for it. This china came from the auction too. Always something new!"

Susan could barely get the words out. "How much?"

"Got to have $295 for it. I think that's a bargain for a piece like that."

"Sold!" Susan had seen a piece similar, but not as ornate, for $500 on line. She would have bought it but it was 'pick-up' only in a state a ten hour drive away. "I think it will fit fine in my van. Can someone load it for me? And do you take Visa?"

"Will meet you up by the desk with your ticket. Let me find my husband. He'll put it in your van." Nancy disappeared as quickly as she appeared.

Susan remembered her *three's the charm* rule and looked around the room. She walked over to a pile of books stacked on a marble top Eastlake table. The book on the very top was titled *Love's Fancy*. The cover was pretty racy with a buxom young blonde passionately kissing a man in a business suit. She picked up the old paperback and flipped through it. It was a 1950's romance. *My third item.* Susan laughed out loud. *Perhaps the universe is giving me a gentle reminder I have work to do.* She looked at her watch. It was almost six. The shop would be closing soon.

"Add this to my total, please." Susan handed the worn book to Nancy and dug out her credit card.

"Book is on the house." Nancy tucked it in a small paper bag. "Ned has the gable by the back door. Would you like to join our e-mail list?" Nancy handed her a pen.

"Thanks for the book." Susan scribbled her address down.

"Have a great night and come back to see us." Nancy smiled at her.

Susan grabbed her package and went to meet Ned to load her van. Nancy and Ned made a cute couple. She felt a tiny tug on her heart. She'd been part of a couple once. She'd put all that behind her, yet lately it was back on her mind.

She thought about the night ahead. There was that e-mail from *Love Me Cupid.* Perhaps someone else had written. There was no guarantee anyone would be online this evening. Her night would be like all the others, just her and Daisy, alone. She wasn't ready for an evening of solitude.

Was Emily right? Should she try to meet someone nice? The thought made her laugh. *Where would I find a guy in tiny Safe Haven?* She started the van to head home. Romance was not in the cards for her, but it would be for Jamie, if *Mr. Wrong* was waiting on *Love Me Cupid.*

14
DETOUR

The day got away from her. If she hadn't enjoyed it so much, she'd be annoyed with herself. It was dark, way past the hour she planned to be home, when she pulled in her drive. The lights were on in the upstairs of her neighbor's house. Susan heard banging and thought she saw a figure moving around. It was too far away to tell. *I wonder why he works so late at night.* She assumed it was a *he*, but she really didn't have a clue. The rest of the street was quiet.

Susan decided she could get distracted easier than a pup in the yard. She took a different country road back to Safe Haven after leaving the antique shop and got side-tracked. A mom and pop style diner caught her attention on the last leg of her drive. The large wooden sign, nailed to a rough post in front of the stucco building, read simply *Myrtle's Home Cooking.* She was happy there were no vehicles behind her. She hit her brakes to slow down and made a left hand turn into the dirt parking lot. She loved hole-in-the-wall type places. The food was always great and she loved to chat with the local folks, full of the most wonderful stories.

A poster-size, hand written sign was taped in the front window. It boasted quite a promise. *The best fried chicken and fried green tomatoes in the state.* The last two words were at an odd angle as space ran out on the poster board. Susan smiled. This was going to be fun! She pulled out her cell and took photos of the sign and building.

She was hungry. She also had a method to her madness. Maybe she could get a freelance article for the magazine. Local diners had a universal appeal. One of her favorite shows on cable TV featured diners across the US.

Susan wanted to taste *Myrtle's* fried green tomatoes. The only fried green tomatoes she had eaten were in a bistro in Atlanta that served up a platter so fancy the tomatoes looked like a delicacy rather than good old southern food. And fried chicken? That was a no brainer.

The interior of the diner was as plain as the outside. Small square wood tables with straight back chairs dotted the room. The cement floor was painted green and the walls were a bright yellow. The place was impeccably clean. She was the only customer when she walked in.

"Have a seat anywhere and I'll be right over." A pretty young girl called out to her from the other side of the room where she was cozied up to a young man. Susan wondered if she had interrupted something.

She sat at a table by the window and looked out. The sun was setting and the colors in the sky were lovely. *Red sky at night, sailors delight. Red sky in morning, sailors take warning.* Her mind rambled off the old sailor's saying. Tomorrow should be another beautiful day.

"Welcome." The young girl appeared at her table holding a small chalk board. "Our specials for dinner." Then she laughed. "We ain't really got no specials, but we like to say we do. Lee thinks it adds something to have the board. Mostly serve our fried chicken and tomatoes. Have grilled pimento cheese and a few other sandwiches, if you're interested."

She introduced herself as Brittany, one of the owners. She looked to be in her early twenties. "The place belonged to my husband's kin, but we got it when they passed." Brittany was shy as she spoke. A pretty girl with long blonde hair pulled off her face and tucked in a bun at her neckline. "Lee, my husband, does most of the cooking. He's in the back right now. Maybe you saw him when you came in. I wait the tables and clean up."

"Order up!" Lee called out from the open widow in front of the kitchen area. Then he walked up to them laughing. "Love to say that! You're our only customer in the last hour." Lee shook his head in disgust. "Folks like to go to the new burger place up the road."

Susan smiled at the couple. So young and naïve. She would definitely write about the diner. Maybe it would help them with business.

"I'm a writer." Susan handed them her card. "I've published a few books and have a monthly dog-column. But, I sometimes do a bit of free-lance work. The diner is charming. I'd love to write something about it for the on-line magazine. I feel certain they'd publish it. Would that be okay? I'd need a few photos of the two of you and of the inside of the diner. I've already taken pictures of the outside."

"That would be so great, Ma'am. Thank you." Lee broke into a big smile. Brittany gave Lee a quick hug.

Susan cringed at being called Ma'am. "Just call me Susan, please."

"Yes, Ma'am. I mean Susan." Lee smiled and nodded at her.

"I'd like to take the pictures over there." Susan pointed to a table with a pretty flower painting on the wall. She herded them to the spot. "That looks good."

"Where's your camera?" Lee had his arm around Brittany, ready to strike a pose for her.

"I use my cell. It has a great camera. I like how you both look. Hold it." Susan took two photos. "You can relax now." She stuffed her phone back in her purse and smiled at the young couple.

The two looked flushed and were holding hands.

"Thanks for taking our picture, Ma'am." Lee spoke. "Sorry, I mean, Miss Susan. Guess you've got me too excited with the article and all."

"I'm going to need some information." Susan asked them some questions about the diner's history and jotted down their answers. "That should do it. If I need anything else, I'll let you know. Now, I think I'm ready to eat. How about that fried chicken and fried green tomatoes."

She watched them head back towards the kitchen. As they pushed through the door, Susan saw Lee squeeze Brittany's butt. She stopped, giggled, and kissed him on the check, then whispered something in his ear. Susan could only image what she said. She figured on slow days there was more than chicken heating up in the back kitchen. Susan wondered if she was suddenly seeing sex in everything because of her book, or was sex everywhere and she was the only one missing it.

The fried chicken was scrumptious. "An old family recipe," Brittany told her. The fried green tomatoes finally gave her a touch of the old south that had been missing in Atlanta. Between bites she had to ask how they were made.

"It's Lee's Grandma Myrtle's recipe." Brittany stuttered on the sentence. "Heap of a lot of words." She smiled at Susan and continued. "It's a family secret, like our chicken. But I can tell you, we use white cornmeal and buttermilk."

"Well, the tomatoes melted in my mouth!" Susan was stuffed to the point of feeling sick. She sipped on the last of her sweet tea and pulled out cash to pay for her dinner.

Lee showed up at her table before she could move. "Our way of saying thanks." He placed a large bowl of peach cobbler piled high with vanilla ice cream in front of her.

Susan didn't think she could eat another bite of anything, but didn't want to be rude. She took a heaping spoonful. "This is wonderful!" She was amazed at how quickly she polished it off. "Myrtle's secret recipe too?"

Brittany nodded and grinned. "Yep, everything is Myrtle's. Comes down the family line of suppers around the farm table and holiday feasts. I've heard stories about the family reunions in the old days that were awesome. Amazing everyone wasn't fatter."

Susan grabbed her stomach and laughed. "I'm stuffed! I'd weigh a ton if I ate like this often. The food is incredible. Myrtle knew how to cook. I'm so glad you are keeping her recipes alive." Susan gave Brittany the money she'd been holding and stood up to leave. "It was great meeting you both."

"It was our pleasure to meet you." Brittany flung her arms around Susan and hugged her goodbye, a good old southern hug. Susan hugged her back.

"Come back and see us soon." Lee hugged her too. "Let us know when your story is up. Got a computer at home. Here's our e-mail address, if you please." Susan took the paper he handed her.

Susan got in her van. The sun had all but vanished and she wanted a nap. The meal made her sluggish and she decided to play a game on the twenty minute drive home. She would count pick-up trucks. By the time she saw her street she had counted six. It seemed as though everyone drove pick-ups, including her neighbors. *A sure sign I'm in the country.* Susan chuckled as she pulled in her drive.

Daisy appeared indignant at being left alone so long. Susan fed her as soon as her feet hit the kitchen, then the two of them went outside for Daisy to do her business. The noise from her neighbor's sounded even louder on the patio. She was glad she couldn't hear it inside the house. *Just a bit late to make that kind of racket in the neighborhood.* Susan shook her head, then stopped herself. *I sound just like the kind of neighbor I want to avoid.* She grabbed Daisy and went back in. Time to see if *Mr. Oh So Wrong* was available.

Susan grabbed her sherry and headed to her computer. She was anxious to check her e-mail to see if anyone else from the dating site had contacted her. Eighty-five e-mails came in. Most were from writing groups she had joined. Every opinion on every conversation was sent to her in-box. Not one personal e-mail. She hated that.

She looked for the earlier e-mail from *Love Me Cupid* and linked back to their site.

Tease&Please had written. *I like your photo. We might have something in common.*

Susan shook her head. The only thing they would have in common was their desire for casual sex. His would be a real desire, hers would be faked. *Kind of like faking an orgasm.* She laughed at the ridiculous nature of her plan.

She quickly read his profile. Tease&Please was thirty. He owned his own consulting business. No kids, no pets. He was not looking for a serious relationship. Casual sex, casual dating, e-mail only. All three categories were checked.

Tease&Please had thick light brown hair. He wore wire rimmed glasses. His smile was friendly. Everything about him shouted nice guy. Clean cut. *Those clean cut guys were the worst.* Susan found that out when she first dated. Those guys looked safe but, were players at heart.

I need a player, not a boyfriend. Susan reminded herself this was research, not real dating. The bigger the player, the kinkier he was, the better for her mission. A touch of perversion would be nice, too.

Susan was just about to send him a reply when a tiny window opened up in the lower corner of her monitor. Someone was trying to instant message her.

Hey Babe, let's chat.

She checked his profile before she answered. A biker. He stood next to a big Harley, a stocky guy wearing a bandanna wrapped around his head, dressed in jeans and a black T-shirt with a skull logo on the front. He had a big mustache and a bigger grin. His handle was Harley69. *That's certainly original.* Susan giggled, nervous and a bit excited. She read the header on his profile page. *Let me take you for a ride on the big one.*

She wondered if that bike was the big one he wanted someone to ride, or did he have something more personal to offer? She sent him a message back. *What's on your mind?*

You are, Babe. Hot photo.

Susan blushed. *Thanks.*

What's a babe like you doing home at this hour of the night?

Susan paused. Here was a chance to test the waters. *I'm writing a book. Erotica. Need some inspiration.*

I've got something that will inspire you. Let me send you a photo.

Before Susan could reply a message popped up from *Love Me Cupid* asking if she would accept photos. She clicked *yes*, took another sip of sherry, and waited.

Just took this photo for you. Like what you see, Babe?

Susan looked at her monitor. Harley69 was standing in his bathroom butt naked. She realized it was his reflection in the mirror. He held his cell in one hand, and his other hand covered his privates. *I hope that is a very large hand.* Susan chuckled to herself. His thighs looked hard and tight. He had a bit of a tummy, and some light blond chest hairs. Now that his bandanna was off, his head was shaved. Her reaction to his photo startled her. She felt a surge of pleasure. All that skin. She had not seen a naked man in far too long. She quickly messaged him back.

Speechless.

Babe, I'm a writer too. Want to play a game? I can help you with your writing skills, if you let me.

Susan was more than intrigued. A writer? Was he for real or just full of BS? She didn't care. He had her excited. The night was far too quiet for her. Now she had someone to play with.

I love games.

Susan remembered the e-mail she had started to Tease&Please. He would just have to wait. Tonight she was taking a ride on Harley69.

Her profile in front of him on Love Me Cupid showed 'online now'. He got up and paced the small room, waiting for her reply to his earlier e-mail. He'd waited all day. He checked his e-mails again, nothing. She was still on the site, but not with him. Rage bubbled up in his chest as he watched the monitor. He clenched his hand into a tight fist, then slammed it hard into the desk. The impact spiraled pain from his knuckles up to his shoulder. He twisted his neck and smiled. Pain always made him feel better. He looked at her photo one last time before he shut down the computer. She was the one, soon she would know that. Once his mind was made up there was no turning back.

15
THE WRITING LESSON

Susan sipped on sherry and wondered how this would play out. She sometimes wondered if her mind left her late in the night. *What the hell am I doing looking at Harley69's naked photo and waiting for my first writing lesson?* She labeled everything stupid late at night as *midnight madness.*

I'm back, Babe. Had to let Hambone out. Hambone was his black lab. Harley69 took a minute to introduce himself properly. He was known to the real world as Franklin, or Frank. He was a graphic design artist, a biker, father of two young boys, and divorced. His secret life was writing erotica for the fun of it and riding his Harley. He apparently enjoyed sharing naked photos of himself with strangers too. She asked him about that.

Love to flaunt it. Find women like to see it too.

She read his words and shook her head. He seemed honest in a rather bizarre way, and Susan was fascinated. He also lived in Arkansas, so no harm could come from toying with him tonight.

Show me what you write? She messaged him back.

She was curious if he told her the truth and quickly Googled the information he shared with her while she waited for his next reply. He was easy to find, his design company was a big deal. He looked tame in jeans and a crisp white shirt on his website. CEO of Franklin World. His art was quirky, edgy. Not unlike the man himself.

Wrote some erotica a year ago and my friends loved it. Lost it when my computer crashed. I'll try to recreate it for you now.

She watched as his words came through on the screen. A few paragraphs that sizzled with sex. Beautifully written, sensual, downright graphic. It seemed more porn than erotica to her, but what did she know about the genre. And there was her problem in a nutshell. The reason behind this crazy idea she called research.

That was pretty awesome writing. Susan messaged him back. *So what is this game you want to play?*

Role playing. Will help you with your writing, I promise. I want you to pretend to be a man entering a bar. You see a beautiful gal. What would you do?

Susan's head started to spin. If she were a guy, she'd be the one with a dick. She thought for a moment and started to write.

The brunette at the bar caught my eye the minute I walked through the door. I don't know what it was about her, not the type I am usually attracted to. Her short dark brown hair looked like she jumped out of bed and forgot to run a comb through it. She was older than the young gals I'm used to. Maybe it was the way she turned and looked at me. My dick liked her approving glance. Her dark eyes drew me across the room.

"Join me for a drink?" Her hand brushed against my arm.

"Sure, why not?" I'm an agreeable sort of guy.

"Hey, Joe, get him whatever he wants." She waved down the bartender. "Put it on my tab."

"What do I owe this pleasure to?" I liked her style.

She cocked her head and grinned at me. "You look sexy with that bald head. Haven't seen sexy in a while in here." Her hand reached up and she gently caressed my head. Another head took notice. My dick tingled in my jeans.

Susan sat back, pleased with what she had sent him. She waited for his response.

Harley69 got right back to her. *Cute, but not hot. Tell me more. I'm not getting worked up over here. My dick is still limp.*

Susan was embarrassed. This was so silly, but she wasn't going to quit. *Hey, I'm doing my best. I've never had a dick of my own before.*

Harley69 sent another message. *I'm waiting…Do I have to do myself while you ponder this?*

Susan stared to type. It was exhausting trying to write so much.

She turned in her chair to face me. Her T-shirt was tight. I could see she wasn't wearing a bra. Her breasts were large and every inch of her peeked through to me. She caught me looking.

"Like what you see?" She pulled the lemon wedge off her glass and took a bite of it.

My mind tried to keep up the conversation, but all I could think of was taking her somewhere and putting my dick in her. "Sure do." I'm man of few words.

She leaned forward, and tugged at her shirt until the tops of her breasts seemed to pop at me. She squeezed the rest of the lemon wedge on her breasts. Her eyes were bright as she smiled at me. "Care to taste?"

My mind went wild. My jeans strangled me. I wanted to free my dick and drip some of that lemon juice on me. Let her lick it off. I held myself in check. "Looks very tempting."

"Joe. Be back in a jiff." She jumped off the bar stool and grabbed my hand. "I've got more than that for you to taste."

We headed for the parking lot. My brain was on autopilot. I wanted to taste every inch of her. I think I was going to get my chance.

Susan took a big gulp of her sherry. She was getting into this game. She was still shy with the words she chose. Damn it.

Harley69 messaged back. *Okay Babe. This is where I take over. Sit back and enjoy.*

Susan let him take the lead. She was tired of owning a dick.

She pulled me to the shed out back. The door closed with a bang and I turned back to look at her. She had taken off her T-shirt. She was luminous in the moonlight.

"I saw you looking at these in the bar. Figured you wanted to see them up close and personal." She had a smile on her face as she came closer to me. "Here, touch them." God, my dick was throbbing. She grabbed my hands and put them on her breasts. "Squeeze me hard. I like that."

I squeezed and she licked my ear. Her tongue probing in my ear made me harder if that was possible. Her tongue had a light touch to it. A touch I wanted to feel lower down.

She pulled back and smiled at me. "I brought this with me." She had the other half lemon tucked in her hand. "Although I think I am still wet from the last one." Her smile told me more than her breasts were wet. As I watched she squeezed the lemon until juice drizzled down her bare chest.

"Taste me now. I'm a little bit tart."

I'm sure there was a pun in there, but my tongue was hungry for her and I buried my face between her flavorful breasts.

Her body swayed towards mine and her hips moved close to my crotch. A moan, almost like a small animal, escaped from her throat.

Her hands were on my belt buckle. She undid it in a flash, unsnapped my jeans, and tugged at the zipper. Her hand reached down inside. I almost exploded with her touch.

"That is one fine hard on." She pushed my back against the wall and knelt in front of me.

Susan had a mouth full of sherry when she realized the instant message stopped.

I want more. She typed quickly. She was just getting into the groove. *Where are you?*

Harley69 disappeared. Was he a dick tease? Got her all frothy with his writing only to take off.

Went to get a beer. Worked up a thirst. He was back. If there was a voice behind the messaging, she knew he was laughing.

You are crazy. But this is fun! She waited for the story to continue.

No. That's all. A little tension and mystery should get you writing that book. Horny now?

Susan giggled. She guessed she was. Every nerve in her body wanted more. *You are the master, I agree.*

I need something from you in exchange now. A favor.

Anything you want. Susan figured he couldn't ask for much from Arkansas.

Hang on a minute while I turn on my webcam.

Susan waited. She sat up straight in her chair when she saw what he was up to. *No!* She couldn't decide if she was horrified or tickled. His dick filled the entire monitor. Full screen. He was still naked. His hand slowly reached to grab it, and in what seemed like an instant, he wagged it around until he climaxed. Susan couldn't move.

His face popped up on the monitor. He winked at her, puckered up, and blew her a kiss, then clicked off. He was gone in a flash.

Oh my. Susan was stunned. *I think that's enough research for…FOR EVER!* She burst out laughing. She wasn't sure who the bigger nut job was. Her writing lesson seemed more like retro porn, but it was funny as hell. Just what she needed to lighten her mood.

Susan crawled into bed, a bit tipsy from her sherry, still chuckling about Harley69. He didn't turn her on, but he got her to relax with the words they exchanged. *I think that's been my problem,* Susan mused. *I'm making this into a big deal, when it just needs to be a good book.*

She kissed Daisy and turned off the light. Jamie's story needed to be spiced up and tomorrow would prove if she learned anything from her teacher tonight.

16
WITCHCRAFT

Jamie looked at Lynn and winked. Lynn was definitely a witch, albeit a good witch. Tom was on the other end of the phone. Only minutes before Lynn rubbed her temples to conjure him up. And, there he was. Only a good witch could work that magic. It never dawned on Jamie that she was the one who cast a spell on Tom when they first met.

Lynn discreetly moved into the living room. She plopped down on the sofa and grabbed a magazine off the coffee table. She wanted to give Jamie privacy, but she wasn't leaving until she got the details of the call when they finished.

"Saturday night, then?" Tom had called to invite her to dinner with another couple he was good friends with. "I hate to make it a double date on our first date, but they are visiting for the weekend and staying at my place. So, it was either all of us, or I'd have to wait to see you. Don't think I can wait."

"That will be great." Jamie wanted Tom to herself, but meeting his friends was a good sign he was very interested in her. She only prayed his friends were a little older than him or she would be the old lady in the group. "See you then." She was being cool, but he made her hot. She hoped she could steal him away Saturday, if only for a few minutes. She wanted to pick up where they left off at the club the other night—in his arms, pressing her body into his, kissing him. Saturday seemed forever to wait for him. She would keep her hands to herself until then and behave. If she didn't satisfy herself before then, she'd have to find a way to let him do it. It was a perfect excuse to be naughty.

"Can I come in now?" Lynn peeked into the kitchen to see if Jamie was off the phone, then barged in. "So?"

"Tom." Jamie grinned at Lynn. "You are a witch you know. You made that call happen."

"I most certainly did not. He liked you the other night, and why shouldn't he? Look at you. Adorable and hip."

"Yes, and probably ten years older than him." Jamie sighed. She wasn't sure how he would feel about the age difference.

"Do you know how old he is? I don't remember your mentioning he told you that while you were kissing in the parking lot."

"He just looks young." Jamie couldn't let it go.

"So do you. You know I can keep this up all day if need be until you drop this stupid idea. Witches don't tire easily." Sometimes Lynn wanted to shake Jamie. She was lovely and talented and appeared ten years younger herself. She knew where Jamie's insecurity came from. She didn't think Jamie really came to terms with Jack's one night stand.

"You are right. I am acting too uptight. I will just be excited we have a date. Dinner with some friends of his from out of town. Did I show you that skirt and top I bought at the resale boutique last week? I went in to talk to them about their ad and came out with a sack full of clothes. Gently used, priced so well."

"Better." Lynn was happy Jamie refocused.

"I've got to stop by the office. Want to come with me and go to lunch?"

"Wish I could, but I have to get home to Ben. I told him we'd have lunch. Husbands can be a bit demanding." Lynn smiled thinking of Ben. She liked to pamper him.

Jamie hugged Lynn goodbye and went back to the kitchen. One more cup of coffee and then she had to get going. She was the editor of the local neighborhood paper. Not *the newspaper* as she corrected everyone who thought she was the editor of the *Jamestown News*. She edited the small monthly paper that circulated her neighborhood. *Edenton Neighborhood News.* Each community had one.

She loved her job. She even had a tiny staff to supervise. Jessica helped bring in the ads, Mike was their photographer, and Lindsey covered the hard core news. The paper came out monthly so there was a crunch the last week to meet deadline. But three out of four weeks her time was more her own. She needed to send out the bills for ad space and leave a note for Jessica to contact the boutique and the new restaurant in town to work up their ads.

Jamie handled their PR in addition to being the editor and was hands on with all other aspects of the paper. She'd lived in the community for fifteen years. When her husband was alive, they were very social. She made some excellent connections during that time that stayed close to her now. Friends and acquaintances that liked her and kept her up to date on the latest community buzz. They supported the paper with ads and were generous in buying space when Jessica contacted them. Jamie included all the local social events in the paper. She posted free ads for fund raising events and art openings. It worked well for everyone. A win-win, although Jamie hated that term.

Jamie had an excellent eye for design, but let her staff do most of the layout. She would help them if they got stuck, but it was a learning experience for them. She gave the final approval before the paper went to the printer. Jessica and Mike were college students. Part of their work gave them class credits, part paid them a salary. They would stay with the paper until they graduated. Then the college would send replacements. It was a system that helped her and helped the kids who wanted some journalism and newspaper experience for their degree. Lindsey was a full time employee. She had initially come on as a student, but when she graduated she wanted to stay with the paper. Jamie was thrilled she could keep her as a permanent employee.

She hired a company to distribute to the different locations around town. The paper was free to its readers. Jamie was paid a modest salary she could live on. Her mortgage had been paid in full when her husband died. She thought buying mortgage insurance on top of life insurance was excessive and had voiced her opinion to Jack. He didn't listen to her. She never expected he would die. It turned out to be a blessing and allowed her to do work she enjoyed. She might be lonely, but she was financially secure.

Her office was part of a small complex. It was a low rise brick building with a parking lot to the side. The building included the *Edenton Neighborhood News*, a yoga studio, a healing arts practice, a wine shop, and a small pub. Edenton was a lovely small town within eight miles of Jamestown, a metro area. The town was small enough to be friendly, but large enough your personal life was private.

She thought about Tom on the drive to her office. She wanted to bed him badly. She hoped her eagerness would be a turn on and not a turn off. It had been way too long for her. Her reaction to Jackson at the bar the other night told her she was ready to do it with any man that came along. Lucky for her, Tom walked in. How nice it would be to have sex with someone she was crazy about rather than to just have crazy sex.

Jamie started to feel an excitement build in her. She kept one hand on the steering wheel and reached down with her other hand. She put a bit of pressure where her legs met her hips and felt a surge of excitement. She couldn't stop thinking about sex.

Jamie parked her car and unlocked the office door. The kids were out pulling together their material for this month's deadline. Jamie locked the door and closed her eyes. She was horny as hell. Tom's voice had an unnerving effect on her. She wanted to call him. She played the conversation in her mind. *Get over here right now. I want to… want to, crap, how do I tell him I want to have sex with him?* She toyed with that idea for a full minute and knew it was not going to happen. She wasn't going to call Tom. But she could take care of the sense of urgency. She wanted to wait for him, but she'd want him a dozen times again before she saw him on Saturday.

Jamie reached up under her skirt and let her hand move down inside her panties. Her bare stomach felt cool to her touch. She leaned back against the wall, opened her legs and slipped her hand where she wanted Tom's to be. How many times had she done this? Today was different. She knew who she wanted. She no longer had a phantom man in mind to pleasure her.

She didn't want to rush. She closed her eyes and caressed between her thighs gently, her fingers a whisper on her skin. She thought about Tom as she rocked her hips and felt a delicious tension build. She moved slowly, teasing herself, barely touching. She imagined him kissing her, touching her, entering her. She couldn't stand it any longer. She moved her fingers with more intensity. Her hand dropped to her side when she was finished. Her legs were weak. She could only imagine what it would be like to be in bed with Tom. She knew what she wanted, and she felt Tom wanted it too.

The spell had been cast. She could not be more intoxicated with desire if she had swallowed a love potion. There would be magic in the nights ahead if she had her way.

17
DESSERT

Jamie heard the doorbell. Tom was right on time. She was a wreck. He was on her mind too much all week long. It was a wonder she got anything accomplished. As soon as she thought about him, she tucked herself away in a private corner and played with herself. *Worse than any guy I've ever dated. I can't keep my hands out of my own pants.* She was a bit horrified that she was out of control, but afterwards, she smiled like a fool, tension gone...until the next time.

A basket case, that's what I am. She had to win his heart tonight. It wasn't just the sex, it was Tom. Something about him made her want him to hang around.

What if I mess this up? What if his friends don't like me? What if he thinks I'm too old? Jamie thought of all the things that could go wrong on their date and then realized Tom was still outside her door. *What if he leaves because I haven't opened the door yet?* She wanted to kick herself. She was a power person, got things done. Her feelings for Tom were something that made her uncomfortable. *Or at least until I know where I stand.*

"Be right there." Jamie called out and hoped Tom heard her through the thick wood door.

She took one last look in the mirror. She had planned every detail in her outfit, down to her skinny black leather pumps with their tiny heels, to wow him. The tight horizontal black and white T-shirt, a bit French looking, the vintage short yellow skirt with a black net lace under slip, very eighties, short and flouncy enough he could slip his hand on her thigh without anyone noticing. *Easy-peasy-lemon-squeezy.*

She loved that phrase from when she was a kid. Only now she was thinking X-rated adult thoughts. She pushed her long blond hair behind her ears to show off the gold loop earrings.

Breathe deeply. All her bravado and bold outfit did not hide the fact she was nervous. She took another deep breath and casually opened the door.

"Wow. You look hot." Tom's face told her he meant what he said. "Adorable might work too. You look adorable!"

Jamie suddenly felt adorable. "Good to see you, Tom. You look great too." She gave him a hug, then stepped back and looked around behind him. "Where are your friends?"

Tom actually blushed. "I hope you don't mind I didn't call you. They canceled out for the weekend. Last minute family issues."

"I think I can live with that. But so sorry your company bailed." Jamie wasn't sorry, she was thrilled. Not that she wouldn't like to meet his friends, but she really wanted a one-on-one date with him first time out.

"Please come in? I seem to have you blocked outside. I'm not a very gracious hostess." Jamie moved back and gave Tom her most inviting smile. She surprised herself with how calm she sounded.

Tom walked in and closed the door behind him. He reached for Jamie and pulled her right to him, touched her face, and kissed her gently on her mouth. "I've been wanting to kiss you again since we parted last week."

Jamie blushed. Her opportunity to finally have sex after a year stood before her. She kissed Tom back, then pulled away. She didn't want a one-night stand with him. She wanted to get to know him. *If they had sex right away would he be gone? Maybe that was all he was interested in.* Jamie's confidence wavered again. *I'm an idiot. God how I hate dating.* She quietly chastised herself. She never knew what to do and when. *I need to do this right so he'll come back.*

"I have reservations at a great place. Dinner is waiting for us, my lady." Tom interrupted her thoughts. He did a dip in front of her and stood back up. "Ready?"

Jamie grinned. Tom was a bit of a clown. She started to relax.

They were going to have a real date. Not just a romp in the bedroom. At least this wasn't about just sex for him either. At least not the wham-bam-thank-you-ma'am kind.

"Let me grab my bag and keys, lock up, and I'm ready!"

Ten minutes later Tom parked his car in front of the charming yellow Victorian house with a huge wrap around porch that Jamie had visited a few days ago. It was not dark yet, but tiny white lights outlined the porch and twinkled in the early evening dusk. It was the new restaurant that just placed an ad with her paper.

"Like?" Tom smiled at Jamie and squeezed her hand. "The house kind of matches your skirt!" He chuckled.

Jamie laughed and rolled her eyes. "How utterly thoughtful of you to find a yellow restaurant to match my yellow skirt!"

"I aim to please. Actually they serve the best seafood. Maybe I should have asked if you like seafood. I'd hate to find out you're allergic and have you keel over on me. I want to make you faint with my charm, not pass out from hives or worse." He winked at her. His dark eyes sparkled against his tan skin.

"No it's fine. I love seafood. Grilled shrimp my favorite."

A young lady came up and led them to a table by the window. "Your waiter will be with you in a minute. Can I get you something from the bar?"

Tom ordered a bottle of Riesling wine. "See. I remember what you like." He smiled and continued. "Some of my students work here and a good friend is the owner."

"Don't tell me your friend is Dale. He just placed an ad in our paper."

"No way. Yes, we've known each other since we were in college. Dale moved back here from Denver a year ago with a dream to have his own restaurant. You are sitting in that dream now."

"Your students? Are you a teacher? I thought you were the student when you said *you had class in the morning* last week at the club."

"You thought I was a student? Do I look that young? They tease me it's my bald head. I shaved it for a play last year and liked the look — are guys allowed to say that, liked the look? — and have shaved it ever since."

"Love the look, and it is fine to say that. What do you teach and, if I may ask, how old are you?"

Jamie knew she was obsessed with this age thing, but better to get it out of the way and relax, or die in the process.

Tom scooted his chair closer to her and kissed her, quickly and gently. "Now why do you want to know my age? Does age matter? I'm pretty young in my actions."

Jamie burst out laughing. "How old do you think I am?" Did he think he was much older than her? *Thanks for the good genes, Mom.*

"I'm thirty-eight." They said it in unison and looked at each other.

"Damn, I thought I must be ten years older than you." Jamie could finally get that fear off the table. "You do look young."

"So do you."

Jamie was charmed that Tom worried he might be too old for her. Boy, they had a lot to talk about over dinner.

"So tell me about your job. I saw you were the editor of the *Neighborhood News* on your business card. Small local paper, but it sure keeps you up on what's happening. Couldn't live without it."

The wine was refreshing, the dinner scrumptious. Jamie made a mental note to write a review for Tom's friend Dale.

"You know you stole my heart at the club." Tom pulled Jamie's hand to his lips and kissed it.

Jamie felt at ease for the first time in a week. Tom would be around. He was as excited about her as she was about him.

"Thanks for coming by tonight!" Dale stopped by the table. "It's been a great week." Dale slapped Tom on the back and reached over to shake Jamie's hand. "Good to see you again. Hope that coupon brings in some more customers. We're going to have live music starting next week. Did I put that in the ad? So busy I don't remember what I do."

"Yes you did. I'm also going to comp you a small article. So fax over the information you'd like included, or call, and I'll send Jessica by."

"I like that plan. You two have fun. Tom, drinks next week old buddy?"

Jamie couldn't decide if the ride home was awkward. The time to make a decision on how far to go was nearing. They would be at her place in ten minutes. She was nervous again and did not like that one bit.

Tom parked in her drive and turned to her. He moved closer and buried his face in her neck and gave her a nip. It was a gesture that send shivers through her. "I've been thinking of this all week." His hand caressed her face and moved down to the front of her T-shirt. His touch electrified her.

"You've been on my mind too." She wasn't going to play coy. "Would you like to come in?"

"Yes I would. Wasn't sure if you were ready for me."

"Hon, I was ready for you when you said hello." *Corny, but too true to ignore.* Jamie didn't want to wait any longer.

They got in the front door, locked it, and then locked into each other. Tom kissed her face, her neck, as his hands moved down her T-shirt, and tugged it out from her skirt. His hands were warm on her skin as he moved across her bra and unhooked the front of it. "Oh you feel good." Jamie heard Tom mumble as he pulled up her T. She raised her arms and her shirt came off and dropped to the floor. It only took a second to wiggle out of her bra. She closed her eyes for an instant and felt heat move through her body.

He held her back and looked at her. "You're beautiful. Even more than I imagined." His hands were back on her full breasts as he bent his head to kiss them. Jamie arched her back and hoped he would nip her there as he did on her neck. She got her wish. She wanted out of the rest of her clothes. She wanted him naked beside her in bed.

Jamie pushed a little at Tom. She hated to move his mouth, but she had plans for him too.

"The bedroom is down the hall. Care to join me?"

Tom followed behind her. His hand reached up under her skirt, caught the skinny edge of her thong. Jamie stopped in her tracks. Her back still towards Tom. She held her breath as his hands moved across her butt, caressing it, and toying with her thong. He tugged at her thong, pulling it up, tightening it between her thighs, and up into her. The movement sent sparks throughout her body. She stood still to see what he would do next.

"You feel good, baby." Tom was behind her, this time on his knees. He moved the skirt and net lace up and pulled her thong down. "Step out of it. Let me look at you."

Jamie obeyed. She moved her feet slightly and stepped away from her lace thong.

"Bend over. I want to see you. All of you." Tom's voice was a whisper.

She was on fire. The feel of her skirt still on made it all more exciting. Why did a bit of clothing seem so much more erotic than being totally naked?

"You're beautiful." Tom's words excited her more. She was still in position, exposed to him. Waiting.

She didn't wait long. His hands moved her legs apart a little further and she felt his tongue slip in between them. She thought she might faint from pleasure and prayed she wouldn't teeter over.

He stopped, stood up, and turned her around. He put both his hands on her face and kissed her. "Now taste me."

Jamie unzipped Tom's jeans and tugged at them until they fell to the floor. Tom stepped out of them. He did not wear briefs. She looked at him, how hard he was, and smiled at him. "You look beautiful, too." Jamie wanted him in bed. She would take care of him there.

She had one last thing to do. She unzipped her badly crinkled skirt, let it drop to the floor. She was totally naked before him and his look told her all she needed to know. She was glad she thought to keep condoms in her night stand. She wondered how many they would need. They went into the bedroom and closed the door.

18
Sweet Rewards

"Yes! Yes! Yes!" Susan looked at her monitor, jumped up from her chair, and did a happy dance around the room. "Woot! Woot!" She was ecstatic beyond words. She'd written a pretty steamy sex scene. Daisy barked and twirled at her feet. "This calls for a celebration!"

Susan popped into the kitchen, opened the pantry, and grabbed the bag of her favorite chocolate cookies. One bite and she was in heaven. The cookie was a sinful pleasure, thick, soft, and loaded with dark chocolate bits and almonds. She hummed as her tongue rolled a large chocolate chip in her mouth, twirling it, before she swallowed the remains.

"Oh God, this is good, so good." She went to take another bite and stopped, the cookie halfway to her mouth. She giggled. *I sound like I'm having an orgasm, not eating a cookie.* Eyes closed she savored another bite. *Chocolate, orgasms, who cares. Both are delish. And right now, all I have is this cookie.* Susan laughed. She knew she was being silly.

"You get a treat too." Susan reached in the vintage pink tin candy container and grabbed a tiny biscuit. "There you go, girl." Daisy grabbed it and disappeared. Susan refilled her glass and headed back to the computer.

I want to be kissed like that. Susan reread the last chapter in a hushed voice. *Damn, Tom has turned me on too.* The words she wrote excited her more than she would admit to any of her friends. She had trouble admitting it to herself. She wanted to be Jamie, feel that intensity and desire again. *I could be Jamie. We look alike except for the color of our hair.*

Susan felt a tug of sadness. *Am I crazy or just lonely?* She felt like there were two of her these days. Susan, and the Susan who wanted to be Jamie. *I'll settle down when I finish this book. At least I am writing it.*

She had Harley69 to thank. His role playing loosened her up. It was bizarre, the words they shared, his final farewell on the webcam. She wasn't sure he fell under the category of inspiration, but he got her cranked up to write.

"Yes, yes, I'm hyper, Daisy." She looked at Daisy staring up at all the commotion she was making. If only she had someone to celebrate with. But it was just her and Daisy. She was having her own party of one, plus dog.

She took another sip from her glass. The sherry felt warm going down. It was time to remove her profile from *Love Me Cupid*. One crazy night was enough. No harm, no foul. She got what she needed. Her profile was a sham and she didn't want to court any trouble. She'd label Harley 69 her one-night-stand.

Susan decided she was just ridiculous. She made a mental note *not* to tell the girls about her latest folly. She was just about ready to hit *delete* on her profile when the instant message icon lit up on her monitor.

Would you like to chat? It was Tease&Please.

Susan never answered his e-mail. She remembered she'd liked his photo when she first saw it. She forgot he lived close by her. The site gave out the mileage between them. She hesitated a moment and then decided to accept the chat. A larger screen popped up where they could type. She saw his message.

Been writing to you. Hoped you would write back. Love your photo.

Susan smiled. Nice enough. She replied. *Sorry, been busy. Have a minute now.* She could delete her profile soon enough. She wasn't ready to sit in quiet by herself on a lonely moonlit night.

And so it began. Somewhat politely. She was restless. There was no one to share her day's work with. A little messaging couldn't hurt. She took a sip of sherry. Her guard was down and she said more than she should in answer to his questions.

Name is Dan. What's yours?

Susan.

Nice name. What do you do?

I'm a writer.

What do you write? Anything I might have read?

Susan chuckled to herself. She thought about her memoirs and dog column. *More chick-lit type of stuff.*

Like what? I might surprise you.

Well, I write a dog column for an on-line magazine. Do you like dogs? My other writing is definitely not for men. Memoirs.

My dog died last year. Big golden. Got out, hit by a car.

Oh, I'm sorry. My dog never goes into the yard alone.

What kind of dog do you have?

Daisy is a small mixed breed. Only seven pounds

Sounds sweet. Does she get along with your roommate?

Susan thought it was an odd question, but she was on a roll. *I live alone. Bought a farmhouse last year in a small town by the college.* She took another sip of sherry.

Have you met many guys here?

No. What about you?

The instant message icon disappeared from her monitor. Susan wondered where he went. Was he writing someone else?

Sorry, had to take care of something. He was back.

Susan wanted to ask him what he had to take care of, but let it alone. Not her business. She was in a chatty mood and not ready for the messaging to end. Maybe she should flirt with him. She sounded pretty dull. She came on *Love Me Cupid* for research, but everyone else was here to hook up. Find romance. Find whatever they were looking for. Whatever turned them on. *It is a dating site*, she reminded herself. People joined sites like this every day. She decided to relax and have some fun with him.

Why the Tease&Please ID? Even though she asked, she figured she knew the answer. Some guys like to think they took more time taking care of a women's needs than most. She wanted to get him a little worked up. This was her last night on the dating site. What could go wrong?

I like to please women. Some men only think of themselves. I like to do what makes a women happy.

It's nice to hear that. Some men just hit and run.

Tell me what you like. He asked at her most vulnerable moment. It was past midnight. The lights in her office were soft and low. She could see the moon through the tall windows beside her desk. She remembered having a man in bed with her and desire started to flood through her.

I like to be touched. God how she missed being touched. She didn't even have anyone to hug. Human touch. So important.

What are you wearing?

A T-shirt and PJ bottoms. That certainly didn't sound sexy. Susan filled her glass again. She wanted to be sexy.

Are you wearing a bra?

No.

Would you like my hands to touch you?

Susan didn't hesitate with her answer. She felt a flush flood over her.

Yes. If she were talking rather than typing, her voice would have been a whisper.

Touch yourself and pretend it's me.

Susan reached under her T-shirt. Her cool hands warmed as she caressed herself, fondled her breasts. She rocked her hips slowly in her chair, increasing the sensation. She stopped and wrote back. *I did.*

How did it feel?

Soft and lovely. Susan was getting excited. Not about him, or her hands, just remembering the last time someone touched her.

Where else do you want me to touch you?

Susan didn't answer. She knew what she wanted, but the words would not come.

He messaged her again. *Reach in your pajamas. Touch yourself there. Tell me how that feels.*

Susan thought about all she'd written for Jamie. She wanted that and more. For the next twenty minutes they sent messages back and forth. He told her what to touch and she touched herself. She told him how it made her feel. It was a fantasy, but it was her fantasy. There was no human voice, just messages on her screen, a photo of a cute guy in her mind, and her hands doing things she wanted a man to do to her.

Come on, baby. Let it go.

She touched herself until she didn't need to touch anymore.

Did I please you baby?

Susan looked at the instant message and got nervous. Her passion gone, reality hit home. What had she done? She didn't want to chat with him anymore. Not later, not ever.

Got to go. Susan sent the last instant message. After all, she was polite and it seemed rude to just click off and disappear. She couldn't believe she was even worried about it. Exasperated, she went to her account settings and erased herself off the *Love Me Cupid* site. Enough was enough. She had been out of control with two strangers in two nights.

Susan clicked off the light by her computer and walked back to the bedroom. Daisy curled up on her pillow. She took off her T-shirt and dropped her PJ bottoms to the floor. She looked at her naked reflection in the dresser mirror. The moonlight made her skin luminous. She thought about Steve and how easy it had been to be with him. It wasn't easy anymore. Dating had changed, she had changed. She thought she had all the answers to go on without him. Now she wondered if she had closed out too much of the world.

Am I lonely? That was a question she asked herself more than she liked since she started writing her new book. Jamie made her think about her own demons. She didn't know what she wanted, but she knew what Jamie wanted. Jamie had been moving her in that direction from the beginning

Susan slipped back into her PJ's and curled into her bed. A new chapter was forming. There were things Jamie needed to sort out to be sure Tom was the one. She pulled her quilt up and let Jamie's story line form as she waited for sleep to take over.

He went back to find her profile. She was gone. Wiped clean. He thought it sweet she thought she could just vanish and be done with him. He knew how to work her. That sappy dog story drew her in. His fake profile worked every time too. She was real, he was not. She told him enough. Susan, a writer, dog column. He found her website, her column, her full name, and her lovely farmhouse. He had saved her photo to his desktop. He looked at her picture. He had pleased her tonight. Now he would take care of himself. His eyes were glued to her photo. Susan, Susan…he kept repeating her name. Soon they would be together.

19
HE LOVES ME,
HE LOVES ME NOT

Jamie couldn't decide if last night was a fairy tale or a chapter out of an erotic novel. Tom was amazing. She looked at her bedside table and counted the empty condom wrappers....three. Two were from last night, and one from first thing this morning before Tom left to catch up with his running buddies. It was an honorable number of wrappers. He took his time with her and if she had any more attention, she might have passed out from exhaustion. She smiled, a Cheshire cat grin, remembering that thing he did that she loved, and fell back on her pillow giggling.

"I think you should insure your tongue," she kidded him last night before they fell asleep. She woke up to Tom's dark eyes watching her. She knew what that look meant.

"I'm not really a morning person..." Jamie looked at the clock across the room as his hand moved down under the quilt and up her thigh.

"Pretend you're asleep and I'll take care of you." He grinned as she looked at him through her sleepy eyes. "I'll pamper you a bit."

"I'm embarrassed to admit it, my body is not used to all this attention." Jamie blushed as she said the words. Every inch of her was sore. "I'd love a massage." *He wanted to pamper her, she'd be a greedy gal and tell him what she wanted.*

"Your wish is my command. Roll over and I'll work some magic."

Jamie was embarrassed to have him see her butt in the morning light, but she wanted to feel his hands relax the tension in her muscles more. She obeyed.

"Beautiful." Tom eased himself over her thighs. He straddled her and leaned down to quickly kiss her butt. Then his hands moved to her shoulders. "I can feel a knot right here." He touched the side of her neck and ran his hand down the length of her shoulder. "You are really tight."

The release last night was wonderful. She had a love hate relationship with her body this morning. She was physically in great shape, but sex after all this time, well, it worked muscles she never used riding her bike. Her neck was knotted up from a week of worry things might not work out well between them. That was a waste of time, it was a perfect evening. They meshed together beautifully, not only with sex, but between their lovemaking, they talked about everything.

Jamie felt her tension ease as Tom worked on her shoulders, gently kneading and stroking, running his hands up the side and back of her neck and down her shoulders and upper back. She moaned when he moved his fingers in deep circles, pushing with his thumb, to go deep into her shoulder muscles.

"How does that feel, baby?"

"Wonderful. What can I say? Just what the doctor ordered."

Tom eased himself back to her side. Jamie turned to face him. She loved his looks. She felt her body heat up again as she reached out to caress his face. His shaved head, dark eyes, and tan skin excited her. His day old chin stubble sent chills up every nook in her body when he rubbed his face against her bare skin. She was ready for what he had started earlier.

"I think something else needs your expert touch now." She winked at Tom and reached for his hand and moved it to her thigh. "I believe this is where we left off."

Jamie closed her eyes and felt a warmth tingle through every inch of her body from her toes to her head. Tom was so sensual. His lips, his hands, she couldn't get enough of him.

"I want you now." She begged him, arching her hips into him as he nipped her neck.

"Your wish is my command." Tom's voice was just a whisper as he moved on top of her.

When they finished they lay next to each other, holding hands. Jamie was exhausted but so happy. He was everything she ever dreamed of in a lover.

"You are good, so good." Jamie sat up and gently punched him in the chest. "Romantic like my favorite novels and naughty like a porn movie." She giggled at the look on his face.

"Nice to know. If you want, I'll text you from my cell and see how worked up I can get you. I'm good with words too." Tom playfully rolled his eyes and kissed her knee. "Got to go now. I'll be late for the jogging group. It's our Sunday morning ritual." He gave her a gentle kiss on the mouth. "I'm thinking it's time to change my Sunday ritual to something else."

Jamie got up and slipped on her vintage white lace robe and walked Tom to the door. He pulled her close and kissed her hard. "We need to do this again soon. I'll call you later today."

"I'd like that." Jamie watched him walk to his car. He turned and waved to her. She closed the door and hightailed it back to get under the quilt. She wanted a quick nap. She'd had very little sleep.

The sound of her cell startled her. She reached for it off the night stand and knocked the condom wrappers to the ground. "Hello." She figured it would be Lynn.

"How was last night?"

"Hang on, I've got to grab something." Lynn could wait a minute. She didn't want to leave the wrappers on the floor and forget to toss them. Thank goodness Tom disposed of everything else.

"So…." Lynn dragged it out, "how was last night?"

"Perfect. I really, really like him. I think he likes me too." Jamie was sure he liked her. It was a great feeling…finally. "I'd forgotten how nice things could be when you were with a guy you liked and who got how you were. Never thought I'd find someone after Jack died."

"Oh sweetie. I'm so happy for you. I'm guessing he spent the night?" Lynn wanted to be polite, but she wanted details.

"Yes he did! And he is great in bed. Happy with that information. I think it's time to toss the vibrator you gave me." *Not that I ever used it*, Jamie thought to herself. Then she wondered if Tom might like to use it with her? She felt her face warm up as she put that thought on the back burner. She didn't want anything other than Tom's hands on her...for now.

"What are you doing later today? I want to run to the bookstore and pick up the new *Prairie Design Interior* decorating book. I hear it is killer. You know me, have to keep up with the latest for my customers."

Lynn owned a small antique shop. "I'm on the cutting edge of the latest trends," she like to boast. She was being modest. She was a trend-setter and her shop had been featured in various magazines over the years.

"Are you asking me to come with you?"

"What do you think? We could meet at the mall. Have dinner in that little Mexican place. I could use a Margarita and some girl talk. Ben is with his poker buddies tonight and I have all the time in the world."

Jamie needed a change of scenery. She hated waiting for her cell to ring. "See you at six. Whoever gets there first orders a pitcher of Margaritas."

Jamie went back to bed. It was that kind of a day. She set the alarm on her cell for three hours, just in case she went into a coma. Her body ached and she was so tired, she felt it could be possible. She wanted her cell close in case Tom called.

The sound of the alarm woke her up. She grabbed her cell and shut it off. It was almost five. She checked her recent calls. Maybe she'd slept through Tom's. The only call was from Lynn earlier. Jamie sat up. She needed to get ready to meet Lynn. She didn't want to be paranoid about Tom so soon. Although this was the critical time. They'd just had sex and she didn't hold back on anything with him. *I don't want to rush things,* Jamie chatted in her mind as she turned on the shower. *I just want to miss the dating drama and jump right to the part where we are a couple.*

Jamie pulled her long blonde hair up into a pony tail, twirled it into a bun and pinned it in place. Out of the way for her shower. The warm water eased the final muscle tenseness she felt. Now if she could only relax about Tom's call.

She slipped into her jeans and looked in her closet for the perfect top. She always watched how she dressed in public. She had an image to keep up for the newspaper. If she ran into one of her clients, she'd hate to be frumpy. She knew Lynn would be as stylish as ever.

She pulled out an altered couture top her friend Angie made for her. That girl had talent. She took vintage clothing pieces and worked magic changing them into fantasy fashions with lace and other adornments. Lynn carried some of Angie's pieces at her shop. This jacket was her favorite. It was a vintage tan linen smocked jacket with large cuffs and big buttons down the front. Angie had added lace across the shoulders and a double tiered lace ruffle at the bottom. It was blousy and looked great over her skinny jeans.

Jamie was also known for her jewelry. Last year it was vintage Mexican Silver, this year she was into assemblage pieces full of rhinestones, antique medals, and old crosses. It was a sickness, but one that kept her healthy.

Some of her favorite pieces came from Lynn's shop, made by local artists, and some from her favorite online shops. She kept her necklaces draped over a French dress form in the corner of her bedroom. It had been a gift from Lynn when she rearranged her store. Jamie almost cried when she brought it over.

"For you hon, know how much you coveted this. Got a full mannequin for the shop and space is tight. This needs a new home."

Jamie knew Lynn was lying. She had plenty of space in the shop to keep both. Lynn was a gift-giver. If she knew you loved something of hers, she found a way to give it to you. She called her on it once.

Lynn's answer made sense. "I am surrounded by beauty all day long and it is fun to share. I have more than I'll ever sell."

Jamie picked a necklace and earrings, then slipped into a pair of her vintage tan leather ankle boots. Satisfied with how she looked, she grabbed her tooled leather Mexican handbag. She felt like a fashionista. Jamie amused herself at times with how much attention she put on the details of her outfits.

She glanced at her watch as she locked the front door. *Why hadn't Tom called like he said he would?* She panicked again. *What if it doesn't work out? What if he doesn't call? Not tonight, not next week.* She'd felt so certain it was a mutual feeling only a few hours ago. Dating. Was anything ever a sure thing? Even in marriage it wasn't written in stone. Jack had let her down once, but they were already married. She and Tom just met.

I'm a crazy lady. Jamie backed out of her driveway. *Margaritas will put this in perspective.* She couldn't wait to talk it over with Lynn. Why did she always want life to be like a fairy tale? She wanted that with Jack, thought she'd had it, until she found the letter. God, she'd put that behind her years ago. Now the thought of a new man dredged up her old worries. Tom. Jack. Maybe all men were alike. She wondered if Tom had a secret.

20
THE LETTER

In a perfect world life would be simple. Jamie sighed. She anxiously picked up her cell, kept checking to see if she'd missed a call or a text. Nothing.

She caught up with Lynn at the Mexican restaurant and immediately started to whine. "It's after six. He said he'd call. He hasn't."

"Relax. You will hear from him. You worried last time and he called."

"Well that was before the sex. Maybe I was too quick to …" Jamie was beside herself.

"Stop it, hon, you're making yourself crazy." *And you're making me crazy.* Lynn wanted to be supportive, but Jamie was being a bit of a drama queen. "You wanted the sex, so relax with it already."

Jamie took a deep breath. "You are right as usual. Sorry I am such a drag. First sex in a year and I am off my rocker. Trying to make Tom into my next big true love."

"And he might be. It was just last night. Settle down!"

"I am an ass." Jamie started to lighten up. She was being ridiculous, she hoped. "But this is why I liked being married. It was so simple. Now things are …well, complicated."

"Your marriage was complicated too, if I may remind you." Lynn held her breath. She was treading on sacred ground. They never spoke of it after that one night when Jamie called her crying.

"Okay. So he wasn't perfect. He cheated on me. Thanks for bringing that up now."

"You make that man into a saint and then expect every other man to live up to him. He was a cheating sack of..." *be nice,* "of garbage. Maybe it was just once, but that first year you were married. I declare. I never forgave him, although you did." Well the cards were out. Lynn held her breath.

"I know. But he really was sorry. And things got so much better after that." Jamie thought back to the night he confessed he'd had sex with an old girlfriend of his that happened to be in town for business. *Monkey business,* is what Jamie decided. Of course he only confessed because of the letter she found in his desk.

She wasn't a snoop. He asked for it. Asked her to go get a copy of his broker's license.

"Where do you want me to check?" Jamie put down her book and looked at Jack, sitting on the couch in his jeans, covered in receipts, working on their taxes. He was so handsome and he was all hers.

"Center drawer of my desk in the office. Should be in a tan envelope." He never looked up when he answered her. He probably had no idea Miss Sherlock Holmes was about to find a clue to change their lives.

Jamie went through the top drawer and couldn't find the envelope. She tugged open the large side drawer and pulled out a stack of papers. On top was a letter postmarked two weeks earlier. The envelope had Sandy's return address on it. *Why is Sandy writing to Jack?*

Jamie was more than curious. She knew Sandy well. A letter meant trouble. She remembered the first night she met Sandy, she was in town for business then too. Jack and she had just gotten engaged. The three of them went out to dinner. Sandy had suggested the restaurant followed by the words, *my treat.* Jack saw a client as soon as they entered the restaurant and popped over to a table across the room. Sandy had the nerve to pull her to the side and remind her she and Jack had *done it* before and it was damned good.

"We were an item for some time. The sex was great." Sandy was pretty, but wore too much make-up. Her face was so close Jamie could smell the wine on her breath. "You know, if I wanted him, I just have to ask." She snapped her fingers like you might call a dog. "But I like you, so I'll back off."

At dinner that night Sandy got so drunk she hit her soup bowl, broke it, and sent broth and china across the table. Then she ran to the bathroom and puked. Jamie was the one holding back her hair as she heaved over the toilet in a stall that was too small, and a testament to how thin they both were to fit in it together. Jack was angry at the scene she made. He also got stuck paying the tab. When they dropped her back at the hotel, Jamie walked her to her room and made sure she got in safely. She slammed the door on her way out. *Bitch.* Then she broke out into a big smile. If there was one thing she knew about Jack, getting stuck with that big dinner tab was a strike against Sandy.

The next day she called to say she had to catch her flight home. Jamie answered the phone. "Sorry I was sick last night. Congratulations on your engagement. Give the boy a hug for me." She hung up and that was that as far as Jamie knew.

Until she found the letter. She opened it gingerly. Part of her felt terrible, like she was breaking a trust, the other part of her wanted to know why the bitch was writing. She almost threw up when she read it.

I hope you got home without any problems. Don't want to disturb your home life. Just wanted you to myself for a few hours. The sex was...incredible. You always knew what I liked and you didn't disappoint. We should have stayed together years ago, but maybe the sex was so damn hot and wet because we didn't. Business went well too. Take care, big guy. Sandy.

Jamie grabbed the letter and ran down the stairs. "How could you..." She was crying so hard she couldn't even get the words out. She just thrust the crumpled paper in his face, stormed upstairs, slammed and locked the bedroom door. She called Lynn and cried until she curled up in bed exhausted.

The next morning she woke up with a new attitude. The bitch was not going to ruin her marriage. Jamie washed her face, held the damp rag on her eyes until the swelling went down, ran a comb through her long hair, and put on lip-gloss. She went downstairs to see what was left of her marriage.

Jack was asleep on the couch. She slipped into the kitchen and turned on the coffee. Then she pulled out a skillet and started bacon and pancakes. She banged the skillet hard on the stove and turned on the small TV over the refrigerator. Within a few minutes Jack appeared in the doorway.

"I don't know what to say." He looked at her, waiting to see if she would listen to him. "I am sorry. That doesn't cut it. I have no excuse. We met for drinks and it got carried away. Was like old times with Sandy, you know how long we dated."

"So, are you seeing her again?" Jamie's voice was cold. She was terrified of his answer, but she would not let him know.

"God no, honey. I love you. I want this marriage to work. Please forgive me." He said it so simply, so sincerely, she forgave him. She would make him wait a little longer to find that out.

"Breakfast is ready. Sit down."

They ate breakfast together like they did every morning. Jamie thought about Jack screwing Sandy as she chomped on her bacon and slowly sipped her coffee. As mad as she was, the vision started to arouse her. She hated that, but it turned her on. *What was it Jack did that Sandy liked so much? Was it the same thing he did to her that she loved?* She watched him like a cat watching a mouse, wanting to pounce. She held off doing or saying anything else. They exchanged a quick peck when he left for work.

"Never speak of last night again." Jamie called Lynn. "It's going to work."

That night she and Jack had make-up sex. It was hot. He did the thing she loved, and for some bizarre reason she loved it more thinking of his doing it to Sandy too. Perverse maybe, but it turned her on. Jack was hers. As mad and sad as she had been last night, she came back with a sexual understanding of herself. She was no longer shy in bed and sex went from something *they did* to something she never wanted to be without. Jamie found her fantasy life and it was the lifeline they shared with each other.

"You get a free pass this time!" Jamie wasn't mad at Lynn. "Jack did have his moments, but you know, the sex was outstanding. Made me forgive him for many things over the years."

"So sorry…" Lynn was relieved.

"No sorry needed. I think you helped me clear my head. What I liked about having a husband was I always had a man in bed. Miss that. And I guess I wanted Tom to be the man in my bed."

"Should I do that thing again where I conjure him up by rubbing my forehead?" Lynn giggled from relief she had not upset their friendship.

"Hold off on your magical powers. I'd like to see what magic I have over Tom. I want the only witchcraft to bring him to me to be my own." Jamie's laugh was soft. "I'm hungry. Do you think we should order?"

Time would tell if Tom and she would have a happy ending.

21
LET'S MEET UP

"At least get out of the house. Take your laptop up to a coffee shop, something." Susan woke up remembering Emily's words. She didn't sleep well. She had a nightmare. She dreamed she was old and alone, sitting in her rocking chair on the porch of her farmhouse. She'd never made new friends and her old friends had gone on with their lives. The years brought them children and grandchildren. Her years brought her...well, loneliness. Susan hated her dream. As she got dressed she decided to revise her dream in her mind. *The years brought her a New York Times best seller.* Susan smiled. That took the edge off the dream. She was almost done writing her book and that was a great reason to be happy, if she would relax. *Dwell on the positive,* Susan reminded herself. Still, she had a feeling of foreboding she couldn't ignore. It was more than the dream.

What triggered that nightmare? Susan pulled on her jeans and T-shirt. *I'm not normally depressed and shit, that was depressing.* She tried to figure it out as she brushed her teeth. Daisy yapped at her feet, anxious to go out.

It seemed harmless at the time, but the encounters on *Love Me Cupid* stirred up feelings she didn't want to face. She'd gotten crazy with two strangers using the excuse it was research. Such BS. She missed sex, real sex. She felt uneasy about the two men she'd let loose with. What did she really know about either of those guys? She'd found Harley69 on Google, but it was only business facts, nothing personal. Her profile was a blatant lie, they had probably lied too. *For all I know they could be serial killers.*

Susan started to annoy herself. She wasn't worried about her safety, but her state of mind, well that could be in jeopardy. Perhaps three years of no sex had made her daft.

Susan had to smile at how silly her thoughts were. *I'm bonkers from lack of sex. I wonder if I could claim that as a medical condition.* She played out a scenario in her mind. She could see herself at a shrink's office with her health insurance card checking in for an exam.

"What are your symptoms?" The nurse handed her a chart to fill out.

"Crazy as shit from lack of sex."

"Oh, honey," the nurse would sympathize. *"My sister had the same problem. It wasn't pretty. We lost her that year."*

"She died?" Susan was horrified. Could lack of sex be fatal?

"No honey, she ran off with a male stripper." The nurse paused. *"Midlife crisis."*

Susan broke out into a laugh. *I'm so pathetic.*

She'd had a different dream a year ago. It was a wonderful dream. She had a vision of her future life when she signed the closing papers for the farmhouse. A movie version of her future, she realized now. That movie version had her house full of her old friends from Atlanta spending the weekends with her. She took classes at the college and had dinner parties for the new friends she'd met at school. She joined a woman's club and garden club, and offered her lovely patio and kitchen for their meetings and luncheons. She wrote and spent time with other authors critiquing their work. Her dream a year ago had her in the middle of wonderful friendships. Her reality was that she was more alone than ever living in her farmhouse.

Susan petted Daisy and they headed towards the kitchen. *I want coffee.* The coffee maker was set up and just needed to be plugged in. She reached up into the cabinet and pulled down the first cup her hand felt. Solid yellow from the fifties, tulip shaped. Not one of her favorites, boring actually. *Just like me.* Then she remembered why she'd bought that cup. The bright yellow color had fascinated her when she found it for a dollar at the thrift store. After all the years nothing had dulled its brilliance. The cup was to be a reminder to stay sunny no matter what. She was pleased with her choice, filled it to the brim, and walked out to the patio with Daisy. She needed to snap out of her gloomy mood and get back to her positive self.

The morning air was heavenly. She loved to sit and look out at her expanse of land. The perennials filled her yard with soft colors everywhere she looked. Tucked in old planters, her annuals dotted the patio with an infusion of color. The fruit trees helped to block the dismal view of the Miller farm. The old rosemary bush that was in such pitiful shape the day she first saw the property, had thrived and was now three feet tall and four feet wide. The rosemary legend was true. A woman did rule on this property. She was that woman.

The warmth of the coffee on her tongue, drizzling down her throat, and the heavy aroma as she inhaled the lovely hazelnut fragrance, were the final calming touches she needed. She put on her thinking cap.

She needed more social activities. Her best buds were an hour away. She had not involved herself in anything close by in a year. Her neighbors were not the answer. She did not have a change of heart about wanting to know anything about them. What she needed was to get back out and do something more than sit at her computer. She didn't need to be a rocket scientist to know the answer.

When she had her shop she joined *Let's-Meet-Up*. It was the perfect online site, not for dating, but to meet groups of people in planned activities with similar interests. There were groups everywhere for just about everything you wanted to do, from dinner out, movies, hiking, exercise classes, and groups to just have fun as friends.

It worked well for her. She joined, paid a fee, and started a garden book club and journaling group. They met monthly in the back room of the shop. Teaching the journaling group gave her the final answer on what she really wanted to do. Write. She loved her shop, and it was great when Steve was alive, but on her own, she wanted to focus on writing. The new owner, Holly, wanted to continue the tradition of groups meeting in the shop at night. Susan stepped down as the organizer and Holly took over. Susan was happy she didn't have to cancel the groups and disappointment everyone.

She visited Holly right before she moved to the farmhouse.

Holly's eye for the older antiques was not like hers. Holly was younger and was more into the newly produced, easy to find items, that had an old look to them. Still, she did a fine job of keeping the feel of the place. It was amazing how close some reproductions looked to the real thing. Susan had to keep herself from purchasing a small tin tabletop chest with tiny drawers, newly made to look like old weathered zinc. It had ten thin drawers that would be perfect to hold her jewelry and it looked so old and used it could pass for the real thing. She stopped herself at the price…$149.00. She still dreamed about that sweet piece. New or not.

That's my problem. Susan laughed out loud at her last thoughts. *I dream about antiques, houses, everything but men and sex.* She could control these other things, she realized, but a man and dating…that was out of control and out of her comfort level. Joining *Let's-Meet-Up* was in her control. She grabbed her cup, called Daisy, and headed inside. There must be a social group up by the school.

Susan went online and typed in *Let's-Meet-Up*. The site came up immediately and she clicked on the link. She put her zip code in the search bar on their home page and clicked on *radius of twenty miles.* A few book clubs, hiking groups, and social media groups popped up on her screen. *Not quite what I'm looking for.* She scrolled down further and a social group 'Beer and Buddies' caught her eye. It was geared to the thirty to forty age group and met every two weeks at local pubs. It was in Arden, right up by Community College. Their next meeting was in two days. Susan planned to be there. But first she had to renew her membership to *Let's-Meet-Up*.

She pulled a small avatar from her documents file on her computer to use as her profile photo. *I think I've about used this to death.* It was on her web, blog, Facebook and Twitter page. Susan shook her head, but she did like the photo. She'd made it using an online program that edited photos to just the right size for avatars

She went back to the 'Beer and Buddies' home page and clicked on *yes* to make her reservation. The other members who had RSVP'd to the meeting were listed, along with their photos. *Friendly faces.* Susan was pleased that the group looked nice. *I could sit and visit with anyone of them. If we don't have anything in common, well at least I am out of the house enjoying being with the living.*

It was a start to open her up for the universe to zip her along to her destiny.

Emily would be proud. Susan resisted the urge to call her. She shared all her thoughts with Emily, well, most of them. Some things were too painful for her to even think about herself. Her move to the farmhouse gave her what she had wanted the most, a clean slate to be whoever she wanted without being bogged down with history and expectations from her old life. It was time to do something with her clean slate.

It was all good. She was where she was meant to be. For the first time in a long time she wondered if there might be a man in her future.

22
THE MILLER FARM

Susan grabbed a glass of tea and headed out to the patio. She was pleased she had somewhere new to go in two days. Filled with a sense of accomplishment, she propped her feet up and took a big sip from her glass. She loved sweet tea in the heat of the day.

She looked across the yard into the Miller property. *I wish I'd seen the house in its day.* She was fascinated with the house. Its history was connected to her own house. She remembered Ann telling her how the property was split when Flora Miller married. She lived in the bridal house that had a happy marriage in it all those years ago.

Susan wanted to know more about the old farm. She would also love to track down the owners and give them a piece of her mind for leaving the house vacant and unattended all these years. It was heartbreaking to see the place going to ruin. It was also damn annoying. The view from her back yard looked straight into the Miller property. It was an eyesore. The overgrowth encroached on her land. Still, in all its decadence, there was something so splendid about the house and grounds. More than once she had driven by the front side of the farm where the house could be seen. It was eerie and hauntingly beautiful.

The house was a Victorian built in 1868. In its glory the porches had detailed railings and lovely mill work. Now they were sadly in decay. The old white paint had worn down to the wood in many places. The shutters were still on the windows, but had come loose and hung at odd angles. The front parlor windows went from floor to ceiling and had been boarded up to keep out trespasses, as had all the windows on the lower floor. Old photos of the house showed a gracious staircase in the entry, tall ceilings both upstairs and down, exposed handmade bricks on the six fireplaces, and southern heart of pine floors.

The *Safe Haven News* had run a story about the farm and its history a few years back. Susan found it online and was amazed to see all the old photos of it and of other points of historic interest in the tiny town.

The Miller Farm was a favorite spot for amateur photographers who had a fondness for abandoned houses. Many photos were posted on Flickr and Tumblr and it was rumored the house would be featured in a book on abandoned farmhouses in the South. While that was exciting, Susan was not fond of strangers prowling the premises and worried someone would venture into her yard. She was glad the old farm fence cut across the back of her property, separating the two.

Susan was romantic about the house. When Emily first came to visit and Susan showed it off from the street, Emily's only remark was, "Seriously creepy!"

The Oakville Cemetery was another draw that brought photographers. One particular marker, belonging to Mrs. Sarah Mae James, the wife of the founder of the downtown area, was said to be haunted. The cement was covered with mildew that had taken years to form. From a distance the mildew looked like a woman's profile. The story went that Mrs. James died before her husband and kept an eye on him after death so no other woman could have him.

"Willies. That gives me the willies!" Emily rolled her eyes when they visited the Cemetery. Susan gave her the three-minute Safe Haven tour that weekend. Emily liked her modern home and didn't get old houses. She most certainly did not want anything to be haunted.

"Does your house have a ghost?" Emily sat in the kitchen at the farm table drinking wine that night. "I think I'll head back to Atlanta if you say *yes!*"

"My house does have quite a history, but I think you're safe. The only thing that haunts this house is my dead dating life." Susan chuckled, but it was true.

"Don't get me started…" Emily paused and took a sip out of her glass. "You wanted to live here away from civilization as we all know it and you don't do anything to try and meet someone. Yeah, this town is dead. I bet there isn't a single man for miles. At least there is life at the college."

Susan kept her mouth shut. She asked for it with her somewhat humorous joke.

Emily's cell rang which ended that conversation. Susan was happy for the distraction.

"Al wants to know how I like the house." Emily winked at Susan and mouthed silently, *he misses me*. "It's fabulous. Just sits in the middle of nowhere."

Susan walked out of the kitchen. She wanted to give them privacy. She loved to roam her house at night and take in all the beauty. Maybe the place was haunted, but not with a ghost. All her dreams for the future filled every room. It was such a relief to walk through the house and feel hope and anticipation. She felt weightless, as if anything could happen here. In her old house she was bogged down with memories. That was the real haunted house.

"You can come back now." Emily's voice drifted in from the kitchen. "Our sex talk is over."

"Did you really talk about sex?" Susan sat back down at the table. "You two are animals. Can't even handle one night apart."

Emily blushed. "Can't help loving that guy."

"Can't say I blame you." Susan reached over and gave Emily a quick hug. They were such a sweet couple. "Think you two will ever get married?"

"Hush your mouth!" Emily held her hands up to form a cross in front of her. "We are fine the way we are. Marriage would complicate things, maybe change things. I'd hate that."

"I stand corrected!"

They both looked at the clock. Emily spoke first. "I think I need to hit the sack." She yawned and stretched her arms over her head. "So sleepy."

Susan recognized that move. Emily wasn't really tired, she was up to no good.

"Are you sure Al is not going to call you back when you get in bed so you can have your long-distance phone sex? You know you can't fool me!"

"Honestly, Susan...." But she couldn't contain herself and burst out laughing. "He is going to call me back. But just to talk." She jumped up and hugged Susan. "I'm gone. See you in the morning!"

Susan watched her dance down the hall and up the stairs. *Please don't trip* was all she could think. Emily had put away some serious wine.

Daisy was in the bedroom. She hated to disturb her, but it was time for her last outing. "Come on, sweetie." Susan reached out and petted her. Daisy rolled over and wagged her tail, then jumped on the floor. It was a lovely evening to sit outside. She heard Emily's laughter drift down from the upstairs window. *What the hell are they up to on her cell?* Susan giggled and wished it were her.

That had been a fun visit with Emily eight months ago. She had been more fun herself then. *I'm getting back on track.* Susan kept reminding herself of that fact. Soon she'd have a new book and in two days she'd start to have a social life.

Susan's tea was finished and she was about to head back to the kitchen when she heard voices coming from the Miller farm. She hated to be nosy, but she wondered who was there. They were pretty close to her property line.

"Hello. Can I help you with something?" She yelled across the yard. Most likely it was a photographer. Couldn't be anything sinister on such a beautiful sunny day.

"Hello, back." A girl's voice came closer.

"I hope it's okay we're here. Drove by and saw the house and couldn't resist walking the property." A man's voice joined in.

Susan stood and watched as a young couple walked up to her fence. She walked over to meet them.

"Hi, I'm Scott." A nice looking guy in his late twenties put out his hand. "And this is my fiancé, Claire."

"I'm Susan."

"Nice to meet you. We *l-o-v-e* this house." Claire stretched out the word love to make her point. She was about the same age as Scott. A pretty girl with short bouncy blond hair. They made a cute couple.

"Do you know who owns this house?" Scott spoke up. "Is it for sale?"

"We're looking for a house to rescue and rehab. This place would be awesome!"

"As far as I know, it's not for sale. It's in terrible shape, do you think it could be saved?"

"I'm an architect, specialize in historic property. Claire is a landscape designer. We really want to find a special old house and bring it back to life. This place is splendid."

"I was told the folks around here rarely sell. But I will give you the name of the agent that sold me this house." She saw their confused looks. "My house for sale was a fluke. The owner, grandson of a grandson of the original owners, moved to the West Coast and didn't want to leave the house vacant. So I lucked out. Hang on, let me get her card. Be right back."

Susan dashed to the kitchen and rummaged through her purse. She had put Ann's card in one of the compartments. *Wouldn't it be wonderful if they could buy the place?* She hated the view from her yard, she disliked that the house would one day rot to the ground if someone didn't come in and love it.

Finally! She found Ann's card. She doubted the owners would sell, but she didn't want to be rude. *It's not going to happen. Nothing ever happens here.* Susan waved her hand in the air and shouted out to them as she pranced back to the fence. "Got it!"

SATIRE IS A LESSON, PARODY IS A GAME
—VLADIMIR NABOKOV

23
THE DOG COLUMN

Susan looked at the calendar with dismay. She was so busy working on her book, she forgot the deadline for her monthly on-line column was three days away. What to write about? She didn't have a clue.

"I'm so off my game." Susan called Emily. "The column is due and I haven't written the first word. Don't even care to. My mind is on my book, not cute dog stories. Help me think. You always have an opinion and I need one, like in ten minutes."

"Settle down, hon, you'll come up with something. You always do." Emily wasn't crazy about the dog column. Thought Susan's writing about her dog, well, as bad as any cat lady jokes. And coming from her, that was quite a statement. She had a great Calico cat that slept with her and Al. She loved Daisy, who wouldn't? Just worried Susan was too focused on her.

"That dog column may be the reason you don't have many dates. What guy wants to date a girl who writes about a talking dog."

Susan let out a hearty laugh. "Daisy doesn't talk in my column. She just has her own view on sharing me with others and I'm the one talking about it." She loved writing about Daisy and her readers always left comments about their dogs. Emily knew that.

"Still the same to me." Emily poked back. "I think it scares guys off . . ."

"Oh my God!" Susan cut her off. She started to giggle. "I don't believe what Daisy just did. She ran out of the office when I called you and now she's back, with my panties in her mouth. I left them on the floor this morning with the laundry and never got back to put them in the washer."

"That is purely disgusting." Emily cringed. "Maybe you should write about that! You know, some doggie erotica. Get your readers ready for the new you, the new book!"

"You know, that might work. I'll be tame and make fun of it, but I think I'll do a bit of doggie porn for this column." Susan's mind started to race with ideas. *Why not take that first part of the book with Jamie, toss in a dog, and test the waters. A bit of humor about sex to break her fans in to what was coming next.*

"Hey, I was just kidding, but it might work. Go for it. If anyone can get readers to like that kind of combination, it's you babe."

"Wish me luck. I'm on it. If this doesn't pan out, I don't have anything to work with."

Susan clicked off her cell. She went and sat in front of the computer. Daisy jumped up and joined her. Susan loved the old wicker barrel chair. It was a great size for her and Daisy curled up between her back and the chair back and slept for hours while she wrote. At first it was uncomfortable, but then Susan realized it improved her posture at the computer.

Feeling like a maestro at the piano, Susan wiggled her hands and fingers in front of her. Then she sat up straighter in her chair, heard Daisy growl with displeasure at the movement, and placed her fingers on her keyboard. She started with her usual introduction.

Dear Readers,

Today I am trying something new. Instead of a real life story about Daisy, I am writing a fictional tale inspired by Daisy's bad behavior earlier this morning. She stole my bikini briefs out of the bedroom and dropped them at my feet by the computer. I don't know what kind of a statement that was from Daisy, but it did put a plan in motion for my column. Those who follow me here and read my books, know I write non-fiction memoir, full of my life and my dog. This year I have a new plan, a new book in mind. I am writing a novel, with a bit of erotica. It is a learning process for me, and I will test the waters here! Let me know what you think! As usual, it is a bit tongue in cheek. Susan

Fifty Shades of Red, An Erotic Tail (typo, Tale)

The author took another sip of Jack Black. Somehow she had to get this right. She needed to get her heroine out the front door, to begin her evening of sex. There was the matter of the dog stealing the scene and, try as she did, the dog would not go away.

Chapter One, Paragraph One:
"I'm not going another night without sex." Jamie looked in the mirror and liked how she looked in her sexy short dress. The bar was not far from her house. It was still early. She could probably find a man to bring home. She stepped out of her thong and let it drop to the floor. She wanted to be free for whatever action came her way. "Later, hon." She called to her dog, Precious, as she grabbed her keys and headed for the door. Precious grabbed the thong, jumped on the bed, and waited for Jamie to return.

The author thought something was wrong with that paragraph. She didn't want Precious to steal the thong. She couldn't believe she typed that. She went back and edited her words.

Chapter One, Paragraph One:
"Honey, I'll be home late tonight," Jamie gave her little dog a kiss on the head and tossed her a biscuit. She stepped out of her lace thong, let it drop to the floor, straightened her short skirt, and headed for the door. Precious watched the thong in anticipation.

No, no, no, no! The author took another sip of Jack Black and reached for the keyboard again. What was it with Precious and the thong? Maybe it would be best to drop the thong from the scene. It could come off later, at the bar. That might make a good plot switch and a juicy scene. Let a guy take off Jamie's thong. Good idea. The author re-wrote the paragraph again.

Chapter One, Paragraph One:
Jamie locked the door and straightened her skirt around her behind. The static cling between her tiny thong and short skirt was driving her crazy. Her skirt seemed to get stuck in a very odd place. Precious curled up on the bed to wait for her mistress to return.

The author looked at the words on the monitor. Better. She reached for the bottle, the hell with the glass, and took a swig of out of it. She moved on to the next chapter.

Chapter Two, Paragraph One:
After an unsuccessful attempt to find a man at the adult bar known as a habitat for casual sex, Jamie returned home a bit tipsy. Precious raced to meet Jamie at the door and, in an odd display of affection, humped Jamie's foot. Jamie, exhausted from her evening out, picked up Precious and headed back to the bedroom. They both curled up in bed and fell asleep quickly. Jamie woke up the next morning with a terrible hangover. Precious had the thong in her mouth.

What the heck? The author was disgusted that the writing had a life of its own. Something had to change. A character had to go. It was the only way. Another shot of Jack Black and the author was ready. A character was killed off.

Chapter Two, Paragraph One:
Jamie locked the back door, eased into her car, and headed to the bar that had the reputation as a pick-up spot for adults wanting to hook up for sex. She felt naughty. The last thing she did before she grabbed her keys was to step out of her thong and drop it on the floor. She needed to meet someone to bring home. The house was empty without her little dog Precious. She missed her, but still, Precious did have a wonderful long life.

Perfect! The author was pleased to have solved the problem of the dog and the thong. She took one last sip of booze, emptying the bottle, and continued to write.

Chapter Three, Paragraph One:
Jamie let the valet park her car. He was hot. Young. His head was shaved. And there was light stubble on his chin. She gave him her keys then heard a yap from the side lot. "What was that?" She looked into the valet's blue eyes. "Did you hear something?"
"Sure did." They both turned towards the dumpster. A small, sad looking dog was digging around the ground trying to find something to eat.
"Oh no!" Jamie dashed to the pup and bent over to pick the little thing up.
"That's quite a view there." The valet called out to her.
Jamie smiled. She guessed she looked adorable saving the dog. A gentle breeze eased up her skirt and she remembered her thong at home and pulled her skirt back over her naked butt.
Now there is fifty shades of red on anyone's color scale!

finis

Susan laughed. *I am out of my mind.* She had no clue how her readers would react. *Sorry, Jamie,* she apologized to her character for putting her in the spoof. She loved Jamie and felt she did a bit of injustice to her in the column. *I had no control over Precious, Jamie.*

She went to her e-mail, attached her column, and sent a brief note to her editor explaining her story-line. They wouldn't care what she wrote about as long as she made her deadline. Her column was a hit on their site and they gave her free license to write what she wanted. This would fly well with them. She hoped her readers would agree.

Susan gave a few biscuits to Daisy, slipped out of the chair, and went to get ready for her first official event with her new group. In the spirit of her latest column, Susan dug out the lace thong from behind her bikini briefs in the back of her dresser drawer. She had purchased it on a whim but never wore it. Instead of her usual jeans, or long skirt, she found a clingy aqua and black print skirt, short and curved at the hemline, a silky blouse, and her black heels. She showered, ran a brush through her long dark hair, and clipped on her favorite vintage Mexican turquoise earrings. The color of the earrings highlighted her blue eyes, or so Emily had told her when they celebrated her birthday last year. The earrings were her present from Emily and she loved them.

Susan grabbed her keys and Daisy ran to the door to watch her leave. She smiled down at Daisy. The scene reminded her of what she had just written and she giggled. It felt good to be thirty-eight and still able to giggle. She spent enough time being serious.

She bent to pet Daisy. "Go back to bed. I won't be late." She adjusted her skirt and pulled at it to be sure where the hem ended if she bent over. She had no plan to be fifty shades of red showing her butt this evening.

I THINK I COULD FALL MADLY IN BED WITH YOU
— AUTHOR UNKNOWN

24
City Pub

Susan was late leaving the house to catch up with 'Beer and Buddies'. Her mind always seemed to be engaged elsewhere when her body needed to head out the door. *Writer's Curse*. She gave it a title to make up for her horrid lack of timeliness. She slammed the front door, locked it, and jumped into her van. She backed out the driveway in a frenzy and almost collided with a white pick-up truck that blocked part of her path. Susan rolled down her window, stuck her head out and yelled, "Sorry." For a second she thought the driver looked familiar, but dismissed it. For all she knew he could be the neighbor next door. She looked at the clock and sped down the road. If she hurried she might just be on time.

The white truck backed up and turned around. Susan switched on her radio and started to sing with a familiar tune. She did not notice the truck was behind her, or that it took every turn she made. Her mind was on the evening ahead.

Susan pulled into the only space left in the lot next to City Pub and walked up to pay the attendant. "How much?"

"Parking is free after six. I'm fixing to head out. The lights shut down when I leave, so watch your step when you come back." He gave her a kindly smile and closed the glass door.

Susan looked around. The lot was jammed. City Pub was the closest bar to the college. She headed to the front door and hoped her group would be easy to find. Then she snickered. *Of course they would be. They would be in their thirties and forties. Older than the students.* She shook her head. She just wanted to meet someone that she could hang out with a bit closer to home. Any age would be fine.

She grabbed the big brass handles and entered the bar. Inside City Pub reminded her of a man cave. Leather couches and chairs lined the sides of the room, small wood tables with modern leather parson chairs flanked the tables. The bar was spectacular. It was u-shaped, brass trimmed with a leather base. The top of the bar looked like marble. The bar stools matched the leather parson chairs at the other tables. Not her style of decorating, but very well done. Combined with brick walls and modern art, the bar looked like it should be in a major city, not in a small college town.

Susan's eyes got used to the low lights quickly and she gazed around the room. In the far corner she saw a sign 'Beer and Buddies'. Ten people were sitting at a longer table. She took a deep breath and walked over to introduce herself to the woman who looked in charge.

"Name tags are required. Some of the folks are regulars, but we have new people all the time, like you." The woman handed her a marker and name tag across the table. "I'm Patti." She continued with her orders. "Just put your first name on the label, pull off the back, and put it where we can see it." She caught her breath and gave Susan a friendly grin.

Patti looked to be early forties. A little on the plump side with long blonde hair pulled back and clipped off her face. Patti turned to reach in a bag behind her and Susan saw her hair clip. It was large, copper color with red rhinestones. It looked like a small jeweled flower basket. *I wonder if it's old,* Susan thought. It reminded her of a Victorian hair clip she had sold when she first opened her shop.

"You hair clip is lovely," Susan couldn't resist commenting on it. "It looks antique."

"Oh, thanks. So glad you like it. Just bought it. New, made to look old. So easy to slip on my hair. Had tried barrettes, but my hair is too thick for the barrettes to sit properly." Patti touched her hair and smiled at Susan again. "You are the first to comment on it. Thanks."

"It's a great reproduction. I'd like to find one myself." Susan pulled her hair back from her face. It was untamed and unruly the first day after she washed it.

"This is what I was digging for." Patti dropped her bag and handed Susan a small ticket. "First timers get a free beer, or glass of wine, if that is more your style. Nice perk from the pub. You can take it to the bar. Then come back and join us!"

A drink will be perfect, Susan thought as she looked around at all the strange faces. Patti was friendly. *Off to a good start,* she mused. First things first, Susan looked for the ladies room. She needed to pee after the drive. She also wanted to do a final check on how she looked. Her outfit fit in well with the others, her heels were a bit out of place, a little too dressy, but it made her feel sexy. Then there was the matter of her thong. It made her feel a bit reckless.

The ladies room was lovely. For a masculine bar, the ladies room was totally feminine. The tiny black and white tiles on the floor were original to the building. The wallpaper was a knock off of a vintage pattern, old pink roses on a white trellis, repeated across the room. It looked antique, but Susan could tell it was a reproduction. The sink was white porcelain with chrome handles that were marked 'hot' and 'cold'. She couldn't decide the age. The counter looked like white marble, but Susan realized it was Formica when she ran her hand across it. She made a mental note on how classy and real it looked in case she decided to update her upstairs bath. Formica was certainly cheaper than marble and to have such a realistic look…maybe she should ask the owners where they got it.

Susan looked at her reflection in the beautiful vintage beveled mirror and shook her head. *Once an antique dealer, always an antique dealer.* She was here to make new friends and instead she was mentally critiquing the bathroom décor. It's the nature of the beast she knew well.

Susan looked at the name tag she still held, pulled off the sticky back, and slapped it on her left shoulder, just over her heart. *There. I am ready to meet new friends.* She grabbed the big brass handle, pulled the door open, and stepped back out to the semi-dark room. The group was filling up quickly. Susan counted twenty-five people sitting and standing in the area. Patti was still handing out name tags. Susan walked towards the bar.

Jim looked up from his beer and newspaper when he heard her order a glass of Riesling. Her voice was soft and captivating right next to him. He couldn't help but stare at her. He'd only seen her from a distance in her yard, but she had looks that were hard to forget. Then he saw her name tag, *Susan*. It really was his neighbor. He couldn't believe she had just walked up to the bar. He had wanted to meet her for a year and couldn't get the nerve to barge in on her at home and here she was! He'd popped in for a cold beer before heading to his apartment. He was not in the mood to drive back to the house. Talk about great timing. She was prettier up close than from the distance at home. She looked to be a bit younger than him, but not by much. She turned to him and smiled. Her eyes were blue, like the ocean water. He now felt like a complete idiot staring at her.

"Hi, I'm Susan. Here with the group 'Beer and Buddies'. Are you a member?" Susan felt she needed to say something. His look confused her, but it was definitely aimed at her, and in a very complimentary way. She liked his face, there was something gentle and strong in it. He was pretty cute too, dark brown hair that curled slightly, tan skin, and a great smile. She just couldn't figure out the befuddled look on his face.

"Jim." He held her hand for a quick moment and then reached back for his beer. "Sorry, bet that was cold and damp. I've been holding this bottle too long!" He wondered if he sounded daft. "I stopped in after class. No, I'm not part of the group to answer your question." He couldn't wait to tell her he was her neighbor, but she cut him off.

"This is my first time with the group. I moved into a farmhouse a year ago not far from here and still don't know a soul around. My fault, I refuse to meet my neighbors. I like my privacy and the town is so small, well, I don't want anyone to know my business." Susan saw his confused look. "Sorry, too much information. But you know how small towns can be." Susan kept rattling off words. She felt she had said something disagreeable and hoped she'd finally come out with something that would make him smile. "I do have a dog. What about you?" That was her final straw to grasp. Maybe he loved dogs. She was drawn to his looks and wanted to get to know him.

Well this sucks. Jim didn't want to scare her off, but clearly if he told her he recognized her, lived next door to her, she'd be gone in no time. He'd just play it by ear, see how they hit it off. There was plenty of time later to figure this out. She'd hadn't told him where the farmhouse was, so he wasn't withholding anything in case they ran into each other back home. His brain backed up to realize she'd asked a question. "I love dogs, but my apartment doesn't allow any. My place is within walking distance and I stop in here some nights." Jim smiled at her. *That part was true.*

"This is a great town." Susan took a sip of her wine and looked at his face. Something made her want to stay and talk to him. "But college towns are always cool. I love it when the town is small. Comfy, but full of intellectual and artistic happenings."

"Well, we are definitely cool here." Jim smiled at her and cursed himself for such stupid small talk. "So what do you do?" An inane question. He knew the answer, but she didn't know that. Anything to keep her talking and at the bar.

"A writer." Susan took a sip of wine. He was cute. She looked back at the group and again at Jim. They could wait. She wanted to get to talk to Jim a bit more. A real live man that appealed to her. Now that was something to write home about. "And you?"

"Instructor at the college." Jim started to relax. "I teach writing. How is that for a coincidence?"

"Have you had anything published?" Susan tilted her head with interest. Her dark hair fell across her face. She pushed it back behind her ears. She had a grace to her movement he found sensual.

"Not yet. I have a book idea." He started to laugh and shook his head. "Everyone I know at the college has a book idea."

"What do you want to write?" She saw his expression. He seemed nervous. "No really, I'm interested. I live for writing. It's my income and my therapy."

"Now don't laugh. I'm a great mystery fan. Have an idea for a mystery series of my own. Takes place in Europe. I am still flushing out the character. I'm in the middle of a project that will bring me money to spend next summer overseas. I hope to work on it then." Jim took a deep breath after his words came out. *Yes, the project is the house next to yours. I want to sell it when I finish renovating it.* But he couldn't tell her that either.

"I'm not laughing. That is very exciting." Susan thought about her book. Maybe she should be writing something of more substance. Romance, sex…no redeeming value other than entertainment. "You have to have a keen mind to plot out a mystery. Are you murdering anyone in your book or does the mystery have to do with intrigue and something more subtle?" She looked at his eyes, his hands as he reached for his beer. He was a sexy looking man. "There are days I think murdering someone in the name of literature would be very cathartic."

"I know what you mean! You can kill the people that annoy you in your writing. The perfect crime. You have the satisfaction of doing them in, yet there is no body." He chuckled and watched her smile at him. *God, she was lovely.* She seemed interested in him, but he worried she would finish her wine and head back to her group. He didn't want her to leave.

"Do you need to head back over to the group, or can I kidnap you for a bit?"

Susan smiled at him. She liked how he made her feel. Something about him was so appealing She felt playful, no it was more than that, she was turned on. She had many desires at the moment, and leaving was not one of them.

"Kidnap me. I'm yours for the taking."

25
FEELS SO GOOD
TO BE BAD

"So what are you writing?" Jim turned in his stool to face her. "I've done most of the talking." He continued to ask a few questions and she zoned out, didn't hear anything more.

Susan didn't want to talk about her book. She really didn't want to talk about anything. She was turned on. Not like the online crap the other evenings, but a feeling that was hard to describe. She was filled with lust, but she liked Jim. The combination was explosive.

She watched him lift his beer, his lips on the bottle. She wanted those lips on her. The sexual tension was thick between them. There was no way to ignore that. She felt a rush, an excitement, to the point she was light headed. She didn't want the moment to pass. She had the urge to reach out and kiss him. She decided to do just that. In the middle of his sentence, words that made sounds, but did not register in her mind, she leaned forward and her mouth found his. At the bar. In front of everyone who cared to notice. She kissed him, softly, gently, but with purpose. Her lips lingered only a moment, then she pulled back. Her blue eyes stared into his. She waited for his reaction.

"Wow." His voice was barely above a whisper. "That was incredible." Jim looked at her. She had taken him by surprise, but she did exactly what he had thought about, kissing, only she kissed him first. He had no clue what to do next. All the stories he'd heard about her being a recluse and now she was in front of him, kissing him. He didn't want to break the flow of the moment. He wanted to know her, in every way possible. Feel her, touch her, smell her, bury his face in her hair, move his mouth down her body.

"You are so kissable. I couldn't help myself." Susan's words broke his thought pattern. She smiled at him, her face turning a soft pink.

This has to go further. Jim's mind raced with what to do next.

I'm so out of practice. Susan fretted. *Why isn't Jim doing anything more? Should I make another move? What would Jamie do?*

Damn girl, she heard Jamie's voice, or was it Emily's voice. It didn't matter. Everyone wanted her to get out and meet someone, if just for the sex. If she were writing this scene and Jamie was at the bar with Jim, she knew what Jamie would do. She and Jamie were more alike than she cared to admit. It was time to live her life somewhere other than her imagination.

Jim looked at her, his mouth open to speak, but didn't have the chance to say a word. Susan placed her finger on his lips. She felt breathless and kissed him again. This time not so gently. She ran her hand down his arm and grabbed his hand and placed it on her bare thigh, just under the hemline of her short skirt. She felt flushed, hot. She turned her head towards him, smiled and raised her eyes to meet his. "Take me somewhere we can be alone."

The bartender watched and shook his head. Mostly kids came in here, kissed at the bar, and left. It was nice to see a couple a bit older getting this worked up in front of everyone. He had their tab on the counter in a matter of seconds. Jim dropped a twenty, grabbed Susan's hand, and they made their way past the students towards the front door.

Patti saw them as she handed out more name tags to the late arrivals. She started to call out and saw the look that passed between Susan and the man from the bar and just shook her head. *Maybe next time,* she giggled and watched them outside the glass doors. His arm was around Susan as they disappeared into the night.

Someone else had watched them kiss at the bar, someone who wasn't happy about it. He pushed to get to the door, but the kids in front of him slowed him down. A pretty young girl grabbed his arm and smiled at him. "What's the hurry? Buy me a drink?" She had already had one drink too many he decided. He pulled his arm loose and looked at her. Her dark hair reminded him of Susan. He nodded and continued to the door.

They were out of sight when he hit the street. He raced to where he had seen her park her car. No one was there. His anger blinded him to anything that made sense. He stormed from alley to alley looking for them.

"My apartment is not far from here." Jim hesitated to sound like he expected she would want to go there, but it was close, and she did tell him to take her somewhere.

Susan turned to face him. She didn't want to wait. She wanted more and she wanted it now. "Kiss me first."

Jim pulled her into the alcove of an old brick office. It was private. The small opening was surrounded by a metal iron picket fence and plants. The office was dark and the outside light had either been turned off or burnt out. They moved to the side of the building, protected by trees, and behind a large brick pillar, hidden from the street. Jim pressed her against the brick wall with his body, his hands moved from her face to her long hair. He pulled back on her hair and his lips met hers. They kissed, parting lips, tongues gently probing. He ran his tongue down her neck and took in her fragrance, a combination of spice and roses, heady, exciting. At the base of her neck he nipped her gently and heard her moan.

"Bite me again." Susan wrapped a leg across the back of his thighs and pulled him closer to her. It was a gentle bite, but it sent shivers through her body and her hips started to grind against his jeans. The sensation between her legs, up inside her, took control of her thoughts. She was reckless with desire. She couldn't wait. He was moving his lips on her neck, but still a gentleman. She wanted him to do more, quickly. Standing against the wall with his weight on her, she wiggled a bit to open her legs slightly and reached for his hand. "Here, touch me here." She ran her tongue on his ear as she whispered to him. Her hand was firmly on his as she moved it under her skirt between her legs. She felt his fingers move up and play with her thong, then reach under the edge and into her. Susan moaned and her mind went blank as she moved in rhythm with his hand, lost in a sensation she had missed for too long.

Jim brought her to a climax and kissed her gently on the mouth. He was rock hard, but her reaction to being touch overwhelmed him. He thought of nothing but pleasing her. "You are something else." That was the most original thing he could think to say and felt stupid after the words were out. He was usually smooth with women, but with Susan he lost his cool.

Flushed, her lip-gloss gone from lips that were slightly swollen from kissing, Susan smiled at him. "I think you made me crazy." She didn't know if she should be embarrassed, but she felt so good, she didn't care.

"At least the cops didn't break in on us." Jim chuckled.

"No way. I didn't even think about that. That would have been ghastly, now." Susan was so overcautious it amazed her she had let go so easily with him.

Jim had his arms around her. She felt perfect tucked in close. He rested his chin on the top of her head and his right hand slowly moved up her side to cup her breast. The fabric of her blouse was thin and silky. His fingers caught on the edge of her name tag, he pulled it off and let it drop to the ground. He wanted to feel more of her. He reached for the top button of her blouse.

"Whoa!" Susan turned to face him. "Enough of me. I think you have been neglected. What should we do about that?" She teasingly cocked her head at him.

"Well, my place is still just down the street..." Jim wanted more of her. He was afraid she'd disappear on him.

"Come to my car." Susan wanted to continue this game, but she did not want to go to his place. After all, they had just met. What did she know about him? For some reason playing in the alcove or car seemed safe compared to going to his apartment. She really was attracted to him and if she went to his place, well she might spend the night and that was off limits too. She used her best, her weakest, but her real life excuse with him. "I have a small dog I have to get home to."

The parking lot had emptied out. The attendant was gone and the lights were off. It was dark except for moonlight. Susan felt fearless tonight and careless, so she did what came to mind as soon as they got in the car, and didn't worry about the consequences.

"Here are the rules. You were good to me, now I am going to be good to you." Susan reached across for his jeans and zipper. She tugged on the zipper, then turned to face him. "I am allowed to do whatever I want to you, but you are not allowed to touch me. If you do, I push you out of my car and leave." She gave him a smile, tossed her hair to the side, and unzipped his jeans. Jim slid down further in the seat and Susan moved her hands past his waist, wiggling her fingers in until she felt him, smooth and hard. She gently pulled him out of his jeans, bent down close until her tongue met skin.

Jim wanted to touch her, as she touched him, but he remembered her warning and kept his hands to himself. He closed his eyes and got lost in the moment. There were worse things that could happen in a dark parking lot than to have a beautiful girl have her way with you.

He turned into the alcove and pushed against the brick wall. He knew he was out of control. He leaned back to catch his breath then he saw it. A small piece of curled paper stuck to a rock on the ground. He bent to pick it up. It was tacky on one side. The other side had Susan written on it in black marker. This is where they went. He imagined them having sex in the very spot he was standing. He pounded his fist on the brick wall and drew blood. Someone would pay for her actions. He sucked the blood off his fist and ran a hand over his head, straightening his thick hair. He thought about the girl who asked him to buy her a drink and headed back to City Pub.

26
THE THINGS WE FORGET

Susan stretched, wiggled her toes, and pulled her pillow over her face. *What the hell was I thinking last night?* She was in a great mood. She inhaled the smell of her perfume off her pillow then tossed it to the end of the bed. She felt giddy, silly, happy, and a touch naughty. Last night at City Pub turned out to be so much more than she expected.

She sat straight up in bed. *OMG. I didn't even say goodbye to Patti.* For her first meeting with the group 'Beer and Buddies' she didn't behave very well. Patti was the only one she spoke to. Susan made a mental note to e-mail Patti through the group site and apologize for her...*for my what? Hasty exit? Indecent exposure in the alley next door?* Susan just laughed at herself. She had no clue how to explain her actions. She had no desire to apologize for anything. The night rocked. *And Jim...* She felt a rush of excitement thinking about his hands up her skirt. His expert touch, gentle and probing, brought her to climax in minutes. She returned the favor when they got to her car. His taste lingered on her lips on her drive home. She blushed remembering how she pushed him towards the car door afterwards and said she had to leave. She was embarrassed she had been out of control. She drove off and left him standing with his shirt unbuttoned in the parking lot. Next time she would go home with him.

Next time. Shit. They had not exchanged last names or phone numbers. How was she ever going to see him again? Her great mood went flat. She thought there had been more than a spark between them, but maybe it was one-sided. He didn't ask for her number. But then, she didn't think about it either.

Susan reached for her cell to call Emily. Daisy circled her feet and headed down the hallway. She needed to let her out. Susan got up to follow Daisy and put her cell back on the bedside table. What would she tell Emily anyway? That she met a cute guy at a bar, let him feel her up outside the pub, then took care of him in her car? She didn't know a thing about him. Didn't even know his last name. It all sounded too crazy now in the morning light.

Jamie got her into this. If she hadn't been so wrapped up thinking about sex for her book, she might have behaved better. Jim's smile made her heart skip a beat, *OK cliché writer's talk,* Susan shook her head. Her fantasy life blurred with real life if she looked at the last few days. She acted out a fantasy last night with Jim. *A great fantasy,* she reminded herself. She just wished he knew how to call her. She hadn't said much about herself at the bar. Her mind was on his lips and hands. What did he tell her? *Name is Jim. Instructor at Community College.* Contacting the college seemed desperate. And if she found him and he wasn't interested, her ego didn't need that.

Susan fidgeted with the coffee maker. She filled the carafe with water and added coffee to the basket. She plugged it in and pulled a hunk of cheese out of the fridge. *I am so stupid.* She bit into the cheese with a vengeance.

She replayed last night in her mind. The sex was amazing, but there seemed to be more between them. She felt like they connected, like he already knew her. For the first time in three years she just went with her feelings and it felt great. Not so great however, that the chances of her seeing Jim again were one in ...*one in none.* She wondered if he woke up this morning slapping himself for not getting her information. Maybe she was just a notch on his belt. *What did she know, really?*

The coffee was ready and Susan grabbed her blue willow pattern English cup from the cupboard and filled it to the brim. She walked outside with Daisy. The sun was up and the air already warm. Everything was quiet. Too quiet for her. She was edgy and wanted a distraction. Even her neighbor was quiet. No renovations this morning.

She knew she was mad at herself and disappointed about last night. The high, the rush of his touch, and the total let down it was over before it started. *If I'd only gone to his apartment...okay, enough of this crap. I don't do this. The reason I don't want to date.* If she rationalized this it might be for the best they couldn't reconnect. She was close to finishing her book and he would be a huge distraction.

"Come on Daisy, let's go." She'd had enough fresh air and her own pity party was disgusting her. A simple solution to the problem, write about last night in her book. Let Jamie handle it. Jamie seemed better with the men than she was.

Susan slammed the kitchen door. *Damn it.* This was crazy thinking. Jamie was her character in the book she was writing. Had she gone totally bonkers now comparing her life with Jamie's, expecting Jamie to find the answers to her problems?

Was it only a few months ago she was happy writing her dog column, working on her essays? This book had opened up feelings she'd put to rest. Her peaceful world she'd worked so hard to create was getting too complicated.

Breathe, breathe deeply. Susan remembered the class she and Emily had taken at the Healing Arts Center when it opened two years ago. "You can control your nerves if you have control over your breathing." The instructor was a perky, thin, exceptionally healthy looking twenty-something, a friend of a friend of Emily's. She'd forgotten how much better she felt after the breathing exercises.

Susan stood by the kitchen counter and closed her eyes. She focused on her breath. The instructor's words came back to her. "Breathe in slowly. Visualize you are breathing in all the positive energy around you and it is filling you up inside. Enjoy the peace generated in your mind. Then breathe out slowly, and feel all the negative energy leaving you with the out-going breath. Repeat the cycle until you feel relaxed and refreshed."

Susan took slow deep breaths. The tension started to leave her body. Within a few minutes she felt calm. She moved her head from side to side, and stretched down to touch her toes. The movement felt good. *I need to get more exercise.* She hated how locked up her shoulders and legs felt after sitting at the computer for a few hours. Emily had lectured her she needed to get up more and move about when she wrote. Jamie kept fit riding her bike. Maybe she should get her butt out of her chair and do the same.

Jamie. She needed to get to work on her book. If she would forget the fact she totally blew it with Jim and take that energy…well, apply it to her book. She might get another great chapter for Jamie. One of them needed a love life. She'd been pushing Jamie to have casual sex, but Jamie seemed to push back. She wanted more. *Maybe I want more?* Susan hated to admit it, but Jim made her want more. Maybe that need had been there longer than she wanted to acknowledge, and Jim, well, he'd opened it up. Now she was raw with desire and emotions. If she didn't channel that into her book, she'd be an idiot.

The sound of her cell interrupted her thoughts. She grabbed it and saw Emily's name. Perhaps she would share her last night's adventure with her. Things were in perspective for the time being. Maybe she and Emily could brainstorm on how to find Jim in a very casual, doesn't really matter, off handed way.

"Hey. Just the gal I want to talk to." Susan's mood had improved.

"Oh, hon, did you see the news this morning? All over TV here. Some girl was murdered up by the college. She was at a pub, what was the name, oh yes, City Pub. They found her body in a parking lot. Said her neck was broken." Emily paused to catch her breath. She always rattled on at rapid speed when she was upset. "They haven't released her name. And they don't have any suspects."

Susan thought about the group and Patti. The calm she felt only seconds before was gone, it had drained out of her body before Emily finished her last sentence. A cold sick feeling flooded her gut and sweat beaded up on her forehead. She had been there. She hoped to God it wasn't Patti. What would the chances be it was? But it was someone who had been in the bar. Someone she might have met and liked if she hadn't met Jim.

If she hadn't met Jim, would that have been her in the parking lot? She shook her head. *This has nothing to do with me.* She decided not to tell Emily about her night. She didn't need a lecture on caution and she knew one would come under the present circumstances.

"I'll go turn on the TV and see what's on our local news." Susan tried to sound casual. "Let me call you later. Need to finish the chapter I'm working on."

"Call me. Okay." Emily hung up.

Susan dropped her cell on the counter. She walked into the office and turned on her TV. The news would be back on in a few minutes. She paced back and forth and stared at the TV. *Come on. Damn it.* She needed to see if they released a name, or details, something. Her lovely night didn't seem so lovely now. And Jim, her worry about the phone numbers. . . Her world which had seemed so bright last night was turning dark.

The news came on. The photo of a beautiful young girl with long dark hair was displayed, along with a name, Liz Jenkins. She was a student at the college. Susan didn't remember seeing her in the bar. She felt sad looking at the picture. *Thank God it wasn't Patti. . .*

Friends said she left with a man right before closing, but no one could identify him. "She'd had a good bit to drink," a young male student offered. Susan shuddered. The poor girl dead not twenty-hours and already her reputation was being tanked

She left with a man from the bar. Those words echoed in her brain. *How stupid am I? I left the bar with a total stranger too.* Susan never thought about her safety, she was just so turned on and Jim seemed so nice.

Her nerves were already on edge, and now. . .

Susan started to cry. While she worried she might not see Jim again, a young girl had been murdered. None of it seemed fair. She thought back to her husband Steve. He was too young to have died. Just like this girl was so young. She died because she was stupid and trusting. Steve was ill. Susan felt guilty about both. *It was not my fault, there was nothing I could have done to save this girl...or Steve.* The girl's body was left alone in the parking lot. Steve died alone in the hospital. She threw a book across the room. Why was she thinking of Steve? That was behind her. She'd lost him. She had been thinking of Jim. Was he gone too? She couldn't trust her heart. She couldn't bear the pain.

Susan bent over, her hands on her thighs, and tried to catch her breath. She stood up and inhaled. No amount of deep breathing could calm her. She was sure it was a panic attack. She had them when Steve died. Feels like a heart attack, but it's not. *Breathe, breathe, breathe.* She couldn't calm herself down. *Write something.* Her brain shouted out to her. *Get to the computer and write something.* Susan inhaled and walked to the computer. She pulled out the chair and eased herself before her monitor. She'd pick up where she left off with Jamie. Surely Jamie was having a better day than she was.

Her hands went to the keyboard, itching to move, to feel something, to write. Susan sniffled. Her head was killing her. Her hands hovered over the keys ready to type, to write her way out of fear into a perfect scene.

She was ready. She needed to be ready. She had to be ready to save her sanity. *I need to write, damn it.* She wasn't sure who she shouted to or how loud a noise she really made. It was just her and Daisy. Daisy did not flinch on the couch. Susan sat and stared at the computer. She put her head down on her desk and cried for someone she didn't know. Or was she crying for herself. She couldn't answer that question as tears rolled down her face.

Life was hard. She'd learned that when Steve died. People left you. The news reminded her that if life wasn't cruel enough on days, there were people who stepped up to the plate to make it worse. Susan sat up, she didn't have a Kleenex. She pulled up the bottom of her T-shirt and wiped her eyes and face with it. She was ready. "Jamie, life does not always have a storybook ending." It was time for the arc in Jamie's story. Susan started to pound on the keyboard.

27
TIL DEATH DO US PART

Jamie was beyond ecstatic. Tom had called. "Can you meet me at the club? I've got to fill in for someone tonight, but when the crowd quiets, I can come sit with you."

She had not seen him since he left her bed three days ago. He hadn't called until tonight. She'd worried herself sick, then kicked herself for being so uptight. Did it go back to Jack? As secure as she thought she was in her marriage, she wasn't. Now she carried the scars she should have faced long ago.

She found her sexuality through his infidelity. She turned her anger into desire, thinking about how he was with someone else in bed. It freed her. She didn't dwell on being crushed, but on learning how to fantasize about sex. It kept them together for twelve years. It was a sham.

I don't want that with Tom. Jamie started to pull herself together, deciding what to wear to the club. She was excited, but in a reflective mode. *Have I changed?* Jamie had made her marriage work, told herself she was happy after that night, but she never felt as happy as she was before. She never wanted to make that mistake again.

Tom took her by surprise, he took her breath away. She wanted it to be pure. Not the sex, she wanted it down and dirty, but the feelings behind it. *I can't go through that again. I want trust. Can I trust Tom?*

Jamie shook her head. *All this self-realization. Why can't I just let nature take its course? Because it is not in my nature to do so.* Jamie was smart. She knew her own mind. She figured out how her marriage had helped her and the hang-ups it left her with. She loved her life and could live without a man, she proved that. Tom just made her want more.

Jamie decided she wanted to try a new look tonight. She pulled a few dresses out of the closet until she found what she wanted. Another vintage item she'd purchased picking up an ad for the newspaper at the resale shop. It was a 1980's Made in USA hippie style sun dress. The dress was very bohemian with its red and purple paisley print, and its built in bra and spaghetti straps. She liked its longer length and pulled her gold sandals off the top closet shelf to wear with it. The dress fit her like a glove on top, hugging her breasts, the thin straps showing off her tan. She felt like a flower-child with her long blond hair and gold hoop earrings. It was stinking hot outside, but the air conditioning in the club might chill her. At least until Tom could come put his arm around her. She reached up to a box in the closet, pulled it down, and found her crochet shawl, big loops of turquoise yarn, and draped it over her shoulders. Jamie smiled at her image in the mirror. *Perfect. Sweet, sassy, and very sexy.*

It was a short drive to the club, but seemed like forever. Jamie pulled the Mustang into the parking lot. A young guy came up to get her keys. "Here is your ticket. Have a great night. I'll bring this baby back when you are ready to leave." He gave the car a loving look and an approving look at Jamie. "You look lovely, Miss…"

"Jamie. Thanks. Is Tom here?" She looked around the outside of the building expecting him to pop out any minute.

"He's inside. One of the waitresses had a problem and he had to go help."

Jamie gave the valet her keys. It had to be Midge. She suspected there had been something between them and her guess must have been right. A spark of jealousy was ignited as soon as she thought about Tom and Midge together. *Maybe I should leave?* Jamie fretted. *I don't want to see something that I might not like.* Her crappy insecurity was rearing its ugly face.

She stood and weighed her options then headed into the bar. If there was something more with Midge, she might as well face it now.

Tom slammed into her as she walked through the door.

"Whoops. That was kismet." He gave her a big smile. His body hit her hard and he captured her as she teetered back Then he kissed her neck. "Came out looking for you. Didn't see you in the bar."

Jamie was off her game, caught by surprise. "Is everything okay inside? The guy said there was a problem." Jamie thought she smelled perfume on him when he came close.

"Under control now." Tom looked a little nervous. He hugged her again.

The perfume was stronger as he pulled her closer. Jamie recognized the perfume from the night Midge served them their drinks. It was a very provocative floral musk fragrance you couldn't miss. Why was Tom covered in it?

"You look amazing." Tom still had his hands on her arms and had stepped back to take her in. "That dress. Keep that shawl on until I get in there. You are just too damn sexy." He kissed her again and took off.

Jamie started to feel uncomfortable. Tom was not acting like himself, or at least the guy she was used to. And that perfume. What the hell had gone on? She walked in and looked around. Midge was not serving drinks. Jamie decided she needed something strong to settle her down. She wanted to be civilized when Tom came back. *Don't jump to conclusions.* She tried to reassure herself it was all fine.

"Well if it ain't Miss Hot Shot."

Jamie looked up after ordering her drink at the bar. Shit. It was Jackson. He was loud and drunk. She ignored him and waited for the bartender to return.

"I said hello. You deaf?"

"Hello Jackson." Jamie looked him straight in the eye. "How are you and your wife doing? Is she here with you?"

"Leave my wife out of this." He stopped talking and took a shot out of his glass. "Actually we are getting a divorce."

"I am sorry to hear that." Jamie softened. She didn't like him, but she could see he was clearly upset and very drunk.

"Don't be sorry. I caught her in bed with my best friend. Go figure."

Jamie tried to keep a straight face. What goes around comes around. He tried to get her to go to his room. How many women did he succeed with?

"You're looking very hot and sexy this evening, pretty lady." Jackson's mood switched as he tried to put on the charm. His hand reached out to touch her arm. "Maybe we should pick up where we left off last time."

"I don't think there was any *last time* to go back to." Jamie didn't want to wait for her drink. She turned to walk away and Jackson pulled on her arm and jerked her back towards him.

"You're coming with me. And if you say anything, I'll break that pretty arm of yours."

Was Jackson crazy? They were in a crowded bar. Why would she leave?

"I'm not kidding." Jackson's breath was hot on her neck. He reeked of alcohol. She felt something cold hit her skin just under her arm. "I'll cut you if I have too."

This was all too surreal. Jamie wasn't sure how to handle the situation, but it was not going to happen. She was not leaving with Jackson. Maybe she was in a bad dream. A b-movie. This didn't even rate blockbuster hit. She sucked in her breath and took her free arm and jammed it back into Jackson's gut. She felt a sharp pain as his knife pierced her arm, but her blow to his chest took him by surprise. He let go of her and bent over. Jamie stepped back from the bar. She had quite the audience.

Midge showed up out of nowhere. "Get Tom in here," the bartender yelled to Midge. She disappeared as quickly as she had appeared. The bartender grabbed Jackson and pulled him to the back office. He returned just as Tom showed up.

Jamie watched the scene unfold and didn't know if she should laugh or cry. Her sexy evening with Tom had taken on a bizarre edge.

"Shit. What is Jackson up to again?" Tom's anger could not be missed, his eyes blazed with the mention of Jackson's name. He looked at Jamie. "Is that blood on your arm?" Tom reached for her, feeling panic set in. "Damn it. Where the hell is Jackson?"

"I put him in the back office. Sam is in there with him. Afraid he might bolt." The bartender frowned at Tom. "He's got to be banned from here. I don't care what your uncle says."

Tom nodded. "I'll talk to him. Did anyone call the police?"

"Not yet. We thought you'd want to handle this."

Jamie reached out to touch Tom's arm. She wanted to assure him she was not going to cause trouble. "Tom..." her words stopped as she got dizzy. No one had realized how badly she'd been cut. The last thing Jamie remembered was Tom's arm going around her, catching her as she tumbled.

If I didn't start painting,
I would have raised chickens.
—Grandma Moses

28
FRESH EGGS

"Back with the living." Susan buzzed Emily. She cringed at her choice of words. *That poor dead girl wouldn't be among the living again.* "So sorry I cut you short yesterday. The murder unnerved me."

"I could tell you were upset." Emily's voice had more concern than usual. "I tried to call you back a few times, but only got your voice mail."

"I went to bed early. I think I'm just exhausted from all my time at the computer with my book and..." Susan hesitated.

"And what, sweetie?"

"It was so senseless and she was so young. That photo of her, well, her hair looked just like mine, long and dark. Made me think about death and...you know..."

"I do know." Emily realized Steve was in that comment. She wished Susan would talk about the night Steve died, but she kept her emotions to herself. She seemed more distant than ever in her farmhouse. *I only hope she'll start to let others back in . . .*

"I'm fine really." Susan's voice was perkier. "Being a drama queen and you know that is not my style. Truth is, my body hates me from all the time at the computer. Everything hurts. My shoulders are tight and my neck clicks when I turn my head! I sound like some old lady." Susan ended her tirade with a chuckle.

"If you're an old lady, then I am too. I'll have none of that, thank you. I have read that you need to take breaks when you sit at the computer hours on end. Get up and move around every hour or sooner if you can."

"Yes, mother Emily. I get up and take breaks. It's just I get so wrapped up with the book that I forget the time until I ache." That was her answer to everything . . . *the book*. Her world was spinning and she had trouble getting her balance back. So many odd things had taken place since she started writing Jamie's story. Susan moved her head from side to side as she held the cell. There it was again, the click.

"Well as long as you are feeling better." Emily decided to let it go. "The good news is we'll be up there before you know it!"

"It will be just like old times, all of us together again. I miss you guys!"

"Are you ready for us to descend? We'll be there overnight. Figure you can show us around the college too. Maybe spend the day in Arden and have dinner there." Emily paused. "You weren't planning on a home style dinner. Haven't turned all Betty Crocker on us and started cooking?"

"Very cute." Susan tried to sound stern, but she burst out laughing. "When have I ever wanted to cook? Queen of take-out. Although I am seriously thinking about putting a hen house in the back yard for fresh eggs."

"Fresh eggs? You never eat a real breakfast as I remember!"

"Well, I might if I had my own eggs. What is a farmhouse without a bit of farm life? And fresh eggs are supposed to be very rich and yummy."

"This is a new side to you? Are you going totally bonkers in that tiny town with no one to talk to?" Emily was convinced they needed to get up to see Susan quickly. *The girl has lost her mind.*

"Maybe it is a little goofy. But you know, I've been fascinated with hens ever since Janet had them in her yard." Janet lived two miles from her old house and had three hens in a coop. She had fresh eggs every morning.

"I remember that. It always surprised me the city allowed it."

"I've been reading up on chicken ordinances. Seems hens are okay. Roosters are not. They make the noise." Susan was excited to share her information.

"Well, you have certainly studied this." Emily laughed nervously. *WTF was going on with Susan?*

"And a hen doesn't need a rooster to lay eggs, only to fertilize them for chicks. Now there are progressive females for you." The entire idea of hens sparked something in her she couldn't describe.

"I'll bring bagels and cream cheese just in case you don't have hens yet. Now I've got to run. Frozen waffles are waiting for me. Can't wait to see you."

I know I freaked her out. Susan giggled. Hens intrigued her, but she exaggerated for Emily. *I don't know why I like to toy with her so much. Maybe because she is such a mother hen with me.*

Susan smirked at her little joke. It felt good to be light hearted again. The last days had been too intense – those online encounters, sex, not knowing if she'd ever run into Jim again, and now murder. *No wonder my nerves are frayed. What can possibly go wrong next?*

She grabbed her coffee and headed to the office. The vanilla cinnamon flavor smelled heavenly. Her cup today was white with a hand painted hen. It seemed so perfect after her conversation with Emily!

Daisy curled up on the chair next to the computer and Susan pulled up her word doc. *Poor Jamie. I took my emotions out on her and now she is in a small pool of blood.* The murder up at the college shaped that last chapter and Susan did not want to think about murder any more today. She looked at her monitor and could not bring herself to work on her book. She hit save and watched her file close.

She needed a break. There was a farmer's market the next town over and if she hurried, she could catch the last hour of it. *Maybe I'll find some fresh eggs.* She quickly got up and grabbed her bag. "Be good, Daisy!" Susan was on her way.

It was an easy drive. Within fifteen minutes Susan pulled her van up to the street with its rows of tables and vendors. It was an intoxicating view. Susan grabbed her cell and snapped a few photos. *Maybe an article if not eggs....*

Susan took pictures of everything. The colors of the vegetables were rich and bright. Not like what she saw at the grocery store. Tomatoes plump and ripe, mouthwatering deep red, bushel baskets full of small potatoes, rows of corn still in husks, every vegetable in season was displayed, along with small boxes of berries.

"Can I help you?" A woman in jeans walked up to her smiling. "The corn does look beautiful, I agree."

"Couldn't help taking pictures. I haven't been here before. It's amazing."

"Everything you see here is from local farmers. On the weekend the crafters and musicians join us. It's a lot of fun and helps the community."

"I came to buy fresh eggs but the corn looks too good to pass up."

"Have you ever eaten organic corn? Farm fresh is so much sweeter than what you buy at the grocery store." The woman reached down for a small basket and handed it to Susan to fill. "Don't be alarmed if you find a worm when you shuck the corn."

"A worm?"

"Happens sometimes. Won't hurt you. Corn earworms are the larva form of a moth, which lays a single egg in the green silk of a corn stalk. When the egg hatches, the worm feeds on the silk of the corn for two weeks."

"Oh my..." Susan wasn't sure she liked that idea.

"It's a creepy surprise, but all you have to do is discard the worm and cut off the area it ate." The woman looked at Susan's face and laughed. "Best corn you'll ever put in your mouth."

"I did look a bit green, didn't I?' Susan smiled. "I'm going to trust you on that. What do I owe you for these? And can you point me in the direction of fresh eggs?"

Susan tucked the brown paper bag with its six ears of corn under her arm and headed to the end of the row of vendors to find the egg man.

Eggs From Happy Chickens. You couldn't miss the sign. The table had rows of eggs in cartons and baskets. The eggs were all colors - white, brown, tan, speckled. Behind the table was a young man in jeans and a black T-shirt and a young girl who appeared to be about six years old.

"I've wanted to try fresh eggs." Susan smiled at them.

"You've come to the right place. I'm Ed and this is my daughter Mandy. She helps me here when school is out."

"Hi Mandy." Susan held out her hand. Mandy shook it and gave her a big grin.

"Let me tell you about our hens and eggs." Ed grabbed a brochure from under the table and handed to her. "Our chickens are fed certified organic grain and are pasture-raised. We like to let customers know they are happy chickens and spend their days where they can forage for grass and fresh insects. We have them in mobile coups and move them around every few days. The eggs have an incredible flavor."

"Well, I'd like to buy a dozen." Susan watched as Mandy filled a crate for her. "I have a small farmhouse and would love to have a few hens myself. How would you suggest getting started?'

"Much easier than you think." Ed handed her another pamphlet. "Directions for building a hen house. We started out with four hens and now look at us!" Ed winked at Mandy. "The coop in the flyer has two nesting boxes and two perches, which will comfortably house up to four hens. All the fresh eggs you could want!"

"Great. Thanks for the information!" Susan tucked the papers into her purse. They would go up on her vision board as soon as she got home. Hens would be in her future.

"We're always in this spot when the market is open. Come back if you have any questions."

"And thank you, Mandy, for picking such fine eggs for me." Susan noted Mandy had placed a variety of colored eggs in her crate.

Susan was exhilarated from her outing. She was relaxed and would be able to get back to work again. She chuckled to herself as hen sayings whirled in her mind on the drive home.

She needed to *shake a tail feather* and finish Jamie's story. That Jackson was a *bad egg*. Jamie had been *walking on eggshells* and look where that got her. She was a *tough old bird* and should pull through. Did Tom have a *cock and bull* story or would he be true to Jamie?

She didn't want to confuse her plot by putting *too many eggs in the basket*. Her readers might think she was a *bird brain*. Don't be a *dumb cluck*, Susan giggled to herself. *I need to quit my squawking*....and get writing!

An idea *hatched* as she pulled into her driveway. The outing left her *sunny side up*. It was time for Jamie to have her happy ending.

29
THE FINAL CHAPTER

Jamie opened her eyes and blinked from the intensity of the light. Where was she? She remembered all the ruckus at the bar. Oh God, she'd been stabbed. She blinked again, she couldn't focus on anything. *Am I in heaven? All the brightness. Did that SOB kill me?* Jamie tried to clear her brain, but she was foggy. Surely this was a nightmare and she would awake at any moment. She didn't convince herself it was a dream. Everything felt too real. That damn light.

I'm not ready to die. Not now. She sat straight up and felt a twinge of pain. "I am not going to die. I want more sex with Tom. Lots of it." She heard her voice, loud, circle the room. She heard a slight chuckle and a hand on her arm.

"It's okay, babe. You're in the ER. The blood made it look worse than it was. You needed a few stitches and they gave you something for pain." Tom's voice was soft, caring, until he burst out laughing. "I'm so happy to know having sex with me is a good reason to live."

His laughter was the jolt she needed to convince her she was alive. Alive and so embarrassed she almost wished she was dead.

"It's the drugs." Jamie whispered sheepishly.

"Well, those were the very words I'd hoped you would shout out." Tom touched her face, leaned forward, and gave her a gentle kiss. "You scared the piss out of me."

Jamie's brain started to clear. Her thoughts focused. "Do I have to stay here? Are they admitting me?" She just wanted to go home. And hopefully with Tom.

"They're pulling the paperwork together. You'll be good to go home shortly. I found Lynn's number in your cell as your emergency contact and called her." Tom sounded very in charge.

"Does Lynn know I'm alive?" She still could not shake the fact she thought she'd been dead.

"Yes. But she is worried shitless. I told her you would be fine. She is going to spend the night with you. I don't want you alone."

Jamie took all this in. Her look must have said what she was thinking.

"I know. I wish I could stay with you, but I've got that nasty business with Jackson to deal with. He's down at the police station. There's a story there and some things I need to tell you. I will be with you tomorrow and we'll talk."

The nurse came in waving paperwork. "Jamie, you are free to leave. Your man has taken good care of you." She smiled at Tom and then back at Jamie. "The wheel chair will be here in a moment."

Tom jumped up. "I'll pull the car around and I'll call Lynn to let her know we are heading back to your place."

Tom was gone in a flash. The entire scene seemed surreal. This would make a great episode for *Crime & Passion*, one of the sleazy shows she and Lynn watched to unwind. Now they could chat about her real life adventure at home tonight.

Lynn was waiting when they pulled up and dashed out to meet them. "Thank God you're all right. Tom scared the hell out of me." She put one arm around Jamie and helped walk her to the front door. "I used my key to get in. I've got a pot of coffee ready. Tom, you might want something before you head down to the jail."

Jamie eased into her favorite vintage wing-chair and looked at the two of them fretting and fussing over her. The two people who meant the most to her in the world. Terrible way for them to meet. But she was glad they had.

"Thanks. But I need to find out how bad this is. I'd like to put the ass away forever for hurting Jamie. Most likely Jackson will get a slap. He has connections here." Tom paused and looked at Jamie. "Unless you want to press charges and escalate this…"

"No. You do what you have to. I don't want to ever see him again.

I don't think he meant to hurt me, at least not with a knife." Jamie felt a chill wondering what he had in mind if he'd taken her away. "He was drunk. I'm fine. More drama queen with my fainting than anything else." Jamie hoped he really hadn't intended to stab her, but the knife lunged in when she jerked her arm back to break loose from him. Still, the man was trouble. Tom would handle it.

"Well, I'm off." Tom looked uneasy. "We'll talk tomorrow. You need to know some things…" He bent and kissed Jamie on the cheek as if she were a fragile butterfly he didn't want to crush.

"Take it easy Tom. I'll take good care of her." Lynn handed him a travel mug full of coffee, gave him a hug, and opened the door. She wanted Jamie to relax and she could tell she was still on edge.

"I wonder what Tom has to tell me?" Jamie was more concerned about that than her wound. "He looks so serious."

"I'm sure he is a wreck. You got hurt and he has to deal with what happened at the bar. That's a lot on the man's plate." Lynn didn't want Jamie to worry. She needed to unwind. Lynn knew just how to change the subject. "He is really hot. I see why you are crazy about him."

"He is, isn't he?" Jamie's face softened. "So where the hell is my coffee? And I think there is cheesecake in the fridge."

"Your wish is my command!" Lynn took off to the kitchen.

Jamie thought back on the night. Tom was weird before the incident with Jackson. He reeked of Midge's perfume. Is that what he wanted to talk to her about? She hoped he wasn't seeing both of them. That would end it for her. She didn't plan on sharing again.

"One cheesecake and coffee up." Lynn pulled a small side table around to the chair and put down the goodies. "Now, tell me everything and then you need to rest. Oh, and Tom said he'll bring your car around in the morning."

Tom was at her front door bright and early. Jamie didn't sleep well, but felt fine. No pain for which she was thankful. She didn't sleep worrying about Tom and Midge and the whole shitty last night.

She heard Lynn call up to her room. She was dressed and ready. She wore tight jeans, a peasant style vintage bohemian blouse that was low cut. She left her shoes off on purpose and headed down the stairs in her bare feet. Her blond hair hung straight and she only wore lip-gloss with a pale shimmer. Innocent and sexy. She wanted to look fragile, yet ready to hop in bed. If Tom had bad news for her about Midge, she wanted him to remember how sweet and vulnerable she looked. She couldn't take a direct hit this morning after all the hopes she had for them. She bit her lip as she walked into the kitchen.

"You look great." Tom jumped up and hugged her. "For a gal who had the night you had, I'm telling you, you look amazing."

Jamie smiled at him and grabbed a cup of coffee. One point for the home team.

"I'm out of here, guys." Lynn put a few muffins on a tray in front of Jamie. "Ben was great about last night, but I need to get home." She knew she would have stayed all day if Jamie needed her, but she was a third wheel now, and wanted to give them their privacy. "Call me later, promise." She hugged them both, then rushed out the door.

"Your car is in the drive way. I drove it over. I've got someone picking me up later." Tom reached over and touched Jamie's hand. "Let's talk about Jackson first."

Jamie listened. Tom's uncle and Jackson went way back. They were old school buddies. Jackson invested cash into the bar in the early days. That loan had been paid back.

"Uncle Charlie is a good man. He knows Jackson has some anger issues. We, well Uncle Charlie, should have banned Jackson a few years ago. But Jackson was seeing Midge on the side and had quieted down." Tom took a sip of coffee and grabbed a muffin. "Then all hell broke out last night. Midge is pregnant with Jackson's baby. Midge knew Jackson sometimes hit on other women, but she thought he'd come through for her, especially since his wife kicked him out and served him with divorce papers. He told her not to count on him for anything. How did he know it was really his? A damn bastard. You showed up in the middle of all of it. I'm so sorry."

"Wow. That is a lot of bad karma." Jamie didn't know what to say.

She figured it would be in bad form to say how relieved she was he wasn't involved with Midge as she'd worried.

"What is going to happen to him now? And what about Midge?"

"Uncle Charlie and his lawyer are with him now. Don't know, don't really care. Worse case scenario, might be a short probation. We have a restraining order for the bar."

"And Midge...?"

"She's a wreck. Gave her notice and is moving back to Alabama to be with family. Think she's going to have the baby anyway."

"Was there something else? You look nervous." Jamie knew there was more coming, and it didn't have to do with Jackson.

"Yes. I haven't been totally honest about my situation." He reached out to grab her hand. "I have a son. His mom, my wife, died five years ago. I've been raising him by myself. He's seventeen."

"Why didn't you tell me?" Jamie was shocked, but only that he had not brought this up on the night they shared everything. *He was a widower with a son.* So much to know about him.

"Teenager. He has some problems. I didn't call you right back last Sunday because he and I had to work out some things. Basically he is a great kid, but at that age when friends can be a bad influence. I'm crazy about you. You don't have kids, your friends don't have kids. I thought you would bolt if I told you."

"We've just met, why would that change anything?" Jamie looked at Tom and wanted to hold him, tell him nothing would change what she felt for him.

"I want you to be here for the long run. This isn't a fling for me. I haven't dated much since Linda died. Work and Sam. Then you popped up at the bar and life changed for me. I want you in my life. You made me think future rather than just day to day. Sam, well, you'll like him if you give him a chance. Having a teenage boy is a handful."

Jamie was still in shock. He had a son. He wanted a relationship.

"When do I meet him?"

"He's picking me up when you kick me out. I'm hoping that will be later rather than sooner." Tom gave her a shy grin.

"Well, I think we need to discuss this in a more private setting." Jamie got up and walked around the table. "I'm crazy about you too. And I love the idea you have a son. Not having kids doesn't mean I don't want a family."

Jamie put her arms around Tom and kissed him. She didn't mind the twinge from her stitches when he grabbed her back and pulled her so close she thought she'd break in half. She felt his hand reach inside her blouse. Tom pulled back and looked at her.

"Are you up for this? You had a rough night."

"I think I'd be better lying down." Jamie reached for his hand and tugged him towards the bedroom. She stopped midway and turned to him. "Do we have time for this? When will Sam arrive?"

"I told him I'd call on his cell when I was ready to be picked up." Tom's hands reached for her and pulled her close again. "I'm not ready until we've done this." He kissed her neck. "And this." He pulled up her peasant blouse. His mouth was hungry on her. "And this." His hand tugged at her jeans. "Damn those are tight."

"Let me help you." Jamie unzipped her jeans and let them drop to the floor. She had nothing underneath them. "Better?" She smiled at him, toying with him, and moved her hand down to where he was staring. "I heard you like to watch."

"Watch hell. I'm going to take care of you now and forever." Tom scooped Jamie up and carried her to the bedroom. "I hope you don't mind being carried. I'm practicing for our honeymoon." He kissed Jamie hard on her lips and kicked the door shut behind him.

finis

SOME PEOPLE GO TO PRIESTS;
OTHERS TO POETRY;
I TO MY FRIENDS
—VIRGINIA WOOLF

30
GIRLS NIGHT OUT

Susan looked at her watch. The girls would be there any minute. She needed to see them and get back in touch with reality. The last chapter of her book was completed and she was almost in tears. Jamie had her happy romantic ending, but she was full of sadness. It was as though a part of her had died as she said goodbye to her story. This was not what she expected. She thought she'd be relieved, excited. But she missed Jamie already… Susan heard her cell and ran to get it.

"We're coming round the corner." Emily knew Susan liked to put Daisy out of harm's way when she opened the front door. That tiny booger had a way of sneaking out.

Emily had volunteered to be the driver for their outing. She loved to take her Jetta on the road, and knew the way. "Works for us!" Diane and Cheryl were happy to sit back and enjoy the view. They perked up when they reached Safe Haven.

"Cute neighborhood." Diane piped in. "It's out of the way, but damn, the houses are charming."

"Yes they are. But look at that downtown. Nothing, Nada. I'm not sure I'd even enter that little café." Cheryl shook her head.

"Well I love it." Diane snapped a picture of the six old buildings with her cell. "Going to document everything for Facebook!" She flopped back on the leatherette seat. "It is adorable, but what the hell does Susan find to do here?"

"Come on girls. We are here to have fun. Let Susan show off the farmhouse. Then we can escape somewhere for a great dinner." Emily waved at Susan as she pulled in the driveway.

"No way!" Diane moved a small annoying strand of red hair away from her eye. "*This* is the farmhouse. What a dream!"

"You're here! All the old gang together again." Susan ran up to greet them.

"Amazing!" Cheryl perked up. "I love this place."

"Looks like it came out of a magazine." Diane sounded more than a little impressed. "Those roses are unbelievable. They look so perfect they could be fake." Diane gave Susan a huge hug. "Missed you, babe."

"And I missed you too." Susan hugged her back. "I've missed all of you. But you are here now! How was the drive?"

"Actually the trip was easy. Would have been here twenty minutes sooner, except for some hold up on the expressway. Construction of some sort. You do remember that crap traffic getting out of Atlanta." Emily smiled at her friend.

Susan grabbed Emily's overnight bag. "Wait until you see the inside." She turned to Emily. "Finally hung the paintings that were stacked up in the dining room."

"Silly, everything looked great last trip. Those paintings were nothing compared to your old place. Couldn't believe how much inventory you kept at home. It was more fun to come dig around your house than most of the shops in town." She smiled and hugged Susan again. "I've really missed you. Those monthly dinners don't cut it and I can't believe I've only been here once since you moved in a year ago."

"Ta da!" Susan flung open the beautiful old carved door and stepped to the side. "Come on in. Enter, *s'il vous plait*," Susan bent down with a flourish. "Maybe I should just do my old southern greeting, *Enter ya'll*. You remember the living room, Em?"

Susan was anxious to see if Emily noticed the change from her last visit. Susan hung the white architectural piece over the sofa and shuffled all the paintings that had been there before into other areas. Thank heavens it had been lightweight, because it was huge to handle. She turned to see Emily's reaction.

"Holy crap. That's new." She pointed above the couch. "Where did you find that Victorian gable? It's magnificent. All the decorative work is in pristine condition." Emily walked over and ran her hand across it. "That old paint is crazed to perfection. It's fabulous, Susan."

"Found it shopping at a little town close by. Five shops in a row with great antiques and architectural pieces. Almost afraid to go back. You know me, no self-control. I figured it would catch your eye immediately."

Diane and Cheryl were behind Emily at the door. They had not moved a step into the room.

"Are you two waiting for a personal invite in?" Susan was happy to see they looked awestruck.

Cheryl's face lit up with a huge grin. "You did well, girlfriend."

"Who needs a man with a house like this? First thing you know they'd want a man cave. Look how fabulous this is?" Diane shook her head and smiled at Susan. "Love this house."

"Guys, get in here." Susan closed the door behind them and ushered them into the middle of the living room. "Yep. This is the room that told me I needed to buy this place. Made up my mind even before I saw the rest of the house." She pointed to the center hall. "Leave your bags there for now. I've got to get Daisy out of the bedroom." Susan spun around and headed down the hallway.

The three of them looked at each other. Diane was the first to speak. "Maybe we should all consider moving here. Find a house close by. Sure beats my condo."

"Yes, but you like men too much to be in such a tiny town." Cheryl teased her. "But I do understand that man cave thing. That's why I like living by myself."

"Well, Al lets me do pretty much what I want with my house. He hasn't pushed to make changes since he moved in. Lucky for me he had very little furniture and he doesn't have a decorating opinion. He only wants a comfortable bed and a woman in it." Emily laughed. "I guess that is one of my favorite things about him! Plus he lets me come and go as I like. And, boy howdy, I like coming home and finding him there."

"Give us a break! You and your love fest at home." Diane rolled her eyes. "I haven't had time to tell you, but I had a quick fling with a young artist last weekend. He came from South Carolina with some paintings for the gallery to look at for a show later this year. I invited him to my place to see my etchings." Diane winked at them. "He was divine. Loved my red hair and even commented when we were in bed, he could see I was a natural redhead."

They all burst out laughing.

"I heard that last one. I see nothing has changed Diane! Doesn't he know a bottle works at both ends?" Susan joined the laughter.

"Well, he certainly appreciated it. You'd have thought he was looking for hidden treasure." Diane chuckled. "Oh, you have adorable Daisy with you!"

"Daisy looks as sweet as ever." Cheryl reached to pet Daisy, still curled up in Susan's arms.

"Anyone need a soda or something? You know I still don't cook, but that kitchen could change that yet."

"I'll come up and cook if we can have a big party here." Cheryl spoke up. "You know me, culinary goddess."

The girls' reaction to the kitchen was the same as the living room. Who wouldn't love the openness and old charm? The skylight made the room sparkle. Rays of sun danced off the glass front cabinets. Susan had placed baskets of freshly cut flowers from the garden on the four window benches. The center piece on the six-foot farm table was a mercury glass bowl full of pink sweetheart roses and deep violet blue hydrangeas. Old restaurant china in creamy white sat on burlap placemats in front of the eight chairs flanking the table.

"Remember her?" Susan pointed to the far corner of the kitchen. A human size vintage cement garden lady was tucked in the open space by the back door.

"I do remember her. Envious as hell when you found her and mad as hell you refused to sell her." Cheryl smiled and shook her head. "I wouldn't have sold her either. She was great in front of your shop. Let everyone know they were entering the Garden of Eden! That shop of yours was as close to Eden as I've ever seen."

Susan found the old statue on EBay with a buy-it-now price of ninety-five dollars. It was in a thrift store in a small town two hours north of Atlanta. She hired two guys to pick it up and followed them in her van to be sure they handled her gently. She was a steal, but even more so, she was unusual. She was a bit of a siren, with a come hither smile Susan could relate too. The statue was old, but her spirit was young.

"There's soda in the fridge. Thought we'd grab lunch on the way to Arden." Susan let Daisy out the kitchen door. "Be right back. Got to keep an eye on her."

"You worry so about that little dog. The yard is fenced, let her have some fun." Emily did not understand the dog thing with Susan. An overprotective mother.

"Most of the yard is fenced, farm fence, but on the side over there," Susan pointed to the stone wall, "there are several gaping holes. I just like to be sure Daisy doesn't get out. Plus the Miller farm on the back worries me there might be critters, coyotes or something. It's abandoned. I jokingly call Daisy *Coyote Bait*, but that is not really funny." Susan wrinkled her nose as if she smelled something rotten.

"It's a great yard. The patio is a dead giveaway this is your house. It looks just like your old shop out here. Why the hell did you ever sell that place?" Cheryl stared at her. "Yes, I know. You sold it to have the money to write."

"It was time for a change." Susan smiled. "And yes, everything outside came from my shop. What didn't sell at the end came home with me."

"I do believe I have the other half of your shop at my place," Emily laughed.

They did the grand tour. Susan was thrilled with all their comments. Perhaps the best comment came from Cheryl who took her totally by surprise.

"Thought you'd lost your marbles when you moved. But this house is so you. I think you needed to be out of that ranch house. That was your place with Steve, but this is all you. I'll bet you even write better up here."

"Thanks, Cheryl. I think I needed to hear that. It *is* all mine here. No more ghosts from my past life. Just a clean slate for me to get into my own trouble!" Susan smiled and winked at them.

"I need to freshen up a bit before we head out." Diane fluffed her hair and picked up her bag. "You never know who we might meet and I want to be ready."

"Ready is your middle name." Cheryl laughed. "But I'd like to hit the ladies room a minute too."

Susan pointed the girls in the direction of her bedroom and bath. "Or you can go upstairs to the guest bath and unpack. I'll be in my office when you are ready. I've got a full afternoon and evening planned for us!"

Emily was the first one to finish. "So where are we going for dinner? Did you pick a spot in Arden, or are we just going to decide when we get there?"

Susan held her breath for a second, then spoke. She was worried Emily would nix her plan. "Thought we'd go for dinner at City Pub. I was there a few weeks ago. Actually, on the night that girl was murdered. But other than that bad news, the pub is really awesome. Best up by the college."

"Whoa, missy. I called you the morning after the murder and you never said you were there that night." Emily frowned. "Why do you want to go back after all that trouble?"

"I really liked it. I think the group I joined will be there tonight too. Want to say hello and make amends for not staying and talking to them more last time." Susan ignored the questioning look Emily shot her way. She never told her about that night and meeting Jim. "Besides, there have been no more incidents there. They haven't found the murderer, but my guess is that it will be pretty safe with the campus cops patrolling the area." Susan didn't want anyone to talk her out of going. In the back of her mind she hoped Jim might stop in and they could reconnect. City Pub was all they had in common.

Susan thought about the murder. It had unnerved her, but she realized it had nothing to do with her. It was a horrible fluke it happened the same night she met Jim. Fear was not going to stop her from going back to City Pub. The only fear Susan had was that she'd never see Jim again.

"Ready to go!" Cheryl and Diane walked in the office. "What's on the agenda?"

Emily looked at Susan and back at the girls. "An afternoon of shopping and then dinner out."

"Shopping! Of goody, good!" Diane clapped her hands like a kid.

Susan locked the front door and turned to the girls. "First stop, lunch at this great diner I found that serves the best fried green tomatoes!"

They all piled into the Jetta. Susan noticed the white truck on her street again as she got in the front passenger seat. She wondered which house it belonged to. Her van was on its last leg and a new car was in her future. *I'd like to have a truck like that,* she mused. *I wonder if I could get a ride in it.*

Susan listened to the girls talk about lunch and shopping. She was on auto pilot until they went to City Pub. Her fantasy du jour was finding Jim at the bar again.

31
ORDER UP

"The area is beautiful, have to admit that." Cheryl spoke from the back seat. "It is calming on the nerves."

Susan turned to Cheryl. "Thanks. I know it's not what you like, too quiet. But the area just makes me happy." She looked out at the old barns that dotted both sides of the winding country road taking them to *Myrtle's Home Cooking* diner.

"Cows!" Diane laughed out loud. "You don't see those in Atlanta, at least not where I live." She paused for a minute and inhaled sweet country air. "God I love your house. Have I said that enough times? If I could find a place like that in Atlanta, ha, I'd help push old Aunt Matilda off the train to get my finances in order."

Emily burst out laughing behind the wheel. "You don't have an old Aunt Matilda!"

"You are so right. What was I thinking?" Diane rolled her eyes and let out a holler. "Oh my God, horses. You know I ride?"

Again Emily joined in. "You don't ride. Unless you call that last big old male stallion you dated a horse."

"Why, I declare, you are making me blush. I am famished back here. Is civilization close?"

"We're almost there. Not civilization, but lunch." Susan reassured Diane. They had been on the road twenty minutes. Susan planned lunch at the diner. She needed a bit more information for her article and she wanted the girls to taste their great food.

"I hope that fried chicken is as good as you said. I'm picturing a lovely crust melting in my mouth." Cheryl sighed.

"Just you wait." Susan grinned at her. "You'll be dreaming about the chicken, I promise you."

The windows were open and the radio hummed in the background. "Okay with you all if I turn the volume up?" Susan wanted to close her eyes for just a minute and listen to the music.

The girls agreed.

She leaned back on her seat, lost in sensation. The sun streaming in the windshield felt warm on her skin. The breeze from the side window blew her hair wildly across her face. She pushed the unruly strands back behind her ear. She was in heaven.

"Hey, don't close your eyes, Sue, Sue." Emily punched her in the shoulder. "I don't know where *Myrtle's Diner* is. Don't want to blow past it."

"Sorry. Lost in the moment." Susan peered out the front window. "Great timing. It's right over there." Her arm shot in front of Emily's nose as she pointed to the left.

"Glad I didn't run off the road with that move." Emily pulled into the lot and parked the Jetta. "Let's go girls."

"It's a dive." Cheryl sounded dismayed.

"It's a diner." Susan gave her a dirty look and laughed. "You and your city ways."

"Why, I think the place looks cute." Diane added her two cents worth. "Doesn't look like they have a liquor license. Moonshine maybe?"

Emily shook her head. "Looks like a great place for some home cooking. Susan swears by it. And you," she stuck her finger in Diane's arm, "can have your Margarita at dinner. We all can!"

Susan swung open the diner's front door. "Come on in, ladies."

"Oh Miss Susan, it's wonderful to see you again!" Brittany ran up and threw her arms around Susan, giving her a big hug. "These must be your friends." Brittany held out her hand to the other girls. "Let me get you seated." She ushered them to a table by the front window and yelled back towards the kitchen. "Lee, guess who stopped by. Get yourself out here a sec."

Susan blushed at all the hoopla. The other folks in the diner stared at them.

"I'll be danged. You came back and brought friends. Am pleased to meet all you lovely ladies." Lee smiled and tipped his white cap. "Got to get back to my orders. Brittany will take care of you." He winked at Brittany and headed back to the kitchen.

"Indeed I will." She squeezed Susan's hand as she put menus on the table. She held up her chalk board with the daily specials.

"Fried chicken for me." Cheryl interrupted. "I hear it's the best from Susan." She handed her menu to Brittany.

"What's on the board?" Susan wanted to support Lee's idea of a chalk board to list the daily specials. She had been charmed with it on her first visit.

"Grilled pimento cheese with bacon and pepper jelly on rye." Brittany grinned at the girls as she read from the board. "Comes with slaw and a drink of your choice. Or, for an extra dollar, we can substitute our famous fried green tomatoes."

"That's for me!" Susan placed her order. "Side of the tomatoes, please."

"We want the special too." Emily spoke for herself and Diane.

"One fried chicken, three pimento cheese specials with our fried green tomatoes." Brittany took their drink orders and disappeared to the back.

"She's adorable." Emily looked around the diner. "And so is this place. Should be on one of those TV shows that specializes in local diners."

"Exactly what I thought! I'm working on a story now. I want to help them get more customers." Susan was thrilled Emily saw the potential in the diner.

Brittany was back with their drinks and a platter of biscuits. "Honey is right there on the table, and I'll bring butter in a minute." She twirled and disappeared again. Susan saw her collecting money at another table.

"Honey is in the back grilling, if you get my drift." Diane winked at them and reached for a biscuit.

"God, these are beyond sinful." Cheryl plopped a hot biscuit covered in honey into her mouth.

"You are so right." Diane stuffed another bite in her mouth.

"Don't talk with your mouth full, dear." Emily shot her a silly look and reached for the last biscuit.

"You'd be surprised what I can do with my mouth full." Diane mumbled to herself.

"Three specials coming up." Brittany held a large tray and put three plates down. Lee was behind her with the fried chicken order.

"Leave room for dessert now." Lee placed the friend chicken in front of Cheryl. "Peach cobbler. House special too."

Susan was thrilled to see her friends eat so much. She thought they would enjoy the diner, but sometimes she guessed wrong. She wanted this day to be perfect.

"What's next?" Diane finished before the others. "I'm stuffed. Ready to walk off a few calories."

"A few calories? You just ate a whole load of carbs." Emily laughed. "I think we all did. The cobbler almost did me in."

"It's another fifteen, twenty minutes to Arden. You'll like it. College town with all the shops you could want. Those students can spend money. I didn't have that kind of cash when I was their age. Dinner is at City Pub."

"Isn't that the place where…" Diane wanted to say *the murder took place*, but Emily cut her off.

"It will be fine. Susan's friends from that group will be there too."

Brittany came back with their change. Susan still had a few questions for her article.

"We're heading to the ladies room and will meet you outside." Emily interrupted. "Don't rush for us."

"When did Lee's family buy the diner?" Susan wanted to include more history of the place, not just the food and service. "And I should have gotten more information on Myrtle. Is there any recipe you can share?"

"Lee's the one you need to talk to." Brittany turned towards the back and called to Lee.

"What's up, Babe?"

Susan watched as his arm circled Brittany and his hand landed on her butt again. She looked around. The diner was empty.

"Miss Susan wants to know if you can share a recipe for her article."

"You know, we like to keep our family secrets. But since you've been so nice trying to help us out, how about Myrtle's Fried Green Tomato recipe?" Lee sat down next to Susan. "Got something to write with."

"Awesome. That will bring some attention to the article and the diner. Thank you so much." Susan was touched by his gesture. She looked up at Brittany who tenderly had her arm around Lee's shoulders as he wrote.

"Hope to have my article done in a few weeks. Been working on my book and that always slows me down for anything else."

"We'll just be pleased when it's done." Brittany turned to Lee, who nodded in agreement. "Really like your friends."

"Well, they loved the diner and food and enjoyed meeting you both. Guess I should get out there and join them. Going up towards the college."

Brittany's face clouded over. "Be careful. You heard a girl was murdered up there. Gives me the creeps."

"I am sure we'll be safe." Susan hugged Brittany and Lee. "See you soon."

She glanced back as she closed the front door. The two were in an embrace that looked pretty frisky.

"Was he grabbing her ass?" Cheryl asked as soon as they got in the car.

"I noticed that too." Diane giggled. "Young love. They sure were cute."

Emily started the Jetta and looked at Susan. "Which way?"

"Make a left as you leave the diner. Then it's a straight shot. You'll see the signs. You'll also notice we'll be back in civilization. Vintage clothing shops, designer shops, gift shops, and a beauty palace."

"Ah, shopping. I'm armed and dangerous with my debit card."

Diane spoke up. "I think I'm going to close my eyes for a minute. All that food made me sleepy."

The others nodded in agreement. Susan looked at Emily. "Do you mind? I think we all over ate. Hate you have to drive."

"It's fine. You all are a bunch of sissies, but I already knew that." She laughed and backed the Jetta past a white pick-up truck in front of the diner sign. "I think that driver is napping too." The truck blocked part of the entrance and she had to make a sharp left to get past it. "Sure are a lot of trucks around here."

"Country living." Susan mumbled, her eyes closed.

"Don't doze off too long." Emily poked Susan's arm as she headed down the road. "Once again, I don't have a clue where we are."

Susan sat up. "So sorry. Don't know what is wrong with me." She yawned and laughed. "Am I getting old or is it a carb reaction?"

"I'm going for carb overdose." Emily looked in her rear view mirror and caught a glimpse of a pick-up truck behind her. "If I didn't know better, I'd say that is the truck that was parked at the diner. But how weird would that be?"

Susan turned around. "Looks like the pick-up that's been at my neighbor's this week too. All white trucks look the same to me." The sign for Arden caught her attention. "Follow the road to the right. Just a few more miles to go."

The town was as charming as Susan remembered from her first visit. "If you follow this road three blocks you'll be in the center of town. There is a big lot next to City Pub. I think we should park there."

Emily found it quickly. She paid the attendant for the afternoon and parked close to the street. "Will be a breeze to find my Jetta when we come back. Now we need a plan. I don't think we all want to hit the same shops."

Let's see if our phones are in sync." Susan pulled her cell from her purse. "Mine says it's three."

"Same here." Diane called out from the back.

"Me too." Cheryl joined in.

Emily looked at her cell. "Same with me."

"I suggest we catch up at O'Leary's Book Store at seven. That's one place I know everyone will want to hit. It's across from the lot. We can load our stash and walk to City Pub." Susan was anxious to get started. Her plans were different than her friends.

The girls spread out as soon as their feet hit the pavement.

Susan set the alarm on her cell for an hour earlier than they arranged to meet. She wanted some time before dinner to freshen up. She felt a little naughty, like she was cheating on her friends. She told them the group 'Beer and Buddies' should be there and she wanted them to meet Patti. She never told them about Jim. What if she ran into him tonight? She couldn't leave with him, but she could slip him her phone number.

It was a long shot for sure. But she felt hopeful. Watching Brittany and Lee grab each other got her excited to be grabbed again herself.

Fate had a way of making things happen. For some reason her mind went back to the murder of that poor girl. Did she know her killer or was she hoping fate would bring her romance? A chill shot through Susan. Jim was a good guy, she could tell. She just knew fate had something wonderful in store for her, if not tonight, then soon.

Susan pulled open the large glass door to the boutique, her first shopping stop. The angle of the door just as it slowly closed caught a reflection in the afternoon sun. A white truck had slowed down in traffic. The window was open and a man wearing sunglasses watched as Susan disappeared inside.

32
CITY PUB PARTIE DEUX

"Wow. This place rocks." Emily was the first to comment as they stepped into City Pub. "Beautiful décor. A bit more masculine for my tastes, but it is so well done."

"The bar is awesome!" Diane shoved Cheryl gently in the back. "I've been waiting all day for a Margarita. Out of my way girls." Diane pushed ahead and strutted up to the bar.

Dark eyes met hers as she leaned on the beautiful marble top. "Margarita, on the rocks, salt on the rim." She gazed back at the bartender and gave him her most beguiling smile. "Don't skimp on the booze."

"You got it, ma'am."

"I got that ma'am treatment from that stud bartender." Diane moaned as the girls joined her. "Now I feel old enough to be his mother."

"Don't be silly. Look at you. Cougar at best." Cheryl winked at Susan and Emily. "Give him both barrels and ignore any future ma'am remarks."

Diane tugged down on her already low cut top. "Better?" She turned towards Cheryl, leaned forward ever so slightly, and wiggled her shoulders.

"X-rated." Cheryl laughed. "Now I need a damn drink. How do you get those things to stand out so?" Cheryl thought of her own bra. She needed more support.

"Got to keep them up and winking." Diane giggled.

"Here is your Margarita..." the bartender stopped as Diane

swung around, her back arched, and smiled at him. "Excuse me, your drink is here young lady." He put the drink in front of her and smiled at the others. "What can I get you girls?"

The *girls* in his remark did not go unnoticed. Susan turned and whispered to Diane. "I think your boobs have made us all young again."

Cheryl, Emily, and Susan ordered wine. By the bottle. "We can share." Emily piped up when they each wanted a glass. "Cheaper. I'll drink what's left if you *girls* don't want more than a glass. Or there is another bottle in our name if we want more, I am sure."

Susan took a slow sip of her wine and looked around the room. Did she really think Jim would magically appear? And what if he did – sitting at a table with another woman. Shit, she hadn't played out that scenario. She did see the 'Beer & Buddies' group and Patti.

"Want to say hello to a friend." She leaned over to Emily. "Be right back."

"Well, I declare. It's good to see you Susan!" Patti was handing out name tags and stopped to give her a hug.

"So sorry about last…" Susan was cut off with another hug.

"Hush. I saw you leave and wished it were me." She giggled.

"Do you know him? Name is Jim. Teaches at the college." She felt she looked desperate, sounded desperate, and anxiously pushed her hair behind her ears. "We went outside to talk. Never got his full name." Susan gave a weak smile. She hoped it wasn't written all over her they had fooled around.

"Don't know him. I did see him later that night. Came in here and had a beer at the bar before he left again." Patti remembered him because she was surprised Susan didn't come back in too.

"He walked me to my car and I left. Did he hook up with anyone else?" Susan felt she was pushing her luck.

"Not that I saw."

Susan sighed and smiled. "Can we join you later? Three of my best buddies are here from Atlanta. I'd like to meet the rest of the folks too."

"Sure hon. Come on over when you finish at the bar." Patti

reached past her and handed out a pen and name tag to the next person in line.

"Hello." The man looked at Susan and smiled. He had very thick hair and glasses and a nice smile. There was something familiar about him. She looked over at the bar and Emily was waving like crazy.

"Patti, see you later. Got to get back to my friends."

"You are welcome to come back and sit with us." Patti leaned across the table and gave her a peck on the cheek. "Don't be a stranger, girl."

"I won't." Susan was in motion to leave when she felt it. Something brushed up against her thigh, right at her skirt hemline. She felt skin on skin. *Did someone touch her?* She swung around to look at the guy next to her. He was busy filling out a name tag and totally occupied. She looked out into the bar. Was Jim there? Did he touch her to tease her? She didn't see him. In fact, no one was around her. *Okay, imagination on overdrive.* She sighed. *I am way too anxious about Jim.*

Patti was still greeting people. "Monica, so glad you made it!" She turned to a group by the table, her voice loud over the crowded area. "Monica is new to the group. Let's give her a warm welcome." Everyone applauded Monica. One guy stood up and gave a loud whistle. Susan smiled at how friendly everyone was and headed back to her friends at the bar.

"Is that the group you joined?" Emily had kept her eye on Susan. She thought Susan seemed a bit squirrelly since they got there. "I think that guy bumped into you."

"What guy?" Maybe Jim had been there after all.

"The one with the thick hair." She went to point at him, but he was nowhere to be seen.

"Creeping me out a bit." Susan sat down on the stool next to Emily. "It almost felt like someone tried to reach up my skirt."

"Well, the guy with the hair seemed to be very close to you. Surely he didn't try to feel you up." Emily crinkled her nose. "That would be seriously disturbing. I don't see him now."

"Hi. I saw you chatting with Patti." The new girl, Monica, came up to the bar by Susan and Emily. "I have a free drink card as a newbie. Monica." She held out her hand.

"I'm Susan. This is my dear friend Emily and the two girls flirting with the server are Diane and Cheryl." Susan reached for Monica's hand and gave it a quick squeeze. "My friends are visiting from Atlanta."

"I was hoping to run into an old friend tonight. He comes in here sometimes after class. But I don't see him. Think I'll go back and mingle with the group. They seem nice. There is a new guy here too. Kind of cute. I don't see him at the moment. But we started talking earlier. I'd like to pick that back up." She grabbed her free beer and smiled at Susan. "Come sit with us if you have time!" Monica waved to the girls at the bar, who had no idea who she was, but waved back. Monica turned and left.

"Who was that? Kind of bitchy looking." Diane shook her head. "Look who's talking, me. The queen bitch. Still she does have a look about her that is not so nice. Don't you think so?"

Susan laughed at her. "She seems nice enough. Yes, her top is lower than yours, if that's what you mean! But hey, the bartender didn't give her the time of day."

"I do declare, you are so right on that."

"Well, be nice. We are going to join them." She waved and whistled to get the others attention. "Let's go to the table over there." Her hand was in the air pointing in the direction of the group in case they didn't catch her words.

Most of the seats were taken when they made it over. Patti had packed up all the pens and name tags and was relaxing with a beer.

"These are the rest of my friends." Susan introduced them to Patti. "We've had a big day hitting all the shops. They have plenty of places to go in Atlanta, but Arden is so charming, I knew they would really like it."

"It's a great college town. I can't believe that girl got murdered here. We just don't get that type of crime around here. Sorry to bring it up, but it still fresh on my mind. Glad it didn't scare you off." Patti frowned briefly.

"We were a little nervous coming into City Pub, but Susan insisted. I'm glad she did." Emily gave Patti a warm friendly smile. "Glad Susan has joined your group. She needs to get out more. Pretty isolated in Safe Haven."

Susan kicked Emily's shin and kidded her. "Thank you mother dear." She hoped Patti wouldn't mention her spending time with Jim, not the group.

"Tell me what you all do." Patti changed the subject and shot her question to all four.

"I am a caseworker for the feds." Emily shook her head in disgust. "Boring, but secure, and I really shouldn't complain, but I do."

"I run an art gallery." Diane cut in. "Love it. Love the art."

"I am currently unemployed." Cheryl smiled. "Happy with every minute of it. Before that I was a legal secretary. About as boring as Emily's job."

Susan laughed. "My friends are all free spirits. I write. Have a few published books and am working on another. I also write an on-line dog column."

"Yes. We love dogs, but her column is too dog oriented for my taste." Emily hugged Susan and laughed. "She's writing erotica now."

"Well, that sounds intriguing." Patti looked at Susan with interest. "Were you doing research the other night?" She grinned, then saw the look on Susan's face, and stopped.

Emily didn't miss it. "What about the other night?"

"I talked to a few men, that's all." Susan did not want to talk about Jim. She still hoped he would come in, but it was getting late and she decided that was a fantasy that was not happening.

"I overheard that. My old boyfriend was a writer." Monica walked up and joined them. "He was a butt though. Hit me a few times. I had to move out." She shook her head and brushed her short dark hair back from her cheek. "I'm a teacher at the college. Art history."

"You should talk to my friend Diane, she works in an art gallery." Susan looked around. Diane was back at the bar flirting with the bartender. "Maybe later. She seems preoccupied."

"I don't blame her. He is a hunk." Monica looked from the bar back to Susan. "I was talking to a cute guy earlier when I first got here. He disappeared. Probably left with someone else. Isn't that the way."

"I think I saw him go to the back of the bar." Patti looked at Monica. "Just FYI in case you want to talk to him."

"Thanks. I think I will. See you girls later." Monica grabbed her beer and took off.

"Patti, when did you start this group? I had two groups on this site when I had my shop. Such a great way to meet people."

"I was sick of the bar scene, you know, going in by myself. I needed more friends, just friends. Seemed like a good idea. Now I can mingle and not feel I am on the prowl. It's not about trying to hook up with a guy for me. Just want to expand my group of friends. If I hit it off with someone, that's good too. Divorced six months ago, still stings."

"I understand completely. Widow. Of course it's been long enough I'm labeled single now."

She and Patti chatted for a good thirty minutes. Patti never had children, had a dog she adored, worked as a physician's assistant, and collected Victorian antiques.

"Your hair is lovely down, but I still remember that fantastic hair clip you wore last meeting. Wish I could find one."

"Wait a minute. I've got something in my purse." Patti bent over and rummaged in a large tote. "Ah, here it is." She handed Susan a hair clip similar to the one she had worn.

"This is a beauty too." Susan held a large butterfly clip in her hand. It was jeweled with blue stones.

"It's yours. I bought several. Was going to use it tonight, but felt like leaving my hair down. Feeling sexy. *Not.*" Patti giggled. "Sometimes my hair just drives me crazy and I like to get it off my face. You take this one. It is a token of our blooming friendship." Patti saw Susan's look and continued. "Reproduction. Cheap. So don't worry. It just has a great look, don't you think?"

"I love it. Patti, you are a doll." Susan hugged her then reached up and pulled her hair back. She twirled it up high and clipped it with the sparkling blue butterfly. "Like?"

"Perfect."

Diane walked up and flung her arm over Susan's shoulder. "You better take me home or I am going home with that young stud. You may never see me again. Isn't that how girls disappear?" Diane had one drink too many but was smart enough to come back to the fold.

"We'd better head out." Susan grabbed Diane's hand. "I'll send you an e-mail. Maybe I can come up and we can meet for lunch." She hugged Patti with her free arm.

The four of them headed back out. Emily took a look behind her as she closed the glass door. Monica was talking at the bar with the guy with the thick hair and glasses. He was cute, but there was something weird about him. *Oh well, not my problem.*

"Okay girls. We have a slumber party to attend." Emily started the Jetta and turned on the radio. "Anyone care to sing with me. You know how I love this song."

It was a perfect evening. One they would never forget.

33
SEEMS LIKE OLD TIMES

"This is just like old times!" Susan opened a bottle of wine and started to fill their glasses. The four of them huddled in the kitchen in their PJ's, drinking and laughing. Same fun, just different location.

"Can we stay in here? I adore this kitchen." Cheryl plopped in a chair at the farm table. "God I love this table. This is the one you traded a load of garden statues for, if I remember."

Susan nodded and finished her sip of wine. "You are so right. Neither of us had a dime that day. Slow week. Amy wanted garden statues for a show she was doing on the weekend, and I needed a big display table. Funny how we could always work things out in this business."

Susan couldn't part with the table when she sold her shop. She bought it home and had it in the little shed outside at her old place. She knew the time would come she'd have room for it. It was six feet long, pine top, and old white painted legs. A wonder in the world of farm tables. The kitchen farmhouse had plenty of room for it, smack dab in the middle of the room. Eight French style antique chairs, with newer white paint, and covered in burlap, fit nicely around it.

The kitchen was cozy at night. She didn't turn on the overhead lights, but clicked on several of the lamps close to the table. The large windows, like all throughout the house, let moonlight peek in. "This is a perfect place to chat. Plus we can raid the fridge if anyone gets hungry."

Emily piped in first. "How is the book coming along? You ignored my question earlier and we all want to know!"

"Yes, can we read some of it? Emily says it pretty risqué." Diane smiled and gave a small giggle. "Can't be too risqué for me. Those paranormal books I read have all kinds of crazy sex in them."

"I'm actually finished with it. Want to tighten it up before I share it. Then I could use some good eyes." Susan knew she was crapping out on her friends, but she just wanted to have girl talk tonight. The book could wait.

"Well, I went up on a dating site this week. *Love Me Cupid*." Diane gave a devilish grin. "It is wild. Can't tell you how many penis photos have popped up. I think that's the dating site you were on right after Steve died." Diane stopped herself. She never knew if mentioning Steve would upset Susan, even after all this time.

"It is! Shared some wild stories with you all back then." Susan debated bringing up her latest experience, but passed on it.

"*Love Me Cupid*. Been there, done that. I got lots of penis photos too" Cheryl started to laugh. "I think that's par for the course on that site."

"Not me! I've got my own penis at home." Emily giggled. "It pops up almost every night for my viewing."

"Show off!" Cheryl gently slapped Emily's arm. "I did that for all of us." She laughed.

"Well, I've got a new guy that wants to chat tomorrow when I get home. You know, I love those instant messages. If you can't have a guy in bed, not bad to have one on the computer to help you through the night." Diane poured another glass of wine. "This guy's profile name is HungShaven. Weird if you ask me."

Susan blushed. She thought about the instant messages she had recently. They can get out of hand.

"You are turning pink." Emily pointed at Susan across the table. "Something we need to know about?"

She just wasn't ready to admit her folly. "I'm getting ready for the rest of the story from Diane. If anyone can find a guy with that user ID, it would be her!" Susan winked at Diane, who shook her head, rolled her eyes, and burst out laughing.

"Do you think he's going to live up to that ID? I've never seen one that has been shaved." Diane gave a silly grin.

"I may not be dating, but I get the scoop from Gloria about her friends. Then there are their kids, so many of them, girls and guys, are doing it." Emily shook her head. "How behind the times am I? I've never had a Brazilian wax, Al likes me the way I am, a natural gal." She winked at the group. "But, geez, I got more information than I needed from Gloria. Snipping, waxing, shaving, tweaking, landing strips, and jewels. So yes, my guess is HungShaven is shaved down there. And with your track record you'll get a photo tomorrow to prove it!"

Cheryl fanned herself. "Lordy girls, this is quite the conversation, even for us!" Cheryl lowered her eyes in shame than let out a raucous laugh. "I haven't had a professional wax, but there was that one night I got a bit drunk and let my old boyfriend shave me. Had a few scrapes in the morning and I thought it would never grow back. Itched like the dickens."

"Was that Bobby?" Emily was curious. "He's the only one you dated for any length of time."

"It was. Aren't you the detective?" Cheryl smiled shyly. "That will not happen again in my lifetime."

Susan was totally relaxed. Her sides ached from laughing so hard. She couldn't keep her antics a secret any longer.

"Okay. I have something to admit." Susan looked at the three of her best friends and snorted. "Let's all have another glass of wine. I'm going to need another to fess up what I've done recently."

Emily, Cheryl, and Diane held out their somewhat empty crystal glasses as Susan opened another bottle of wine.

"Truth is, I was on *Love Me Cupid* too." She looked at Diane. "Didn't meet a HungShaven, but found a freak or two of my own. I was trolling for a pervert and my profile clearly spelled that out."

Emily spoke first. "Why would you want to look for a pervert? They are everywhere online. Couldn't you have tried to find a nice guy?" Emily shook her head and let out a laugh. "Looking for love in all the wrong places!"

"The point is, I don't want to meet anyone at all. I wanted to find some inspiration to write the sex scenes in my book." She paused and batted her eyes at her friends. "It worked. We all know how they like to talk sex."

"And flash their junk." Diane cut in.

"Can't you just date like a normal person?" Emily shook her head. "No, you have to get some guy worked up on the computer and then use him…" Emily paused and smiled, her mind was clearly in a thought pattern. "Never mind, use him. Isn't that what most men do with their dates?"

"You don't know what most guys do, you've got Al." Diane jumped in. "But nothing wrong with leading a guy on and dropping his ass once you've got what you want. I like that."

"Dating is not fun like it used to be when we were in our twenties." Cheryl sighed. "I'd like to find a good guy and settle back down. It's just so hard to meet anyone of substance."

"Or who will call back." Diane winked. "Someday my prince will come, in the meantime a girl's got to have a little action."

Emily turned to Susan. "Details please. You've tossed out a teaser. I believe I speak for all here at the table." Emily looked around as Diane and Cheryl nodded in agreement.

"Well it wasn't really that much, although I did get the penis photos, a little bit of live action on a webcam from one, and all the trash talk I needed for my book." Susan went on to tell them about the two guys, leaving out her personal participation with each. "It was pretty raunchy, but that is what I wanted."

"Can they contact you again? The guy in Arkansas, well, he's too far away. But the one here…" Emily crinkled her nose, "you don't want him showing up on your door step. It might have been research for you, but you know how some guys can get. Wouldn't want him tracking you down."

"You worry too much. And I love you for it." Susan reached over and squeezed Emily's hand. "If you were in the dating scene you'd know this is normal for lots of people online. It never leads to anything more than what it is. I've deleted my profile so I am off the site. I'm safe. No pervert will come looking for me."

"Well, if he does, give him my number!" Diane raised her glass and smiled. "Whew, I am hungry now. Anything good in the fridge?"

"Me too, I could use something to munch." Cheryl chimed in.

Emily joined in. "Me three. We never ate dinner tonight."

Susan was happy to change the subject. She opened the door to the fridge and pulled out two wedges of Brie, a huge bag of grapes, and a container of dip. "Can someone grab the chips and crackers from the pantry?" Susan then opened her microwave and pulled out a tray of chocolate cupcakes. "Baked them this morning." She saw their expressions and smiled. "The microwave is a great storage place. Hey, shut up. You know I don't cook. I think I should get kudos for baking these."

The girls clapped their hands and reached for the food.

"This is the strangest assortment of goodies." Diane looked at everything on the table. "You'd think we'd been smoking pot."

"Interesting comment from you." Emily looked at Diane.

"Just saying…reminds me of college days." She winked at the others and took a huge bite of a cupcake. "This is simply divine."

34
THE KILLER WITHIN

He gripped the edge of the counter to steady himself. It was good to be home. The evening did not go as planned, nothing had that week. He was off his game. Monica paid the price for his ineptness. The vision of her on the ground, lifeless, was burned into his brain for all eternity. Just like the others. Pleasure? Regret? It was more relief. His anger was gone afterwards.

He was quick. She never knew what happened. One moment alive, the next dead. In as little time as a blink of an eye, the casual snap of fingers, a life was snuffed out in seconds. He looked at his hands, big strong hands, tan, with short clean nails. Women liked his hands. They told him so. They told him what they wanted him to do with his hands, where they wanted to be touched. Monica told him what she wanted him to do within minutes of meeting him at City Pub.

She spoke first when he walked up to the bar for his free beer. "Come sit by me. I saw you sign in with the group. I'm here with 'Beer and Buddies' too." She patted the stool next to her and smiled at him through lips that were red, ruby red.

He nodded and sat down. He needed to blend in. He wasn't with any group, he'd tracked Susan and landed back at the damn bar from last time. Now he'd signed some sheet, been given a name tag, and a ticket for a beer. The name tag was crumpled in his jean's pocket. No sense to pass up a free beer.

"First meeting," he mumbled. He turned and scanned the room. Susan was at the door with the others, hugging the overweight blonde that insisted he sign the member's list. She was with her friends and there was no way to get between them. He watched as the four of them left the pub. His fists clenched under the bar and his breath shortened. Anger bubbled up in his chest. Anger he had to do something about. He turned back to the woman at the bar. This would be easy. He couldn't miss that she had followed him around the pub earlier in the evening. He already had her interest. Now he had to put it to work. He should be polite. "And you?"

"First time for me too. I teach at the college." Monica smiled and leaned close. "You look familiar. Are you in one of my classes?"

"No. I just have that kind of face." He had run into her as he crossed campus to get to the rooming house. He was dressed in old jeans and a tattered sweat shirt that day. He hadn't shaved in a week and his hair was unruly. You might notice him, but you would forget him. He was a master of disguise, blending in with the crowd so he wouldn't stand out.

He rested his elbow on the bar and gently ran a finger down her bare arm. "Feels nice." He smiled at her, a smile he practiced in front of his mirror at home. She noticed his smile, she did not notice his steely cold eyes. Eyes void of any emotion.

"That gives me chills." Monica reached out and put her hand over his. "I'll bet those hands could give me goose bumps all over."

These hands can do a lot more, he thought to himself. *Just wait.* His mouth felt dry and he took a sip of beer.

"What's your name?" He toyed with her fingers and hand. She was soft to the touch. She was also pretty drunk, so much the better.

"Monica." She smiled. "I think I am a bit tipsy." Then she giggled. A youthful sound like a bell chiming in his ears. "And you are?" She circled her finger in front of his face and pushed it into the center of his chest.

"Dan. But my friends call me Tease&Please." He watched her reaction. It told him all he needed to know.

"Well, howdy Dan. That's quite a handle to live up to." Monica put her hand on her thighs and eased back in her bar stool, pivoting it to face him. "I'd like for you to tease and please me." She hiked her short skirt up and moved her knees apart in an inviting way. "Like what you see?"

He ran his tongue over his parched lips. "Lovely legs." His mind was on Susan's legs. He touched her earlier, so quickly, so gently, she wasn't even sure it had happened. It had put him on fire. Now he was here with Monica as she chattered away.

"They go all the way up to a place you might like to visit." Monica gave him an inviting smile. "And I'm not wearing anything under my skirt."

"Maybe you'd like to go somewhere?" His fake smile warmed a bit. He was close. She had no idea what he wanted from her. It had started and he would not turn back.

Monica stopped for a moment and wondered if she was ready to do this. She'd hoped Jim would come in tonight, but it was late and he hadn't. She didn't know what she would say to him if she saw him. Apologize? Tell him to go F off? She was still livid he made her move out. She hated that, hated him for it. She got even telling stories about him, but it wasn't enough to make her feel better. She still thought about him and missed him, even after all this time. She wondered who he was sleeping with now. Thinking about him with another woman made up her mind. Sex was her answer to questions that made her crazy.

"I'm done here." She tilted her head in his direction. "My car is next door. Let me get something out of it and I'll go with you." She pulled a wad of ones out of her purse and dropped them on the counter. "We can please each other. Ready?"

They walked out to the parking lot. The lights had gone off. There was no one in sight. Monica's car was in the back corner. He smiled remembering there were no security cameras.

Monica stopped and ran her ruby red lips over his. "My keys." She dug into her bag, pulled them out, and jangled them in front of him. "In a second we can leave and you can tease me all you want." She turned her back to him to unlock her car door.

He slipped on his gloves, reached out with his hands, and grabbed her neck. With a quick twist it was over. Dead. She dropped to the ground never knowing what hit her. He'd learned how to snap a neck watching crime shows on the television. He never understood why some people thought TV was a waste of time. It was his salvation.

He moved quickly, stepped to the side to avoid her body, tucked the gloves in his pocket, and walked to the street. He hit the sidewalk and kept going. Two couples said hello as he passed them, he looked up and smiled pleasantly. No one would suspect him of anything. No one ever had.

There was a chill in the warm night. He zipped his jacket and went to find his truck. He was pleased with tonight. The release was enormous. Right up there with sex. Sometimes better. He was very particular who he wanted sex with. Monica was a drunk slut. He'd never want her the way he wanted Susan. But she served him well in her own way.

The pick-up truck was up the block on the other side of the street. The truck started without a hitch and he drove the five miles home.

He grabbed a beer from the fridge and looked around the room. Susan would hate it. She had antiques and art and flowers. He read that on her blog. His bed had only a sheet on it. A tall rotating fan stood in the corner. The desk might appeal to her. He got it at a thrift store. It was an old pine table that he used for his computer. His TV was in the corner by a Herculon sofa he'd had since the late seventies. Maybe Susan would help him decorate. She would be spending all her time in the apartment after he brought her home.

A little over an hour had passed since he left Monica in the parking lot. Maybe it was on the news. He turned on the TV and headed for the kitchenette. His hands felt dirty. He put them under the hot running water and scrubbed them with soap and a stiff brush. He scrubbed until his skin was tender, but not enough to bleed. He had it down to a science. Then he reached in the cabinet, pulled out rubbing alcohol, and doused his hands with it. The alcohol stung, but it left him feeling cleansed of his sins.

He pulled a straight back chair in front of the television and turned up the volume. The late night news had just come on.

"*Monica Ryder, an instructor at City College, was found dead late tonight by her car in Arden. Police have no leads at the moment. There did not appear to be a struggle. Her neck was broken. She was last seen at City Pub with the 'Beer and Buddies' group. This is the second murder in Arden . . .*"

He heard enough and turned off the TV. He got up and walked into the bathroom. He liked the murder was their lead story. Now he needed to change some things. In twenty minutes his light hair was dark brown. He spiked it with gel, a looked he found agreeable. He went to the bedroom. His night stand held many styles of glasses. He pulled out a thick dark pair. A change of clothes was in order before he could be seen in public. He found his sweat pants and a thick sweat shirt with City College's logo on it and put them on the edge of the bed for later.

He walked over to the thin mirror nailed to his closet door and looked at his naked body. He was aroused. Monica had taken care of his anger, but Susan would take care of this. His fingers circled the demon that controlled him. His eyes were glued to the mirror as he watched his hand work, his grip tightened until he dropped to his knees. He liked pain and didn't stop until it was so intense he could climax. Women were too gentle with him, he wanted more from them. He would teach Susan what he needed. She would learn to love the pain too.

He stood up and went to wash his hands again. Then he turned off the light and crawled into bed. Tomorrow his dreams would come true.

35
Another Murder

Daisy barked, jumped off the bed, and headed out the hallway. Susan sat up and heard sounds coming from the kitchen. *The girls must be up.* She glanced at the clock across the room. A little after eight. Pretty early considering the late night they'd had. Dinner at City Pub and then girls' night in her kitchen. *Hard core, they are a hard core bunch. How many bottles of wine did we go through?*

Susan rolled out of bed, wiggled her toes, and let her feet hit the floor. She liked the blue polish on her toes. That was another thing they did yesterday afternoon. Pedicures. She grabbed her robe, slipped in the bathroom to brush her teeth, and make herself more presentable. Her hair was a tangled mess. She looked around and found a rubber band, slipped her hand through it, and pulled her long dark tresses up high in a ponytail. *Better.* She leaned towards the mirror and took a closer look. She looked relaxed and happy. She always felt great around the girls. She saw the hair clip on the counter. Patti had been so sweet with her gift. She knew they would become good friends.

"Coming to join you!" Susan yelled down the hallway. Daisy ran back to meet her halfway. "And you, you little booger, what do you have to say for yourself dashing off like that?" Susan bent and grabbed Daisy up. She ran her hand over Daisy's head. Daisy squirmed moving up Susan's chest until her tongue reached Susan's chin. She slathered kisses all over her face. "Enough already." She put Daisy back down. She needed coffee, not kisses!

"Hey, got a pot of coffee ready." Emily handed a cup to her. "I think this is the cup I gave you for Christmas last year." It was a sweet cup with ivy hand-painted on it. "Seemed like a good choice for a sunny morning. I know you and your cup fetish."

"I like to pick a cup for my mood. You did a fine job anticipating my mood this morning. And if you recall when you gave me the cup, I told you that ivy stood for friendship in the Victorian *Language of Flowers* book. It was a perfect gift." Susan hugged Emily.

"I'm soaking the wine bottles from last night in warm water in that glorious old sink. I saw the bottle tree outside and figure you'll want to add these."

"God you are good this morning! Anticipating my every mood."

"BFF's. I *know* your every mood." Emily smiled at her and put an English muffin in the toaster. "No, this is for me. You toast your own. I did find the marmalade in the fridge."

"Where are Cheryl and Diane? Are they up yet?"

"In your office. They wanted to catch a bit of TV. Some guy from one of those vampire movies is supposed to be on the Good Morning Show." Emily shrugged her shoulders. "Go figure, vampires?"

"Oh God!" Diane let out a shrill yell from the office. "No. No. No. Emily, get in here. Get Susan too. Oh my god. This is horrible."

Susan dropped her cup on the counter and raced behind Emily. *What the hell was wrong? Diane sounded on the verge of tears.*

"Oh Sue. This is just awful! Look at the news."

Susan turned to look at the TV. Emily put her hand on Susan's arm and let out a little gasp.

A photo of a young woman was on the screen. Susan could barely hear the words ...*murdered, found dead late last night.*

"Isn't that the girl we talked to at City Pub?"

"I think so." Susan looked at the TV with horror. "Turn up the sound."

From WAVE, this is Jack Taylor reporting on the murder of Monica Ryder. The police have no leads at this time and hope someone may have seen something and will come forward. There was no sign of struggle. The lot does not have security cameras, which was a topic of conversation at a recent town hall meeting. Ms. Ryder was an art teacher at Community College. She was a well-known figure on campus. Ms. Ryder's neck was broken...

"That *is* the girl from the bar." Susan looked from Emily to Cheryl and Diane. "She was so nice. She was talking to a guy at the bar when we left. Remember? God what happened?"

"I can't believe this is the second girl murdered up by City Pub. Does not bode well for going there again." Diane shook her head.

"Maybe we should have stayed and walked her to her car?" Cheryl looked at her hands and fiddled with her rings.

"No, she was with that guy. I hope he didn't do it. Do you think the police have questioned him? Should we call them?" Diane sat in a chair on the far side of the room, her eyes glued to the TV.

"She did rag on about her old boyfriend. A teacher at the college too. Said he roughed her up a bit." Cheryl turned to Susan. "Maybe it was him."

"Look, there's another photo up." All four heads turned to look at the screen.

"A former love interest of the victim, Jim Johnson, has been brought in for questioning." The reporter continued.

Susan looked at the photo and let out a small gasp that strangled itself before it popped out.

"Are you okay? That was a really creepy sound." Emily turned from the TV to Susan.

Susan started to cry. First silent sobs, that stuck in her throat and made her choke. She sat on the couch and put her head in her hands. Sobs racked her body. It couldn't be, but it sure seemed to be…Monica's old boyfriend, the one brought in for questioning, was her Jim from the other night.

"Hon, what's wrong?"

"I think I'm going to puke." Susan jumped off the couch and ran to the bathroom, slammed the door, and dropped to the floor. She couldn't believe he was the killer. *Could he have killed her?* Susan's head felt like it would implode on her.

"Are you okay, Sue, Sue?" Emily rapped hard on the old door. "Open up and let me in. What is wrong with you? We're all upset."

Susan didn't want to open the door. Not now. Maybe never. How could she tell the girls about Jim? Her perfect romantic lover, the one whose name she never got, was linked to a murder. *At least I have his full name now.* She could not wrap her mind around the situation.

"Open the damn door or I swear I'll call the police to pull you out." Emily was furious and troubled by Susan's reaction.

Susan knew her friend meant what she said. She didn't want the police anywhere near her. She never wanted to admit she knew Jim, or had ever met him. She prayed Patti wouldn't see that photo and tell the police they had met. Was it only last night she asked Patti about him... Too many thoughts crossed her mind.

She unlocked the door. She was a wreck.

"Honey, what is wrong?" Emily put her arms around Susan. "Come on, sit down. Cheryl bring her a shot of something from the bar."

Cheryl brought a shot glass of sherry. "This is what they do in the movies when someone is upset, but I think it is with stronger stuff." Cheryl gave the glass to Susan and she downed it quickly.

Susan was not to be comforted. "Are any of us safe?" Tears rolled down her face.

"These things happen everywhere. Crime is everywhere. Did you think it would disappear if you moved to a smaller town? It's random, or it's personal to Monica. It has nothing to do with you, babe."

"Turn off that damn TV, please." Susan had enough.

"Sure babe." Emily talked to her like she was a child. Emily looked at Cheryl and nodded towards the TV. Cheryl got up and switched it off.

Susan wanted to tell them about Jim. The words wouldn't come. She needed to get out, get some air. She had no idea what she was thinking. Let Emily say it wasn't her fault. Maybe it was. Jim seemed so perfect when she was with him, so gentle, loving. Was there a side to him she didn't know? A violent side. It was too much to comprehend. In her heart she wouldn't believe he did this, but her mind was reeling with questions.

"Let's get out of here for a bit. I need some air." Susan jumped up and pulled away from Emily. "Going to get dressed. Why don't you all do the same and let's go for a ride."

Susan felt nervous leaving Daisy, but she needed to run away from the farmhouse and everything she held dear. She so wanted to get to know Jim and now this...not the normal dating obstacle.

Fifteen minutes later they were sitting in a cafe eating biscuits.

"Glad to see you have an appetite." Emily watched Susan eat a chicken biscuit, then took a big bite of her own.

"I'm not hungry. But you know me, I eat when I'm nervous. My stomach feels rancid. Hope the biscuit will settle it down."

"This is the cutest place. I like how they made it look retro and old." Diane had pancakes drenched in syrup.

"They didn't make it look old. This is old." Cheryl punched her gently in the arm. She looked at Susan and her red puffy eyes. *Why is she taking this so hard?* She hated to see Susan so upset.

"Can you guys spend another night? I just don't want to be alone tonight." She shot a pleading look at Emily, Diane, and Cheryl.

"I've got an appointment late afternoon." Emily hated she couldn't say yes. She had volunteered to help a co-worker with papers for Monday's meeting. There was no way to beg off now. "And the girls are at my mercy since I drove. Why don't you grab Daisy and come back with us? You can stay with me and Al. Might help to talk about this with a guy. You know Al. Best listener ever. Then we can all go out for dinner when I get back. I can drive you home whenever you want."

"Think I will come to your place. But I'll drive down later." Susan felt like small rodents were tracking in her head. She needed to take a nap. "What if I get there by five?"

"Are you up to driving?"

"I'm not an invalid – just upset. I'll be fine. It will do me good to break away for a night."

"I can stay with Susan and drive down with her later. That way she won't be alone." Diane looked at Susan, but her words went out to the group.

"I really don't want to be a pain. But I need to just be left alone for a bit. I promise I'll be there by five. Thanks Di, but you head back with the others."

They got home from the cafe in less than ninety minutes. The girls grabbed their bags and loaded the Jetta.

"Don't change your mind. That's an order." Emily hugged Susan. The others were already in the car. "It will be all right. It's horrible this is so close to home and that we talked to Monica last night. But we didn't really know her. She could have been involved with anything. There was no struggle, so maybe she knew whoever killed her."

"Maybe so." Susan felt her gut twist. *Jim. Jim knew her.*

"Her old boyfriend was cute in that photo. The kind of guy a girl dreams of meeting. Is that the one Monica said hit her?"

"I don't know." Susan's body got stiff. "See you later. I really need to do something about this headache."

Susan waved goodbye to her friends and went back to the bedroom. The chill she felt was deep in her bones. She grabbed Daisy and her quilt and curled up on the bed. She couldn't shake the feeling everything around her was shattering. She refused to believe Jim was a killer. He'd had plenty of time to kill her if murder was on his mind. Maybe Jim could help the police. There was a killer on the loose and something triggered him to kill twice in a few weeks. *I wonder what set him off.* Susan fell asleep before she could take that thought further.

The sound of her cell pulled Susan out of a deep sleep. She flung her hand over to grab it off the table.

"Hello?" Susan felt confused. She had to think a minute to remember the day.

"Where the hell are you?" It was Emily. Susan sat straight up. *What time was it?* She didn't have a clue, but from Emily's tone, she must have missed their dinner date.

"It's after six. I just got home from my meeting and expected to see you and Al sharing a glass of wine waiting for me. Cheryl and Diane already called Al to see what was going on." Emily caught her breathe. "Are you okay?"

"Shit. I fell asleep after you left. Your call just got me up. Sorry I worried you."

"Damn straight you did. You were a mess when we left."

"I'm sorry. And I am really sorry, I think I am just going to stay here tonight. I don't have the energy to get dressed and drive an hour. Are you all right with that?"

"Sure, hon. I'll miss you. But if you feel better that's all I want to hear. The girls are on their way over. I'll update them. Relax tonight and we'll talk tomorrow. Love you."

"Love you too."

Susan got up and paced the room. *I'm not relaxed, not at all.* The picture of Jim on the TV never left her thoughts. She had to find a way to talk to him. Maybe she could figure this out tomorrow. She went into the bathroom, pulled the rubber band off her pony tail, brushed her hair, and piled it back up. She washed her face. It was early and she was hungry.

Her usual big night was ahead. Dinner with Daisy and work on her book. She needed to edit a few of the chapters.

Susan looked at her reflection in the mirror. *Some things never change.*

He looked at his watch. It was only seven, too early to drive to her neighborhood. That would be later, when it was dark, and the neighbors were asleep. His plan was in place for tonight. He wouldn't fail. He took out a frozen dinner and nuked it in the microwave. Then with deliberate patience he sat down and slowly took small bites. Susan's photo was on his monitor. It filled the full screen. He watched her with greedy eyes. He needed to stay calm for what was ahead.

36
A Person of Interest

Monica. She'd haunt him from the grave. He felt terrible she had been murdered. He never wished her any harm, never caused her any. He leaned forward in the old wood chair and fiddled with his hands. *Why doesn't someone come over here?* He wanted to make his statement, answer whatever questions they had, and get the hell out of there.

The trip to the police station brought back memories of Monica and all the trouble she stirred up for him. *I hope to God they don't think I had anything to do with this.* They'd ask him to stop by to look at a list of people who might have a beef with Monica. *Ask her last boyfriend,* he wanted to say. He decided to keep his mouth shut until he saw what they wanted.

"Thanks for coming in, Jim." The big, overweight officer put out his hand. "Sorry you had to be dragged into all this."

"Officer James." Jim stood up and shook his hand.

"Chet. You don't have to be so formal here."

"Thanks. I just wasn't sure. It's good to see you again, even if the situation is worse than before."

Officer Chet James was the policeman who questioned him when Monica made those horrible accusations. He sized Monica up quickly. She'd made a play for him in the middle of his investigation, and when he turned her down, as nicely as possible because of a conflict of interest, she turned on him and caused a huge scene in the station.

"She was something else. Makes that stalker gal in the old movie look sane, can't remember the name, but you know it." Chet shook his head. "Almost got me in as much trouble as you." He smiled at Jim. "Don't mean to speak ill of the dead, but she was trouble with a capitol T."

"Tell me about it. I'm glad to offer what I can, but I've stayed clear of her since that incident. She moved in with someone shortly after we broke up. Another instructor. Don't know his name. Caused a bit of trouble with him too. I heard she moved out. Have you contacted him?"

"Know who you're talking about. Not yet. He's on our list. Neighbor said he flew to Iowa last week. His mother is ill and he went to check on her. Don't think he's our boy. Pretty solid alibi."

"I don't have a clue who could have killed Monica." Jim drew a deep breath. He felt sad more than angry. Unless this turned on him. "You know, she was screwed up to date, but her students loved her. Maybe you should check with them. I remember when we were together she would catch up with a few of her favorites for drinks before she came home."

"Got to ask, Jim." Chet pushed back in his chair and looked directly into Jim's eyes. "It's just routine. Where were you last night?"

"In my apartment. I had a student conference at seven. Didn't feel like driving to the house, so just crashed there." Jim felt a headache coming on.

"I talked to the bartender. He remembers Monica being in there most of the evening. First talking to a group of four gals up from Safe Haven and then some guy new to the place. She signed up for a group that met there."

"Max keeps up with the bar chatter." Jim almost jumped when Safe Haven was mentioned. He wondered if Susan might have been back. He really wanted to see her. Did she see his photo on the news? A strike for the home team. How the hell would he get past being her neighbor and a person of interest in a murder investigation?

"Thanks for coming in, Jim." Chet stood up. "I've got another person waiting that was in the bar last night too. Don't worry about this visit. Just needed to check you off the list." He shook Jim's hand. "If you think of anything, however, call me. Maybe when this is over we can meet for a beer."

"You got it. Thanks, Chet." Jim was glad Chet was the officer to talk to him. He needed a familiar face in the middle of this mess.

Jim got in his car and tried to decide if he should drive to Safe Haven or just go back to his apartment. He was zonked. He didn't know what to do about Susan. *Tell her, don't tell her. If she saw his photo on TV...*the thought made him sick...*would she think he was a killer?* They didn't mention he lived in Safe Haven, just up at the college. For some reason he felt relieved. She didn't need to find out he was her neighbor listening to a news report that connected him to his dead, murdered, ex-girlfriend. God this was fucked up.

He pulled up in front of the apartment and shut off the ignition. The apartment complex was small. He liked that. There were only twenty townhomes. The complex was built in the late seventies. Washed out yellow brick, two story units with parking outside the front door. He moved in the apartments when he first got hired by the college. He never moved out. He loved teaching and the apartment was just off campus. He also knew the old house would be his someday, but he was in no hurry for it. He liked that he and his Dad had reconnected and, when he moved up to Arden it was easy to visit him at the assisted living home.

A knock on the car window startled him. It was his neighbor Barry, another instructor at the college, who lived next door almost as many years as Jim had been there. Jim motioned for him to step back, and eased himself out of the car.

"Heard you had to talk to the cops today." Barry gave him a wry smile. "What a bitch of a situation." He smacked Jim on the shoulder. "She was a nut case. But I know you buddy. If I can help let me know. I drove in about ten last night from Anna's and parked next to your car if you need me to tell the cops that."

"Thanks, Barry. I think I'm good. But glad to know someone

knows I was home last night."

"Well, call me if you need me. Anna will be over shortly. I think she thinks we're getting serious." Barry shrugged.

"So are you? I like her." Jim smiled and felt the tension ease out of his back.

"Working on figuring that out. See you later, buddy."

Jim grabbed a beer from the fridge and sat in the leather chair next to his plasma TV. He reached for the remote and turned on the set. There was no mention of the murder, and he was relieved. *Just let me be in peace tonight.* He took another sip of beer, placed the bottle on the pine table next to him, closed his eyes, and dozed off.

Susan... Jim woke with a start. The room was dark except for the moving color from his TV and the lights from the lot outside. He got up, pulled the blinds, and turned on all the lamps. He'd had an awful dream and Susan was in it. He couldn't remember any of the details but it left him on edge. Maybe he should drive to Safe Haven. Even if he couldn't talk to Susan, he could keep an eye on her place. He needed to figure out how to approach her. This was making him crazy.

Why the hell didn't I tell her that night? He felt so stupid. *I didn't tell her because she didn't give me a chance.* She'd gone down on him in the van, then opened the door, and practicality pushed him out. He watched her spin out of the parking lot standing there with his shirt open. He'd barely had time to zip his jeans.

Jim shut off the TV, turned off most of the lights, and got back in his car. He had no clue why he felt he needed to be next door. She wouldn't know. He wouldn't see her. She wasn't in any danger. The two murders had to do with the college. He had no idea what the connection was and why they were murdered. His gut just told him he needed to be close to Susan.

It was almost midnight when he pulled in. Susan's house was dark. He imagined she was asleep. *I wonder if she dreams of me.* He couldn't get her out of his mind. He thought there was something between them that night, more than sex. He knew how he felt about her. He swore it was mutual. Then this fucked up *I don't want to meet my neighbors* situation screwed everything up. *Yeah, now let's add a murder investigation into the mix.* Jim didn't know if he was disgusted or just happy to be close to her.

He grabbed a beer and headed upstairs. He wanted to work on a design for the bathroom. He was too keyed up to sleep and needed a distraction. The air was cool. He opened the windows and looked down on Susan's back yard. *One day soon I am going to be there with her.* He walked back to his desk and went to work.

37
We Meet Again

Damn that Daisy. Susan was furious with her little dog. *I am not in the mood to get up.* Daisy had jumped off the bed, run down the hall, and went ballistic with noises outside. Third time this week. *What it is with her?* Tiny dogs and their Napoleon complex. Her killer instinct was in protective mode and she was on a mission. Susan knew exactly where she'd find her - by the doggie door in the kitchen.

She'd made the mistake of letting Daisy jump through it once, and once was enough. Daisy was obsessed with it and ran to it every time she heard something. The pine floor was scratched from her tiny nails digging in as she pranced back and forth. The door stayed on lockdown.

Susan could see the clock across the room. Just after midnight. Most nights she'd still be at her computer. Of course tonight was different. She tried to distract herself with her book edits, but her nerves were shot. She was exhausted from everything that had happened. *I should have pushed myself harder to go to Emily's.* She wanted to tell her why she was so upset about Monica. About Jim. . . *Maybe I'll call her tomorrow. She'll help me clear my head.*

She didn't know what to think about Jim. He wasn't a killer, she felt that in her heart, but what happened last night? Would there ever be answers? The whole situation was a damn mess. She felt crushed. What else could go wrong? Her peaceful life was fractured. *Nothing is what it seems.*

The huge Victorian windows filled the room with moonlight. She eased off the bed. Her sweater was exactly where she'd left it, tossed on the old painted rocker. She grabbed it and pulled it over her thin cotton night shirt. Not that it was cold, she just felt chilled. "Coming sweetie." Susan whispered more to herself, than Daisy, as she padded in bare feet towards the kitchen. She just wanted to grab Daisy, go back to bed, and pull the covers over her head.

The quiet as she neared the kitchen took on a strange air. It was dead quiet. She didn't hear any sound at all. Susan felt uneasy again. The house was too quiet. Yet the noises outside seemed to escalate in the dark. Everything took on a different feeling with two murders so close to her.

"Daisy." This time she called loudly as she walked into the kitchen. Her voice echoed back at her. She started to get annoyed again. *Where the hell was Daisy?* The moonlight told her all she needed to know. The doggie door was open and Daisy was gone.

She unlocked the ornately carved door and stepped out to the patio. The smell of honeysuckle was thick in the air, but did nothing to calm her tonight. Her private yard seemed ominous, no longer her sanctuary, but the beginning of her worse fears. Daisy was nowhere to be seen. She looked out into the dark, the play of light and shadows from the full moon made her tremble. *Please don't let anything happen to Daisy.* Susan filled up and said a silent prayer.

How did the doggie door get open? Did one of the girls do it? They all knew Daisy wasn't allowed out by herself. Now her little dog was gone.

"Daisy." Her call was just above a whisper. Something was so wrong. Susan felt panic as she wrapped her arms tightly across her chest and tried to calm her breathing. She wanted to run inside and lock the door, but she wasn't going to move until Daisy came back.

Susan looked at her yard, it seemed to stretch on forever in the darkness. She didn't have a clue where to start to look for Daisy. The Miller farm was so overgrown it was like a dark black hole at the back of her yard. She was terrified to go down to the creek. The only open flat space was by the stone wall. Daisy was not there.

I wanted privacy. I brought this on myself. Susan held back her tears, she needed to stay focused for Daisy. She looked around at all the darkness and shivered. She was totally isolated from everyone. *Who would hear me if I screamed? I don't even know my neighbors.*

Susan moved towards the center of the patio. She heard a noise. The crunch of leaves, twigs? She wasn't sure. "Daisy." She called out softly, expecting to see her little dog run out of the shadows into her arms. Nothing. Daisy was gone. Susan started to cry.

He watched her as she called for her little dog. Tall, thin, with long dark black hair pulled up and pinned off her face. This was not his first night in her yard, but it was the night he would finally own her. The doggie door was his answer. All he had to do was open it and wait. Pity she was crying.

Her night shirt left little to the imagination. He could see the outline of her large breasts under her thin shirt until she pulled her sweater close. A gesture he thought sweet. He eyed her long lean legs with anticipation. He savored the moment, her innocence of what was to come. Perhaps she would enjoy it. He knew he would.

Susan heard the sound again. It didn't come from her yard, it was directly behind her. Her heart raced as though it would explode in her chest with the realization she was not alone. A guttural male voice whispered her name and a thick rough rope lassoed her, pinning her arms down tight. With one quick movement he jerked her back until she slammed into his chest. He licked her neck, and whispered "I've been waiting for you." She felt his hand, cold, slide down her bare stomach and inside her briefs. Fear hit her like an orgasm as her body shuttered and she felt a dampness flood down her legs.

Another smell caused her nostrils to flare. It was sickeningly sweet, not like the exotic softness of the honeysuckle. A thick cloth covered her mouth. Her last thought was of Daisy. Then she could think no more.

38
SHOTS IN THE NIGHT

Jim put down the plans for the bathroom remodel and cocked his head. The barking of the little dog next door seemed louder than usual, closer somehow.

He moved to the window and looked out into Susan's backyard. Something caught his eye, a shadow, or his imagination on overdrive. It had been that kind of day. The hairs on the back of his neck bristled. What if Susan was in danger? His mind told him the last thing he needed was to burst into her yard and have her call the cops. His gut told him there was trouble.

Jim went with his gut. He needed to check outside. If he were wrong, well, he'd been called an ass for less things. Jim went to his safe, put in the code, and pulled out his gun.

The Glock felt at home in his hands. He inherited it from his Dad. He was surprised when he bought it fifteen years ago, but it gave them a chance to bond at the range. Some of the best times he'd had with his father were with that gun.

Georgia law did not require registration, but he did get a permit to carry. He'd spent a few weeks visiting the local range, firing the gun, getting used to the trigger, and tightening up his shooting skills. Then the gun went back in the safe where it stayed. Until now. He checked the 17-shot magazine to verify it was full, heeled in the clip, stuffed the gun in the right front pocket of his vest, and headed downstairs.

He heard whining and scratching outside the door. Damn, the dog *was* there. Jim felt a surge of panic. Only one way that dog would be loose. He opened the door and a small ball of fluff ran in and twirled around his feet. He had no idea what the dog's name was and bent to look at her tag. Daisy. *Okay Daisy, what the hell are you doing here?* Daisy seemed frantic, pawing at his ankles, and yapping. Jim picked her up and carried her to the couch. "Stay here. I'm going to check on your owner." Daisy panted and watched him. Jim's skin prickled. He knew Susan was in trouble.

The white pick-up truck in her driveway made him move quietly towards the gate to her backyard. He'd seen that truck too many times this week. Thought it was someone visiting Mildred. It was always parked on the street. Now it was too close to Susan to be a coincidence.

He heard a man's voice, a raspy whisper that made him sick to his gut.

"Susan, my Susan. My beautiful Susan."

Who the hell was back there? Jim bent down low and quickly flipped the latch on the gate. He saw a man huddled over Susan's body. She was tied in rope and blood pooled out next to her head on the patio. The man had his hand on her thigh, moving up her leg.

Jim wasn't sure what to do. Did the man have a gun? He didn't want Susan to be hurt any further. His mind stopped, frozen on what was the best way to handle the situation. He decided to go for it. He stood up, his Glock aimed, and shouted. "Stop! I've got a gun and I'm ready to use it." Jim shuddered. He sounded like a damn character on TV. Only he wasn't acting. Susan's life depended on him.

The man sprung up from Susan's body and turned to face Jim. He was younger than Jim and about his size. He wore a City College sweatshirt. A shock of thick hair poked out from the dark baseball cap on his head. If looks could kill, Jim would be dead. The man glared at him, his eyes wild, his hand reached in his pocket.

Jim saw a glint of metal and a shot fired off. The damn idiot had a gun too. Jim dropped to the ground and rolled over towards the shrubs. The man reached down, grabbed the rope around Susan's body, and pulled her onto the grass. He fired another shot in Jim's direction. The sound of the shots were deafening. Jim hoped a neighbor would hear and call the cops.

A small blood trail trickled across the patio. Jim could only imagine how scraped Susan was as he watched in horror. The truck was outside, but he blocked the path to it. The man was headed towards the Miller farm. The scene was surreal. Jim panicked he would lose Susan forever if they disappeared into the thick overgrowth of the deserted farm.

Jim jumped up, fired, and caught the man in his leg. He didn't stop. Jim aimed again, this time at the shoulder. The impact startled him. Jim watched as he dropped the rope around Susan and grabbed at his arm. Blood oozed through his fingers. Jim took a breath, perhaps the chase would be over.

The man looked at Jim, his features clear as a bell in the moonlight, the snarl on his face chilling. Then he smiled, a crooked, deranged smile, and pointed his gun down at Susan's head. He whacked her temple and swung back and fired at Jim.

Christ. The guy was a maniac. He could shoot Susan if he didn't stop him. The blood on the patio was dark as Jim moved over it. "Stop, you bastard." He knew it was fruitless. He ducked another bullet, then jumped up. It was now or never. Jim stood firm, aimed a strait shot to the man's chest, and fired. He watched him tumble to the ground.

Jim dashed into the yard. The shooter's lifeless body had dropped next to Susan, his chest covered in blood. Jim kicked the gun into the darkness. The police could find it later. He tucked his Glock into his vest pocket and turned to Susan, fearful she might be dead too.

Susan felt cold in his arms as he carried her back to the patio and gently put her on the ground. He knelt down next to her and put his face close to hers. Her breath was warm and sweet. *Thank God, she's alive.* Jim's nerves were raw.

He spoke quietly to her. "Susan, you're safe." He knew she couldn't hear him, but he wanted to talk to her, reassure her. He wanted to reassure himself. He grabbed at the old rope, still tightly wound around her body, and pulled out the pocket knife he'd carried since he was a kid. He wanted to free her and get her somewhere warm.

The sound of sirens and a flash of activity burst through the gate. Police ran in and lights filled the dark shadows of the yard.

"Halt what you are doing!" A deep voice shouted at him.

Jim stopped. His back was to the gate. He raised his hands.

"The guy you want is in the back. Dead. I'm sure of it." Jim hoped they would listen.

"Officer, officer. That's Jim, our neighbor. Don't hurt him." A familiar voice echoed through the air across the gate. It was Mildred. God bless her.

"Who are you lady?" The policeman turned to Mildred.

"I'm the one who called 911. Sounded like the street was exploding." Mildred was breathless.

The officer looked at the scene and shook his head. "McCabe, get out to the yard and check it out." He turned to Jim, his voice kinder. "Tell me what happened."

Jim didn't move from the spot on the ground next to Susan. He reached for her hand as a team of medics swarmed over her.

"Don't touch me!" Mildred's voice was on edge as she pushed past a policeman and ran up to Jim's side. "Is Susan dead?" She started to sob.

"She should be fine as soon as she comes around." The female medic tried to calm Mildred.

"So what happened back here?" The officer questioned him. Jim started with Daisy at his door. . .

"I've heard enough. This gives me the chills. Bless you, Jim. I'm going inside, make some coffee." Mildred walked straight into Susan's house as though it were her own.

Jim tightened his grip on Susan's hand and watched for her to move. He knew he was in the way as the medics worked around him. He just couldn't let go. Not yet. Not until he knew she was fine. Not ever.

39
AFTERMATH

"What happened?" Susan's voice was barely a whisper. She tried to focus on the faces around her, but her vision was blurred. "My head and my body…" Susan couldn't finish the sentence she hurt so badly. Then she remembered someone had grabbed her in the yard. A cold sick feeling flooded over her and she tried to scream out, but sobs came instead.

"Steady." Jim's voice calmed her. "You've had a nasty experience, but you're safe. The police are here."

"Everything is okay." The female medic handed a blanket to Susan. "You're bruised, but thank goodness, nothing serious."

Susan pulled the blanket close and choked back her tears. Jim's face was clearly in view now. *This must be a dream. Why is Jim here?* She looked out past the patio at all the activity. Lights flashed, yellow tape ran across the far end of her yard, she heard loud voices that made her head spin. Policemen were everywhere. *Daisy.* That's what happened. She had come out to find Daisy. Panic set in again. "Where is my dog?"

Jim touched her cheek gently. "Daisy is safe at my place."

Susan stared at him. "What are you doing here? And how did Daisy get to your place?" She started to cry again. None of this made any sense. The details were not coming to her. Her hand reached for Jim. "Take me inside, please."

Jim helped her up, his arm around her.

"Let us take you to the hospital." The female medic reached for Susan.

"No. I'm fine. I want a shower and my dog." Susan wanted Daisy more than anything.

"You need some medical attention . . ."

Susan cut her off. "I said I'm fine. Please leave me alone."

"I've got her." Jim assured the medic. He was worried about Susan's bruises, but her mental state had him more concerned. "Would you tell the police she's gone inside."

Mildred was in the kitchen making coffee. She reached out for Susan's arm and smiled at Jim. "I'll take her from here." Then she smiled at Susan. "You've got some ugly scrapes. Let's take care of you."

Susan turned to Jim. "Daisy? Can you bring her to me?"

Jim smiled. "I'll be right back."

Susan let Mildred guide her down the hall. She rested against her shoulder and thought about her own mother, gone now for so long. Mildred had a motherly quality about her. She'd seen her across the street, but had never said hello. "Thank you." Susan's voice was weak. "I don't know what happened, but I know your face." Susan thought it was the kindest face she had ever seen.

"You've been through a lot, hon." Mildred touched Susan's cheek gently. "I heard what Jim told the police. Jim was quick to realize you were in danger and quicker with his gun. Didn't know he packed heat in that house, but thank God for it. You were tied up in that nasty rope, out cold. He knocked you out with something. What is it they use in those crime TV shows? Any rate, I'm sure that pervert wanted his way with you. Jim got there just as he was trying to get you off the property. Then, lord knows what would have happened to you child. Shots were flying all over the place. Never had nothing like this happen here before. That man won't bother you again. Jim had no choice with what he had to do."

"Does Jim live here?" Susan was very confused. She thought he lived up by the college.

"He's your neighbor on the other side of the stone wall, hon. I thought you knew that? I think he's been sweet on you for some time."

He was her next door neighbor. The renovator? Jim had some explaining to do.

"Your little dog is a hero. Ran up to Jim's front door and barked like the dickens. She's a fine little alarm."

Susan heard a thud of tiny paws track down the hall and Daisy burst into the bedroom. "Oh Daisy, Daisy." Susan picked her up and almost crushed her, she hugged her so tight. She kissed the top of Daisy's head and Daisy licked her back like crazy. "You had me so worried." Susan kept her close and Daisy's head was damp from tears.

"I think the police want to talk to you." Mildred saw Jim down the hallway with two men in uniform. "Are you up to it?"

"Yes, but I want a shower first, get this caked blood off me." Susan looked at her wounds. She also wanted to put on some clothes.

"I'll tell them." Mildred gave Susan a quick hug, patted Daisy, and closed the door.

Susan turned on the hot water and let it pound on her. She scrubbed her thighs and face, happy to discover she had only surface abrasions. The lump on her forehead still hurt and had started to turn blue.

Susan got out of the shower and looked at her face in the mirror. It could have been so much worse. She winced. *I could be dead or with that maniac.* That reality made her tremble. She slipped into jeans and a light sweater, and headed to the kitchen.

"Have a cup of coffee, hon." Mildred placed a steaming hot mug on the farm table. "These nice policemen have been waiting to talk to you."

"Your neighbor filled us in on the details of the shooting. Do you know why he came after you?" The policeman's question only confused Susan more.

"I don't have a clue. But he knew my name and knew I had a dog." Nausea flooded over Susan as she remembered being tied up.

"We ID'd the body. Sonny Watkins. He's been on our radar for some time. We think he's the one that killed those girls up by the college. Been showing his photo around and people remembered him talking to them. His DNA will finalize everything."

They handed a photo to her. "Do you recognize him? Maybe there is a connection on why he came here."

Susan looked at it and gasped. "That's the guy from *Love Me Cupid*." It wasn't the same photo, but it was him. She recognized his face and hair.

"*Love Me Cupid*?" The officer looked perplexed.

"Dating site." Susan blushed. "I never met him in person, but we did message each other one night online. He used a different name." She would tell Jim about it later.

"He's a real predator. We've been looking for him in connection with a murder last year. You're a very lucky lady you weren't number four."

Susan started to shake listening to the policeman. Jim reached over and grabbed her hand.

"I think we've got all we need for now. Do you want to go to the hospital? Ambulance is out front." The officer gave her his card. "In case you have any questions."

"I'm fine. Thanks to my neighbor, I believe." She smiled at Jim and then at the policemen. "And thanks to the Safe Haven police."

"We're cleaning up the place and as soon as the reports are done, your yard will be your own again."

Mildred showed them out then turned to Susan. "Do you need me for anything else, hon?"

Susan looked at Mildred. "I think I've got all I need for now. Thank you so much. I want to get to know you better and the others around here. I've been a butt ignoring everyone."

"I'm sure you had your reasons. Don't you worry. We like to think of everyone as family in Safe Haven, even if we get a little nosy at times. So happy you are safe, my dear."

Mildred gave her one more hug and then closed the door as she left.

Susan and Jim sat across from each other at the farm table. Susan sipped her coffee and looked at him. He had the same effect on her as he had at City Pub. She was drawn to him in a way she couldn't explain. He tugged at her heart and now he was her hero.

Daisy pawed at Jim's leg and he lifted her onto his lap. "Well, one female here likes me." He grinned sheepishly at Susan.

"Make that two. But I have a lot of questions for you."

"I'm sure you do. But if you hadn't been so dang annoying telling me you never wanted to meet your neighbors that night at the bar, well, we could have been dating. I spend time at the apartment, but am here more often than not. I recognized you the minute you sat down. If I had told you who I was, would you have stayed to talk to me?"

"Probably not. But there was something about you that I couldn't ignore. I don't usually pick up men in bars and, you know, fool around with them in the parking lot." Susan blushed. In spite of the horrific evening, she found herself getting excited remembering his kisses and touch. They never actually had sex.

Jim grinned back at her. He seemed to read her mind. "We never finished what we started."

"And we were never properly introduced. Last names and all." Susan tilted her head and narrowed her eyes. "Except I did see you on the news. Sorry about your old girlfriend."

"That's a long story for when we get to spend more time together. Did you think I killed her?" Jim frowned with concern.

"No. I knew you couldn't have done anything to her. Seeing you on TV, well it was a hell of a way to find out your last name. Of course, tonight wasn't exactly my idea of a great way to meet up again. I think we should start over and properly introduce ourselves."

"Jim Johnson." Jim held his hand across the table. "I am your neighbor so you will see a lot of me."

"Susan Meyers." Susan grabbed his hand and held it tight. "I certainly hope so."

Jim got up and to walk around the table. Susan met him halfway. He put his arms around her and kissed her, gently at first. He wanted to be sure she was ready. She'd had a night of it.

Susan pulled back. She wanted to take a good close look at the man she was going to take to bed.

"I hate unfinished business."

"Me too." Jim looked surprisingly shy.

Susan reached for his hand and moved it up under her sweater. His rough hand on her skin brought back all the heat of that night they met. She forgot how her body hurt. She ached in a different way now. A good way.

"Are you sure?" Jim was in no hurry if she needed time to get over the evening.

"Touch me all over." She whispered in his ear and took a tiny nip on his lobe. "And don't let me stop you this time." She was ready for him, had been ready for him for as long as she could remember.

LIFE ITSELF
IS THE MOST WONDERFUL FAIRY TALE
—HANS CHRISTIAN ANDERSON

EPILOGUE
EIGHT MONTHS LATER

Susan stretched in bed and rolled over to kiss Jim. She loved waking up to find him next to her. She poked at his bare chest and slipped her hand under the quilt, down his leg. Susan knew exactly how to wake the man!

She heard a groan and smiled. Worked every time! She nuzzled his neck. "Wake up silly. The girls will be here in an hour. And you know Mildred, she'll be here way too early." She looked at the clock and cringed. They'd better hop to it.

"Do we have time for this?" Jim rolled on his side and reached for a lovely breast.

"Not now. The tables, chairs, and flowers are set up, but there is still so much to finish before the wedding. I am not getting caught with my pants down." She loved to tease him. Ever since she finished her book, she liked to talk in sing-song to him, make him think she was thinking of sex, even if something else was on her mind. She didn't have to think about sex any more, it was hers at every turn since Jim moved in. She never believed in fairy tale endings, but she was living proof they happened.

"Shower is mine first!" Her feet hit the floor as she ran to the bathroom. When they moved the master bedroom upstairs, Jim renovated the old bathroom to include a walk-in shower.

"Not on your life." Jim was right behind her. "We do have time for this." He turned on the shower and pulled her in next to him. The water ran down their bodies and they moved together in harmony that came from knowing each other well.

Susan blew her long dark hair dry and slipped into her vintage pink lace garden party dress. It's not every day your best friend gets married. Emily and Al decided to tie the knot and asked if they could have the ceremony at the farmhouse. They wanted a Valentine's Day wedding. It would be a huge celebration with all their friends bringing wine and gifts. Susan loaned Emily the butterfly hair clip for *something borrowed, something blue.*

The weather was perfect for an outdoor wedding. It was extremely warm for February, but that was not unusual for Safe Haven. The sun was out and the day promised to be glorious.

Jim came up behind her and put his arm around her waist. He nuzzled her neck. "I have a gift for you. It is the most romantic day of the year according to the media."

Susan turned around and looked at him. "You know, every day is the most romantic now that we are together. Don't look for a present from me! The wedding has kept me busy." She laughed and threw her arms around his neck.

Jim pulled her arms down and gave her a serious look. "I don't need a present. Just an answer." He reached in his pocket and handed her a small red velvet box. "Will you marry me?"

Susan was speechless. They never talked about getting married. She opened the box, her hands shaking. A platinum setting with a lovely pear shaped diamond sparkled back at her.

"It's vintage. Actually belonged to my grandmother. I know how you like history in everything."

Susan thought her heart would burst. "Yes. Of course, yes."

Jim grinned and slipped the ring on her finger. He kissed her gently on the mouth, then pinched her butt. "Don't want to get too sentimental. We have a house full of folks on the way." He mouthed *I love you* as he turned and left to go downstairs.

I love you, too. Susan whispered gently to Jim's back.

She was in awe at how her life had changed.

Her book was a success. Early reviews praised her for a smooth transition in writing genres. Her dog column fans loved that she added more spice to her on-line stories. There was a threesome in bed now. Daisy liked to sleep between her and Jim most nights.

Susan thought back to the day she decided to write her book. Jamie did more than fill the pages, she allowed Susan to find her way back to happiness and love. Jamie was the hidden part of her that wanted a relationship again.

A new book was in the works. She and Jim decided to combine their talents. The details were up in the air, but it would be a murder mystery set in Europe. The sale of Jim's house next door gave them the money to travel this summer for research.

A great gay couple in one of Jim's classes jumped at the opportunity to own an old house in a quiet little community. In fact, Evan and Dick were into organic gardening. Susan gave them the plans for her hen house and made them promise to share any eggs.

The guys loved Daisy and dubbed themselves her *dog nanny*. "Travel far and often, we'll take care of her while you're gone."

"Hey, get that cute ass down here." Jim yelled from the stairs. "It's getting crazy. Daisy won't stand still for her ribbon. Mildred has a ton of freshly baked cookies. Emily called, the girls will be here in ten minutes, and Cheryl has the food. Al is coming with the groomsmen. Patti just showed up with her new boyfriend. And if the clock is right, the neighbors and folks from the university are due any time now." There was a pause, then Jim called back up. "Claire and Scott just arrived. Claire has a huge bouquet of flowers."

Claire and Scott did get to buy the Miller farm. The owners were horrified after her incident and worried an empty house would bring more crime. They were in the middle of an enormous renovation.

Susan looked at the copy of her book on the bedside table. *Through Jamie's Eyes*. She'd brought on a predator with her research but found her own Prince Charming. Writing about sex was a thing of the past. A murder mystery sounded more fun. What could possibly go wrong with that?

She blew a kiss to the mirror and headed downstairs. Life was grand!

Myrtle's Famous Fried Green Tomato Recipe

Ingredients

6 green tomatoes
1 beaten egg
1 cup buttermilk
½ cup white cornmeal
1 cup self-rising flour
½ teaspoon salt
Bacon drippings

Directions:

Cut tomatoes horizontally into ¼" slices. Salt the slices, set them aside to dry a bit. Mix egg and buttermilk in a shallow bowl. Mix flour, cornmeal, and salt into another shallow bowl (add cracked pepper if pepper is desired).Dip the slices in buttermilk mixture then give them a good coating of the cornmeal mixture. Heat bacon drippings in skillet to 375 degrees

Brown one side before flipping to the other side. Tomatoes should not touch each other in skillet.

Remove carefully when browned to avoid breaking off any of the breading. Place on paper towel lined plate or rack. Serve immediately.

Acknowledgements

Thank you to my characters for giving me the ride of my life. I sat at the computer and they spoke to me. As a memoir writer, most days I talk to myself. Now I know I am not alone . . . there are voices in my head!

On the name dropping side, I want to thank Pam King, PD King Design, for her cover and book design. She saw my vision and captured it perfectly.

And to my mother, Audrey Frank. She is an author at eighty-five and an inspiration that tells me anything is possible at any age. She is fearless.

Finally, thank you to all the readers who buy books – hard-back, paper, or e-books. You keep the writing community whole!

About the Author

Barbara Barth is the author of *The Unfaithful Widow*, a memoir on the first year on her own. Her book placed as a finalist in the 2011 USA Best Book Awards. Her work has appeared in *On Purpose Woman* magazine and on many on-line sites, including *The Balancing Act* with Lifetime TV, *Skirt.com, Silver & Grace*, and *The Red Room*.

Author, blogger, sometimes antique dealer, and dog whisperer, although some days she has to bark to be heard. She lives in the metro Atlanta area with six dogs from local animal shelters.

Danger In Her Words is her first work of fiction.

Available on Amazon and Kindle.

Visit her on the web:
WWW.BARBARABARTHWRITER.COM

AUTHOR'S NOTES

I am fascinated with the theme of rebuilding a good life after a loss and how creativity and friendships are healing factors to mend a broken heart. Imagine being in a long term relationship where you took for granted that sex and love would always be there, and then it was gone. Susan and Jamie are strong women who have dealt with grief and pieced themselves back together. A little flawed, vulnerable, but full of life and laughter. I hope you will love them like I do.

My own life took a twist some years back and my saving graces came in the form of dogs I rescued who rescued me.

Atlanta is the only real city name in my book and it is to ground you in Georgia. All other places are fantasies in my mind. Safe Haven is a composite of all the towns and farmhouses I have looked at over the past few years. The change in the countryside within an hour of Atlanta is amazing with its small rural communities and awesome antique shops!

Like Susan, I have a farmhouse fantasy. She had the courage to move, I am still thinking about it!

Life will always surprise you if you open your heart. Dream big!

Barbara
"WRITER WITH DOGS"

TRUE LOVE IS AROUND THE CORNER
AT YOUR LOCAL ANIMAL SHELTER.
YOU CAN MAKE A DIFFERENCE:
ADOPT, DONATE, VOLUNTEER!

www.ingramcontent.com/pod-product-compliance
Lightning Source LLC
Chambersburg PA
CBHW070102260626
47160CB00004B/1289